A CHATTO & WINDUS PAPERBACK

CWP 28

THE CAPTIVE

PART ONE

Marcel Proust's continuous novel *À la Recherche du Temps Perdu* (REMEMBRANCE OF THINGS PAST) was originally published in eight parts, the titles and dates of which were: I. *Du Coté de Chez Swann* (1913); II. *À l'Ombre des Jeunes Filles en Fleurs* (1918), awarded the Prix Goncourt in 1919; III. *Le Coté de Guermantes I* (1920); IV. *Le Coté de Guermantes II, Sodome et Gomorrhe I* (1921); V. *Sodome et Gomorrhe II* (1922); VI. *La Prisonnière* (1923); VII. *Albertine Disparue* (1925); VIII. *Le Temps Retrouvé* (1927).

Du Coté de Chez Swann has been published in English as SWANN'S WAY: *À l'Ombre des Jeunes Filles en Fleurs* as WITHIN A BUDDING GROVE: *Le Coté de Guermantes* as THE GUERMANTES WAY: *Sodome et Gomorrhe* as CITIES OF THE PLAIN: *La Prisonnière* as THE CAPTIVE: *Albertine Disparue* as THE SWEET CHEAT GONE: and *Le Temps Retrouvé* as TIME REGAINED. The first seven parts were translated by C. K. Scott Moncrieff; the eighth was first translated by Stephen Hudson, but is now reissued in a new translation by Andreas Mayor.

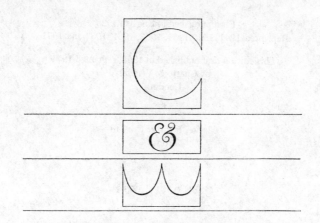

THE CAPTIVE

PART ONE

MARCEL PROUST

Translated by
C. K. Scott Moncrieff

CHATTO & WINDUS
LONDON

First published in English 1929
Reprinted 1941, 1949, 1951, 1957, 1961, 1967 and 1971

This edition first published in 1968, reprinted 1971
by Chatto & Windus
London

*

Clarke, Irwin & Co. Ltd.
Toronto

ISBN 0 7011 1065 1

Reproduced and Printed in Great Britain by
Redwood Press Limited
Trowbridge & London

TRANSLATOR'S NOTE

MARCEL PROUST, before his death on November 18, 1922, had delivered to his publisher, M. Gaston Gallimard, the typescript of this volume—planned originally as a continuation of *Sodome et Gomorrhe*—but had been unable, in his feeble state and in his preoccupation with the more important task of completing his work while life remained, to revise and correct the text. After his death, the typescript was entrusted, for revision, to his brother and heir-at-law Dr. Robert Proust and to the late Jaques Rivière, at that time editor of the *Nouvelle Revue Française*; on November 14, 1923, the original edition of *La Prisonnière* passed through the press, and by the beginning of the following year the book reached the public. The care of these two editors has doubtless eliminated many errors present in the typewritten version, itself a transcript from Proust's almost illegible hand: indeed I have found myself obliged to make fewer than one hundred and fifty corrections of the published French text, as compared with over three hundred in that of *Sodome et Gomorrhe II*.

These corrigenda, of course, differ widely in importance and in kind. Some are to be numbered among those printer's errors which will survive the most careful proof-reading; others are innocuous in themselves but depart from precedents established in earlier volumes: such as the name " Doville " which cannot be allowed to stand, though it recurs a dozen times, after the careful labelling of the place by Brichot with its etymology in *Sodome et Gomorrhe II*, (ii, 137-8: see *Cities of the Plain*, II, 49-50). Of this sort is a curious confusion of persons on page 21 of *La Prisonnière*, I (*The Captive*, I, 13). It is evident here that the author is speaking not of Françoise and Albertine but of Céleste and Françoise; and I should be prepared to wager that the typescript named Céleste. The editors, knowing that the fictitious Françoise was to a certain extent modelled upon the real Céleste Albaret, and forgetting that Proust had introduced Céleste Albaret by name, as a foil to Françoise, in *Sodome et Gomorrhe, II* (ii, 77-83: see *Cities of the Plain, I,* 341-347), may have made this alteration in good faith, thereby saddling Françoise with a speech that Céleste and only Céleste could have made.

Of the transposition of paragraphs or sentences, which I have noted somewhere as being necessary in *Le Côté de Guermantes, I,* I find but one occasion here, in *La Prisonnière, II,* 15-16, (*The Captive, II,* 9-10), where the sentence:

> Ne mentionnons ici que pour mémoire le désir de paraître naturel et hardi, le geste instinctif de cacher un rendez-vous secret, un mélange de pudeur et d'ostentation, le besoin de confesser ce qui vous est si agréable et de montrer qu'on est aimé, une pénétration de ce que sait ou suppose—et ne dit pas—l'interlocuteur, pénétration qui, allant au delà ou en deçà de la sienne, la fait tantôt sur et tantôt sous-estimer, le désir involontaire de jouer avec le feu et la volonté de faire la part du feu.

must be transposed so as to come between the sentences that follow:

> Tout autant de lois différentes agissant en sens contraire dictent les réponses plus générales touchant l'innocence, le " platonisme ", ou au contraire la réalité charnelle des relations qu'on a avec la personne qu'on dit avoir vue le matin quand on l'a vue le soir.

and: Toutefois, d'une façon générale, disons que M. de Charlus, etc. Here I guess that the stray sentence was written in the margin of the typescript, and enclosed in a " kite " whose " string " appeared to the editors to be tethering it to the wrong place on the page.

Another problem arises in the first chapter (*La Prisonnière*, I, 139-140):

> Peut-être dans sa famille riche, mais provinciale, en trouverait-on l'équivalent dans quelques boutiques de la Place de l'Évêché, où certaines sucreries passent pour " ce qu'il y a de meilleur."

I have translated this, rather freely and not to my satisfaction, (*The Captive*, I, 132) but am still in ignorance of its meaning. It has occurred to me as possible that the sentence ought to be carried bodily twelve lines higher, so as follow:

> Pendant que j'adressais à Albertine des reproches que je n'aurais pas dû, elle avait l'air de sucer avec délices un sucre d'orge.

But this is no real improvement. I conclude that the " en " of " en trouverait-on " refers to Andrée's affection for Albertine, which, if not absolutely genuine, might pass as genuine in the absence of anything better.

A second instance in this volume (and there have not been many in the earlier volumes) in which I have found myself unable to read what was in the author's mind occurs in *La Prisonnière*, II, 170 (*The Captive*, II, 168) where Brichot says of Charlus that

> il commente son catéchisme satanique avec une verve un tantinet charentonesque et une obstination, j'allais dire une candeur, de blanc d'Espagne et d'émigré.

My friend " Stephen Hudson " has suggested that " blanc d'Espagne " should be " Grand d'Espagne " and I should hasten to agree with him did I not feel that " blanc " was required by the preceding " candeur " ; but what, on that assumption, is the " obstination " of Spanish white, which is eminently friable? Once again, I must throw myself on the mercy, and invite the collaboration of those readers, in every part of the world, who have borne so patiently with me and have so encouraged me by their letters of appreciation during the last seven years.

As soon as the English text of *Le Temps Retrouvé* has gone to the printer, I hope to find time to prepare a supplementary volume containing a critical emendation of the French text as a whole, which may, I venture to hope, be of service to future editors of Proust in his own country—and also an index, or "Who's Who" of the characters that figure in the story, each of them studied, as far as possible, in historical sequence, so that the reader may trace the history of (let us say) Madame Verdurin from the earliest mention (in time) of her in *Le Temps Retrouvé* in a pastiche of the Goncourt journals to her final appearance, as Princesse de Guermantes, in the same volume.

C. K. S. M.

Rome, Ferragosto, 1929.

CONTENTS

✻

THE CAPTIVE

CHAPTER I

Life with Albertine

A T daybreak, my face still turned to the wall, and before I had seen above the big inner curtains what tone the first streaks of light assumed, I could already tell what sort of day it was. The first sounds from the street had told me, according to whether they came to my ears dulled and distorted by the moisture of the atmosphere or quivering like arrows in the resonant and empty area of a spacious, crisply frozen, pure morning; as soon as I heard the rumble of the first tramcar, I could tell whether it was sodden with rain or setting forth into the blue. And perhaps these sounds had themselves been forestalled by some swifter and more pervasive emanation which, stealing into my slumber, diffused in it a melancholy that seemed to presage snow, or gave utterance (through the lips of a little person who occasionally reappeared there) to so many hymns to the glory of the sun that, having first of all begun to smile in my sleep, having prepared my eyes, behind their shut lids, to be dazzled, I awoke finally amid deafening strains of music. It was, moreover, principally from my bedroom that I took in the life of the outer world during this period. I know that Bloch reported that, when he called to see me in the evenings, he could hear the sound of conversation; as my mother was at Combray and he never found anybody in my room, he concluded that I was talking to myself. When, much

I

later, he learned that Albertine had been staying with me at the time, and realised that I had concealed her presence from all my friends, he declared that he saw at last the reason why, during that episode in my life, I had always refused to go out of doors. He was wrong. His mistake was, however, quite pardonable, for the truth, even if it is inevitable, is not always conceivable as a whole. People who learn some accurate detail of another person's life at once deduce consequences which are not accurate, and see in the newly discovered fact an explanation of things that have no connexion with it whatsoever.

When I reflect now that my mistress had come, on our return from Balbec, to live in Paris under the same roof as myself, that she had abandoned the idea of going on a cruise, that she was installed in a bedroom within twenty paces of my own, at the end of the corridor, in my father's tapestried study, and that late every night, before leaving me, she used to slide her tongue between my lips like a portion of daily bread, a nourishing food that had the almost sacred character of all flesh upon which the sufferings that we have endured on its account have come in time to confer a sort of spiritual grace, what I at once call to mind in comparison is not the night that Captain de Borodino allowed me to spend in barracks, a favour which cured what was after all only a passing distemper, but the night on which my father sent Mamma to sleep in the little bed by the side of my own. So it is that life, if it is once again to deliver us from an anguish that has seemed inevitable, does so in conditions that are different, so diametrically opposed at times that it is almost an open sacrilege to assert the identity of the grace bestowed upon us.

When Albertine had heard from Françoise that, in the darkness of my still curtained room, I was not asleep, she had no scruple about making a noise as she took her bath, in her own dressing-room. Then, frequently, instead of waiting until later in the day, I would repair to a bathroom adjoining hers, which had a certain charm of its own. Time was, when a stage manager would spend hundreds of thousands of francs to begem with real emeralds the throne upon which a great actress would play the part of an empress. The Russian ballet has taught us that simple arrangements of light will create, if trained upon the right spot, jewels as gorgeous and more varied. This decoration, itself immaterial, is not so graceful, however, as that which, at eight o'clock in the morning, the sun substitutes for what we were accustomed to see when we did not arise before noon. The windows of our respective bathrooms, so that their occupants might not be visible from without, were not of clear glass but clouded with an artificial and old-fashioned kind of frost. All of a sudden, the sun would colour this drapery of glass, gild it, and discovering in myself an earlier young man whom habit had long concealed, would intoxicate me with memories, as though I were out in the open country gazing at a hedge of golden leaves in which even a bird was not lacking. For I could hear Albertine ceaselessly humming:

> For melancholy
> Is but folly,
> And he who heeds it is a fool.

I loved her so well that I could spare a joyous smile for her bad taste in music. This song had, as it happened, during the past summer, delighted Mme. Bontemps, who presently heard people say that it was silly, with the result that, instead of asking Albertine to sing it, when she had a party, she would substitute:

A song of farewell rises from troubled springs,

which in its turn became " an old jingle of Massenet's, the child is always dinning into our ears."

A cloud passed, blotting out the sun; I saw extinguished and replaced by a grey monochrome the modest, screening foliage of the glass.

The partition that divided our two dressing-rooms (Albertine's, identical with my own, was a bathroom which Mamma, who had another at the other end of the flat, had never used for fear of disturbing my rest) was so slender that we could talk to each other as we washed in double privacy, carrying on a conversation that was interrupted only by the sound of the water, in that intimacy which, in hotels, is so often permitted by the smallness and proximity of the rooms, but which, in private houses in Paris, is so rare.

On other mornings, I would remain in bed, drowsing for as long as I chose, for orders had been given that no one was to enter my room until I had rung the bell, an act which, owing to the awkward position in which the electric bulb had been hung above my bed, took such a time that often, tired of feeling for it and glad to be left alone, I would lie back for some moments and almost fall asleep again. It was not that I was wholly indifferent to Albertine's presence in the house. Her separation from her girl friends had the effect of sparing my heart any fresh anguish. She kept it in a state of repose, in a semi-immobility which would help it to recover. But after all, this calm which my mistress was procuring for me was a release from suffering rather than a positive joy. Not that it did not permit me to taste many joys, from which too keen a grief had debarred me, but these joys, so far from my owing them to Albertine, in whom for that matter I could no longer see any beauty and who was beginning to bore me, with whom I was now clearly conscious that I was not in love, I tasted on the contrary when Albertine was not with me. And so, to begin the morning, I did not send for her at once, especially if it was a fine day. For some moments, knowing that he would make me happier than Albertine, I remained closeted with the little person inside me, hymning the rising sun, of whom I have already spoken. Of those elements which compose our personality, it is not the most obvious that are most essential. In myself, when ill health has succeeded in uprooting them one after another, there will still remain two or three, endowed with a hardier constitution than the rest, notably a certain philosopher who is happy only when he has discovered in two works of art, in two sensations, a common element. But the last of all, I have sometimes asked myself whether it would not be this little mannikin, very similar to another whom the optician at Combray used to set up in his shop window to forecast the weather, and who, doffing his hood when the sun shone, would put it on again if it was going to rain. This little mannikin, I know his egoism; I may be suffering from a choking fit which the mere threat of rain would calm; he pays no heed, and, at the first drops so impatiently awaited, losing his gaiety, sullenly pulls down his hood. Conversely, I dare say that in my last agony, when all my other "selves" are dead, if a ray of sunshine steals into the room, while I am drawing my last breath, the little fellow of the barometer will feel a great relief, and will throw back his hood to sing: "Ah! Fine weather at last!"

I rang for Françoise. I opened the *Figaro*. I scanned its columns and made sure that it did not contain an article, or so-called article which I had sent to the editor, and which was no more than a slightly revised version of the page that had recently come to light, written long ago in Dr. Percepied's carriage, as I gazed at the spires of Martinville. Then I read Mamma's letter. She felt it to be odd, in fact shocking, that a girl should be staying in the house alone with me. On the first day, at the moment of leaving Balbec, when she saw how wretched I was, and was distressed by the prospect of leaving me by myself, my mother had perhaps been glad when she heard that Albertine was travelling with us, and saw that, side by side with our own boxes (those boxes among which I had passed a night in tears in the Balbec hotel), there had been hoisted into the "Twister" Albertine's boxes also, narrow and black, which had seemed to me to have the appearance of coffins, and as to which I knew not whether they were bringing to my house life or death. But I had never even asked myself the question, being all overjoyed, in the radiant morning, after the fear of having to remain at Balbec, that I was taking Albertine with me. But to this proposal, if at the start my mother had not been hostile (speaking kindly to my friend like a mother whose son has been seriously wounded and who is grateful to the young mistress who is nursing him with loving care), she had acquired hostility now that it had been too completely realised, and the girl was prolonging her sojourn in our house, and moreover in the absence of my parents. I cannot, however, say that my mother ever made this hostility apparent. As in the past, when she had ceased to dare to reproach me with my nervous instability, my laziness, now she felt a hesitation—which I perhaps did not altogether perceive at the moment or refused to perceive—to run the risk, by offering any criticism of the girl to whom I had told her that I intended to make an offer of marriage, of bringing a shadow into my life, making me in time to come less devoted to my wife, of sowing perhaps for a season when she herself would no longer be there, the seeds of remorse at having grieved her by marrying Albertine. Mamma preferred to seem to be approving a choice which she felt herself powerless to make me reconsider. But people who came in contact with her at this time have since told me that in addition to her grief at having lost her mother she had an air of constant preoccupation. This mental strife, this inward debate, had the effect of overheating my mother's brow, and she was always opening the windows to let in the fresh air. But she did not succeed in coming to any decision, for fear of influencing me in the wrong direction and so spoiling what she believed to be my happiness. She could not even bring herself to forbid me to keep Albertine for the time being in our house. She did not wish to appear more strict than Mme. Bontemps, who was the person principally concerned, and who saw no harm in the arrangement, which greatly surprised my mother. All the same, she regretted that she had been obliged to leave us together, by departing at that very time for Combray where she might have to remain (and did in

7

fact remain) for months on end, during which my great-aunt required her incessant attention by day and night. Everything was made easy for her down there, thanks to the kindness, the devotion of Legrandin who, gladly undertaking any trouble that was required, kept putting off his return to Paris from week to week, not that he knew my aunt at all well, but simply, first of all, because she had been his mother's friend, and also because he knew that the invalid, condemned to die, valued his attentions and could not get on without him. Snobbishness is a serious malady of the spirit, but one that is localised and does not taint it as a whole. I, on the other hand, unlike Mamma, was extremely glad of her absence at Combray, but for which I should have been afraid (being unable to warn Albertine not to mention it) of her learning of the girl's friendship with Mlle. Vinteuil. This would have been to my mother an insurmountable obstacle, not merely to a marriage as to which she had, for that matter, begged me to say nothing definite as yet to Albertine, and the thought of which was becoming more and more intolerable to myself, but even to the latter's being allowed to stay for any length of time in the house. Apart from so grave a reason, which in this case did not apply, Mamma, under the dual influence of my grandmother's liberating and edifying example, according to whom, in her admiration of George Sand, virtue consisted in nobility of heart, and of my own corruption, was now indulgent towards women whose conduct she would have condemned in the past, or even now, had they been any of her own middle-class friends in Paris or at Combray, but whose lofty natures I extolled to her and to whom she pardoned much because of their affection for myself.

But when all is said, and apart from any question of propriety, I doubt whether Albertine could have put up with Mamma who had acquired from Combray, from my aunt Léonie, from all her kindred, habits of punctuality and order of which my mistress had not the remotest conception.

She would never think of shutting a door and, on the other hand, would no more hesitate to enter a room if the door stood open than would a dog or a cat. Her somewhat disturbing charm was, in fact, that of taking the place in the household not so much of a girl as of a domestic animal which comes into a room, goes out, is to be found wherever one does not expect to find it and (in her case) would—bringing me a profound sense of repose—come and lie down on my bed by my side, make a place for herself from which she never stirred, without being in my way as a person would have been. She ended, however, by conforming to my hours of sleep, and not only never attempted to enter my room but would take care not to make a sound until I had rung my bell. It was Françoise who impressed these rules of conduct upon her.

She was one of those Combray servants, conscious of their master's place in the world, and that the least that they can do is to see that he is treated with all the respect to which they consider him entitled. When a stranger on leaving after a visit gave Françoise a gratuity to be shared with the kitchenmaid, he had barely slipped his coin into her hand before Françoise, with an equal display of speed, discretion and energy, had passed the word to the kitchenmaid who came forward to thank him, not in a whisper, but openly and aloud, as Françoise had told

9

her that she must do. The parish priest of Combray was no genius, but he also knew what was due to him. Under his instruction, the daughter of some Protestant cousins of Mme. Sazerat had been received into the Church, and her family had been most grateful to him: it was a question of her marriage to a young nobleman of Méséglise. The young man's relatives wrote to inquire about her in a somewhat arrogant letter, in which they expressed their dislike of her Protestant origin. The Combray priest replied in such a tone that the Méséglise nobleman, crushed and prostrate, wrote a very different letter in which he begged as the most precious favour the award of the girl's hand in marriage.

Françoise deserved no special credit for making Albertine respect my slumbers. She was imbued with tradition. From her studied silence, or the peremptory response that she made to a proposal to enter my room, or to send in some message to me, which Albertine had expressed in all innocence, the latter realised with astonishment that she was now living in an alien world, where strange customs prevailed, governed by rules of conduct which one must never dream of infringing. She had already had a foreboding of this at Balbec, but, in Paris, made no attempt to resist, and would wait patiently every morning for the sound of my bell before venturing to make any noise.

The training that Françoise gave her was of value also to our old servant herself, for it gradually stilled the lamentations which, ever since our return from Balbec, she had not ceased to utter. For, just as we were boarding the tram, she remembered that she had forgotten to say good-bye to the housekeeper of the Hotel, a whiskered dame who looked after the bedroom floors, barely knew Françoise by sight, but had been comparatively civil to her. Françoise positively insisted upon getting out of the tram, going back to the Hotel, saying good-bye properly to the housekeeper, and not leaving for Paris until the following day. Common sense, coupled with my sudden horror of Balbec, restrained me from granting her this concession, but my refusal had infected her with a feverish distemper which the change of air had not sufficed to cure and which lingered on in Paris. For, according to Françoise's code, as it is illustrated in the carvings of Saint-André-des-Champs, to wish for the death of an enemy, even to inflict it is not forbidden, but it is a horrible sin not to do what is expected of you, not to return a civility, to refrain, like a regular churl, from saying good-bye to the housekeeper before leaving a hotel. Throughout the journey, the continually recurring memory of her not having taken leave of this woman had dyed Françoise's cheeks with a scarlet flush that was quite alarming. And if she refused to taste bite or sup until we reached Paris, it was perhaps because this memory heaped a "regular load" upon her stomach (every class of society has a pathology of its own) even more than with the intention of punishing us.

Among the reasons which led Mamma to write me a daily letter, and a letter which never failed to include some quotation from Mme. de Sévigné, there was the memory of my grandmother. Mamma would write to me: "Mme. Sazerat gave us one of those little luncheons of which she possesses the secret and which, as your poor grandmother would have said, quoting Mme. de Sévigné, deprive us of solitude without affording us company." In one of my own earlier letters I was so inept as to write to Mamma: "By those quotations, your mother would recognise you at once." Which brought me, three days later, the reproof: "My poor boy, if it was only to speak to me of *my mother*, your reference to Mme. de Sévigné was most inappropriate. She would have answered you as she answered Mme. de Grignan: 'So she was nothing to you? I had supposed that you were related.'"

By this time, I could hear my mistress leaving or returning to her room. I rang the bell, for it was time now for Andrée to arrive with the chauffeur, Morel's friend, lent me by the Verdurins, to take Albertine out. I had spoken to the last-named of the remote possibility of our marriage; but I had never made her any formal promise; she herself, from discretion, when I said to her: "I can't tell, but it might perhaps be possible," had shaken her head with a melancholy sigh, as much as to say: "Oh, no, never," in other words: "I am too poor." And so, while I continued to say: "It is quite indefinite," when speaking of future projects, at the moment I was doing everything in my power to amuse her, to make life pleasant to her, with perhaps the unconscious design of thereby making her wish to marry me. She herself laughed at my lavish generosity. "Andrée's mother would be in a fine state if she saw me turn into a rich lady like herself, what she calls a lady who has her own 'horses, carriages, pictures.' What? Did I never tell you that she says that. Oh, she's a character! What surprises me is that she seems to think pictures just as important as horses and carriages." We shall see in due course that, notwithstanding the foolish ways of speaking that she had not outgrown, Albertine had developed to an astonishing extent, which left me unmoved, the intellectual superiority of a woman friend having always interested me so little that if I have ever complimented any of my friends upon her own, it was purely out of politeness. Alone, the curious genius of Céleste might perhaps appeal to me. In spite of myself, I would continue to smile for some moments, when, for instance, having discovered that Françoise was not in my room, she accosted me with: " Heavenly deity reclining on a bed!" "But why, Céleste," I would say, "why deity?" "Oh, if you suppose that you have anything in common with the mortals who make their pilgrimage on our vile earth, you are greatly mistaken!" "But why 'reclining' on a bed, can't you see that I'm lying in bed?" "You never lie. Who ever saw anybody lie like that? You have just alighted there. With your white pyjamas, and the way you twist your neck, you look for all the world like a dove."

Albertine, even in the discussion of the most trivial matters, expressed herself very differently from the little girl that she had been only a few years earlier at Balbec. She went so far as to declare, with regard to a political incident of which she disapproved: "I consider that ominous." And I am not sure that it was not about this time that she learned to say, when she meant that she felt a book to be written in a bad style: " It is interesting, but really, it might have been written *by a pig*."

The rule that she must not enter my room until I had rung amused her greatly. As she had adopted our family habit of quotation, and in following it drew upon the plays in which she had acted at her convent and for which I had expressed admiration, she always compared me to Assuérus:

> And death is the reward of whoso dares
> To venture in his presence unawares. . . .
> None is exempt; nor is there any whom
> Or rank or sex can save from such a doom;
> Even I myself . . .
> Like all the rest, I by this law am bound;
> And, to address him, I must first be found
> By him, or he must call me to his side.

Physically, too, she had altered. Her blue, almond-shaped eyes, grown longer, had not kept their form; they were indeed of the same colour, but seemed to have passed into a liquid state. So much so that, when she shut them it was as though a pair of curtains had been drawn to shut out a view of the sea. It was no doubt this one of her features that I remembered most vividly each night after we had parted. For, on the contrary, every morning the ripple of her hair continued to give me the same surprise, as though it were some novelty that I had never seen before. And yet, above the smiling eyes of a girl, what could be more beautiful than that clustering coronet of black violets? The smile offers greater friendship; but the little gleaming tips of blossoming hair, more akin to the flesh, of which they seem to be a transposition into tiny waves, are more provocative of desire.

As soon as she entered my room, she sprang upon my bed and sometimes would expatiate upon my type of intellect, would vow in a transport of sincerity that she would sooner die than leave me: this was on mornings when I had shaved before sending for her. She was one of those women who can never distinguish the cause of their sensations. The pleasure that they derive from a smooth cheek they explain to themselves by the moral qualities of the man who seems to offer them a possibility of future happiness, which is capable, however, of diminishing and becoming less necessary the longer he refrains from shaving.

I inquired where she was thinking of going.

"I believe Andrée wants to take me to the Buttes-Chaumont; I have never been there."

Of course it was impossible for me to discern among so many other words whether beneath these a falsehood lay concealed. Besides, I could trust Andrée to tell me of all the places that she visited with Albertine.

At Balbec, when I felt that I was utterly tired of Albertine, I had made up my mind to say, untruthfully, to Andrée: "My little Andrée, if only I had met you again sooner! It is you that I would have loved. But now my heart is pledged in another quarter. All the same, we can see a great deal of each other, for my love for another is causing me great anxiety, and you will help me to find consolation." And lo, these identical lying words had become true within the space of three weeks. Perhaps, Andrée had believed in Paris that it was indeed a lie and that I was in love with her, as she would doubtless have believed at Balbec. For the truth is so variable for each of us, that other people have difficulty in recognising themselves in it. And as I knew that she would tell me everything that she and Albertine had done, I had asked her, and she had agreed to come and call for Albertine almost every day. In this way I might without anxiety remain at home.

Also, Andrée's privileged position as one of the girls

of the little band gave me confidence that she would obtain everything that I might require from Albertine. Truly, I could have said to her now in all sincerity that she would be capable of setting my mind at rest.

At the same time, my choice of Andrée (who happened to be staying in Paris, having given up her plan of returning to Balbec) as guide and companion to my mistress was prompted by what Albertine had told me of the affection that her friend had felt for me at Balbec, at a time when, on the contrary, I had supposed that I was boring her; indeed, if I had known this at the time, it is perhaps with Andrée that I would have fallen in love.

"What, you never knew," said Albertine, "but we were always joking about it. Do you mean to say you never noticed how she used to copy all your ways of talking and arguing? When she had just been with you, it was too obvious. She had no need to tell us whether she had seen you. As soon as she joined us, we could tell at once. We used to look at one another, and laugh. She was like a coalheaver who tries to pretend that he isn't one. He is black all over. A miller has no need to say that he is a miller, you can see the flour all over his clothes; and the mark of the sacks he has carried on his shoulder. Andrée was just the same, she would knit her eyebrows the way you do, and stretch out her long neck, and I don't know what all. When I take up a book that has been in your room, even if I'm reading it out of doors, I can tell at once that it belongs to you because it still reeks of your beastly fumigations. It's only a trifle, still it's rather a nice trifle, don't you know. Whenever anybody spoke nicely about you, seemed to think a lot of you, Andrée was in ecstasies."

Notwithstanding all this, in case there might have been some secret plan made behind my back, I advised her to give up the Buttes-Chaumont for that day and to go instead to Saint-Cloud or somewhere else.

It was certainly not, as I was well aware, because I was the least bit in love with Albertine. Love is nothing more perhaps than the stimulation of those eddies which, in the wake of an emotion, stir the soul. Certain such eddies had indeed stirred my soul through and through when Albertine spoke to me at Balbec about Mlle. Vinteuil, but these were now stilled. I was no longer in love with Albertine, for I no longer felt anything of the suffering, now healed, which I had felt in the tram at Balbec, upon learning how Albertine had spent her girlhood, with visits perhaps to Montjouvain. All this, I had too long taken for granted, was healed. But, now and again, certain expressions used by Albertine made me suppose— why, I cannot say—that she must in the course of her life, short as it had been, have received declarations of affection, and have received them with pleasure, that is to say with sensuality. Thus, she would say, in any connexion: "Is that true? Is it really true?" Certainly, if she had said, like an Odette: "Is it really true, that thumping lie?" I should not have been disturbed, for the absurdity of the formula would have explained itself as a stupid inanity of feminine wit. But her questioning air: "Is that true?" gave on the one hand the strange impression of a creature incapable of judging things by herself, who appeals to you for your testimony, as though she were not endowed with the same faculties as yourself (if you said to her: "Why, we've been out for a whole hour," or "It is raining," she would ask: "Is that true?"). Unfortunately, on the other hand, this want of facility in judging external phenomena for herself could not be the real origin of her "Is that true? Is it really true?" It seemed rather that these words had been, from the dawn of her precocious adolescence, replies to: "You know, I never saw anybody as pretty as you." "You know I am madly in love with you, I am most terribly excited."—affirmations that were answered, with a coquettishly consenting modesty, by these repetitions of: "Is that true? Is it really true?" which no longer served Albertine, when in my company, save to reply by a question to some such affirmation as: "You have been asleep for more than an hour." "Is that true?"

Without feeling that I was the least thing in the world in love with Albertine, without including in the list of my pleasures the moments that we spent together, I was still preoccupied with the way in which she disposed of her time; had I not, indeed, fled from Balbec in order to make certain that she could no longer meet this or that person with whom I was so afraid of her misbehaving, simply as a joke (a joke at my expense, perhaps), that I had adroitly planned to sever, at one and the same time, by my departure, all her dangerous entanglements? And Albertine was so entirely passive, had so complete a faculty of forgetting things and submitting to pressure, that these relations had indeed been severed and I myself relieved of my haunting dread. But that dread is capable of assuming as many forms as the undefined evil that is its cause. So long as my jealousy was not reincarnate in fresh people, I had enjoyed after the passing of my anguish an interval of calm. But with a chronic malady, the slightest pretext serves to revive it, as also with the vice of the person who is the cause of our jealousy the slightest opportunity may serve her to practise it anew (after a lull of chastity) with different people. I had managed to separate Albertine from her accomplices, and, by so doing, to exorcise my hallucinations; even if it was possible to make her forget people, to cut short her attachments, her sensual inclination was, itself also, chronic and was perhaps only waiting for an opportunity to afford itself an outlet. Now Paris provided just as many opportunities as Balbec.

In any town whatsoever, she had no need to seek, for the evil existed not in Albertine alone, but in others to whom any opportunity for enjoyment is good. A glance from one, understood at once by the other, brings the two famished souls in contact. And it is easy for a clever woman to appear not to have seen, then five minutes later to join the person who has read her glance and is waiting for her in a side street, and, in a few words, to make an appointment. Who will ever know? And it was so simple for Albertine to tell me, in order that she might continue these practices, that she was anxious to see again some place on the outskirts of Paris that she had liked. And so it was enough that she should return later than usual, that her expedition should have taken an unaccountable time, although it was perfectly easy perhaps to account for it without introducing any sensual reason, for my malady to break out afresh, attached this time to mental pictures which were not of Balbec, and which I would set to work, as with their predecessors, to destroy, as though the destruction of an ephemeral cause could put an end to a congenital malady. I did not take into account the fact that in these acts of destruction, in

which I had as an accomplice, in Albertine, her faculty
of changing, her ability to forget, almost to hate the recent
object of her love, I was sometimes causing a profound
grief to one or other of those persons unknown with whom
in turn she had taken her pleasure, and that this grief I
was causing them in vain, for they would be abandoned,
replaced, and, parallel to the path strewn with all the
derelicts of her light-hearted infidelities, there would open
for me another, pitiless path broken only by an occasional
brief respite; so that my suffering could end only with Albertine's life or with my own. Even in the first days
after our return to Paris, not satisfied by the information
that Andrée and the chauffeur had given me as to their
expeditions with my mistress, I had felt the neighbourhood of Paris to be as tormenting as that of Balbec, and
had gone off for a few days in the country with Albertine.
But everywhere my uncertainty as to what she might be
doing was the same; the possibility that it was something
wrong as abundant, vigilance even more difficult, with
the result that I returned with her to Paris. In leaving
Balbec, I had imagined that I was leaving Gomorrah,
plucking Albertine from it; in reality, alas, Gomorrah was
dispersed to all the ends of the earth. And partly out of
jealousy, partly out of ignorance of such joys (a case
which is rare indeed), I had arranged unawares this
game of hide and seek in which Albertine was always to
escape me.

I questioned her point-blank: "Oh, by the way, Albertine, am I dreaming, or did you tell me that you knew
Gilberte Swann?" "Yes; that is to say, she used to
talk to me at our classes, because she had a set of the
French history notes, in fact she was very nice about it,

and let me borrow them, and I gave them back the next time I saw her." "Is she the kind of woman that I object to?" "Oh, not at all, quite the opposite." But, rather than indulge in this sort of criminal investigation, I would often devote to imagining Albertine's excursion the energy that I did not employ in sharing it, and would speak to my mistress with that ardour which remains intact in our unfulfilled designs. I expressed so keen a longing to see once again some window in the Sainte-Chapelle, so keen a regret that I was not able to go there with her alone, that she said to me lovingly: "Why, my dear boy, since you seem so keen about it, make a little effort, come with us. We can start as late as you like, whenever you're ready. And if you'ld rather be alone with me, I have only to send Andrée home, she can come another time." But these very entreaties to me to go out added to the calm which allowed me to yield to my desire to remain indoors.

It did not occur to me that the apathy that was indicated by my delegating thus to Andrée or the chauffeur the task of soothing my agitation by leaving them to keep watch over Albertine, was paralysing in me, rendering inert all those imaginative impulses of the mind, all those inspirations of the will, which enable us to guess, to forestall, what some one else is about to do; indeed the world of possibilities has always been more open to me than that of real events. This helps us to understand the human heart, but we are apt to be taken in by individuals. My jealousy was born of mental images, a form of self torment not based upon probability. Now there may occur in the lives of men and of nations (and there was to occur, one day, in my own life) a moment when we need to have within us a superintendent of police, a clear-sighted diplomat, a master-detective, who instead of pondering over the concealed possibilities that extend to all the points of the compass, reasons accurately, says to himself: "If Germany announces this, it means that she intends to do something else, not just 'something' in the abstract but precisely this or that or the other, which she may perhaps have begun already to do." "If so-and-so has fled, it is not in the direction *a* or *b* or *d*, but to the point *c*, and the place to which we must direct our search for him is *c*." Alas, this faculty which was not highly developed in me, I allowed to grow slack, to lose its power, to vanish, by acquiring the habit of growing calm the moment that other people were engaged in keeping watch on my behalf.

As for the reason for my reluctance to leave the house, I should not have liked to explain it to Albertine. I told her that the doctor had ordered me to stay in bed. This was not true. And if it had been true, his prescription would have been powerless to prevent me from accompanying my mistress. I asked her to excuse me from going out with herself and Andrée. I shall mention only one of my reasons, which was dictated by prudence. Whenever I went out with Albertine, if she left my side for a moment, I became anxious, began to imagine that she had spoken to, or simply cast a glance at somebody. If she was not in the best of tempers, I thought that I was causing her to miss or to postpone some appointment. Reality is never more than an allurement to an unknown element in quest of which we can never progress very far. It is better not to know, to think as little as possible, not to feed our jealousy with the slightest concrete detail.

Unfortunately, even when we eliminate the outward life, incidents are created by the inward life also; though I held aloof from Albertine's expeditions, the random course of my solitary reflexions furnished me at times with those tiny fragments of the truth which attract to themselves, like a magnet, an inkling of the unknown, which, from that moment, becomes painful. Even if we live in a hermetically sealed compartment, associations of ideas, memories continue to act upon us. But these internal shocks did not occur immediately; no sooner had Albertine started on her drive than I was revivified, were it only for a few moments, by the stimulating virtues of solitude.

I took my share of the pleasures of the new day; the arbitrary desire—the capricious and purely spontaneous inclination to taste them would not have sufficed to place them within my reach, had not the peculiar state of the weather not merely reminded me of their images in the past but affirmed their reality in the present, immediately accessible to all men whom a contingent and consequently negligible circumstance did not compel to remain at home. On certain fine days the weather was so cold, one was in such full communication with the street that it seemed as though a breach had been made in the outer walls of the house, and, whenever a tramcar passed, the sound of its bell throbbed like that of a silver knife striking a wall of glass. But it was most of all in myself that I heard, with intoxication, a new sound rendered by the hidden violin. Its strings are tightened or relaxed by mere changes of temperature, of light, in the world outside. In our person, an instrument which the uniformity of habit has rendered silent, song is born of these digressions, these variations, the source of all music: the change of climate on certain days makes us pass at once from one note to another. We recapture the forgotten air the mathematical inevitability of which we might have deduced, and which for the first few moments we sing without recognising it. By themselves these modifications (which, albeit coming from without, were internal) refashioned for me the world outside. Communicating doors, long barred, opened themselves in my brain. The life of certain towns, the gaiety of certain expeditions resumed their place in my consciousness. All athrob in harmony with the vibrating string, I would have sacrificed my dull life in the past, and all my life to come, erased with the india-rubber of habit, for one of these special, unique moments.

If I had not gone out with Albertine on her long drive, my mind would stray all the farther afield, and, because I had refused to savour with my senses this particular morning, I enjoyed in imagination all the similar mornings, past or possible, or more precisely a certain type of morning of which all those of the same kind were but the intermittent apparition which I had at once recognised; for the keen air blew the book open of its own accord at the right page, and I found clearly set out before my eyes, so that I might follow it from my bed, the Gospel for the day. This ideal morning filled my mind full of a permanent reality, identical with all similar mornings, and infected me with a cheerfulness which my physical ill-health did not diminish: for, inasmuch as our sense of wellbeing is caused not so much by our sound health as by the unemployed surplus of our strength, we can attain to it, just as much as by increasing our strength, by diminishing our activity. The activity with which I was overflowing and which I kept constantly charged as I lay in bed, made me spring from side to side, with a leaping heart, like a machine which, prevented from moving in space, rotates on its own axis.

Françoise came in to light the fire, and to make it draw, threw upon it a handful of twigs, the scent of which, forgotten for a year past, traced round the fireplace a magic circle within which, perceiving myself poring over a book, now at Combray, now at Doncières, I was as joyful, while remaining in my bedroom in Paris, as if I had been on the point of starting for a walk along the Méséglise way, or of going to join Saint-Loup and his friends on the training-ground. It often happens that the pleasure which everyone takes in turning over the keepsakes that his memory has collected is keenest in those whom the tyranny of bodily ill-health and the daily hope of recovery prevent, on the one hand, from going out to seek in nature scenes that resemble those memories, and, on the other hand, leave so convinced that they will shortly be able to do so that they can remain gazing at them in a state of desire, of appetite, and not regard them merely as memories, as pictures. But, even if they were never to be anything more than memories to me, even if I, as I recalled them, saw merely pictures, immediately they recreated in me, of me as a whole, by virtue of an identical sensation, the boy, the youth who had first seen them. There had been not merely a change in the weather outside, or, inside the room, the introduction of a fresh scent, there had been in myself a difference of age, the substitution of another person. The scent, in the frosty air, of the twigs of brushwood, was like a fragment of the past, an invisible floe broken off from the ice of an old winter that stole into my room, often variegated moreover with this perfume or that light, as though with a sequence of different years, in which I found myself plunged, overwhelmed, even before I had identified them, by the eagerness of hopes long since abandoned. The sun's rays fell upon my bed and passed through the transparent shell of my attenuated body, warmed me, made me as hot as a sheet of scorching crystal. Whereupon, a famished convalescent who has already begun to batten upon all the dishes that are still forbidden him, I asked myself whether marriage with Albertine would not spoil my life, as well by making me assume the burden, too heavy for my shoulders, of consecrating myself to another person, as by forcing me to live in absence from myself because of her continual presence and depriving me, forever, of the delights of solitude.

And not of these alone. Even when we ask of the day nothing but desires, there are some—those that are excited not by things but by people—whose character it is to be unlike any other. If, on rising from my bed, I went to the window and drew the curtain aside for a moment, it was not merely, as a pianist for a moment turns back the lid of his instrument, to ascertain whether, on the balcony and in the street, the sunlight was tuned to exactly the same pitch as in my memory, it was also to catch a glimpse of some laundress carrying her linen-basket, a bread-seller in her blue apron, a dairymaid in her tucker and sleeves of white linen, carrying the yoke from which her jugs of milk are suspended, some haughty golden-haired miss escorted by her governess, a composite image, in short, which the differences of outline, numerically perhaps insignificant, were enough to make as

26

different from any other as, in a phrase of music, the difference between two notes, an image but for the vision of which I should have impoverished my day of the objects which it might have to offer to my desires of happiness. But, if the surfeit of joy, brought me by the spectacle of women whom it was impossible to imagine *a priori,* made more desirable, more deserving of exploration, the street, the town, the world, it set me longing, for that very reason, to recover my health, to go out of doors and, without Albertine, to be a free man. How often, at the moment when the unknown woman who was to haunt my dreams passed beneath the window, now on foot, now at the full speed of her motor-car, was I made wretched that my body could not follow my gaze which kept pace with her, and falling upon her as though shot from the embrasure of my window by an arquebus, arrest the flight of the face that held out for me the offer of a happiness which, cloistered thus, I should never know.

Of Albertine, on the other hand, I had nothing more to learn. Every day, she seemed to me less attractive. Only, the desire that she aroused in other people, when, upon hearing of it, I began to suffer afresh and was impelled to challenge their possession of her, raised her in my sight to a lofty pinnacle. Pain, she was capable of causing me; joy, never. Pain alone kept my tedious attachment alive. As soon as my pain vanished, and with it the need to soothe it, requiring all my attention, like some agonising distraction, I felt that she meant absolutely nothing to me, that I must mean absolutely nothing to her. It made me wretched that this state should persist, and, at certain moments, I longed to hear of something terrible that she had done, something that would be capable of keeping us at armslength until I was cured, so that we might then be able to be reconciled, to refashion in a different and more flexible form the chain that bound us.

In the meantime, I was employing a thousand circumstances, a thousand pleasures to procure for her in my society the illusion of that happiness which I did not feel myself capable of giving her. I should have liked, as soon as I was cured, to set off for Venice, but how was I to manage it, if I married Albertine, I, who was so jealous of her that even in Paris whenever I decided to stir from my room it was to go out with her? Even when I stayed in the house all the afternoon, my thoughts accompanied her on her drive, traced a remote, blue horizon, created round the centre that was myself a fluctuating zone of vague uncertainty. "How completely," I said to myself, "would Albertine spare me the anguish of separation if, in the course of one of these drives, seeing that I no longer say anything to her about marriage, she decided not to come back, and went off to her aunt's, without my having to bid her good-bye!" My heart, now that its scar had begun to heal, was ceasing to adhere to the heart of my mistress; I could by imagination shift her, separate her from myself without pain. No doubt, failing myself, some other man would be her husband, and in her freedom she would meet perhaps with those adventures which filled me with horror. But the day was so fine, I was so certain that she would return in the evening, that even if the idea of possible misbehaviour did enter my mind, I could, by an exercise of free will, imprison it in a part of my brain in which it had no more importance than would have had in my real life the vices of an imaginary person; bringing into play the supple hinges of my thought, I had, with an energy which I felt in my head to be at once physical and mental, as it were a muscular movement and a spiritual impulse, broken away from the state of perpetual preoccupation in which I had until then been confined, and was beginning to move in a free atmosphere, in which the idea of sacrificing everything in order to prevent Albertine from marrying some one else and to put an obstacle in the way of her fondness for women seemed as unreasonable to my own mind as to that of a person who had never known her.

However, jealousy is one of those intermittent maladies, the cause of which is capricious, imperative, always identical in the same patient, sometimes entirely different in another. There are asthmatic persons who can soothe their crises only by opening the windows, inhaling the full blast of the wind, the pure air of the mountains, others by taking refuge in the heart of the city, in a room heavy with smoke. Rare indeed is the jealous man whose jealousy does not allow certain concessions. One will consent to infidelity, provided that he is told of it, another provided that it is concealed from him, wherein they appear to be equally absurd, since if the latter is more literally deceived inasmuch as the truth is not disclosed to him, the other demands in that truth the food, the extension, the renewal of his sufferings.

What is more, these two parallel manias of jealousy extend often beyond words, whether they implore or reject confidences. We see a jealous lover who is jealous only of the women with whom his mistress has relations in his absence, but allows her to give herself to another man, if it is done with his authorisation, near at hand, and, if not actually before his eyes, under his roof. This case is not at all uncommon among elderly men who are in love with young women. Such a man feels the difficulty of winning her favour, sometimes his inability to satisfy her, and, rather than be betrayed, prefers to admit to his house, to an adjoining room, some man whom he considers incapable of giving her bad advice, but not incapable of giving her pleasure. With another man it is just the opposite; never allowing his mistress to go out by herself for a single minute in a town that he knows, he keeps her in a state of bondage, but allows her to go for a month to a place which he does not know, where he cannot form any mental picture of what she may be doing. I had with regard to Albertine both these sorts of sedative mania. I should not have been jealous if she had enjoyed her pleasures in my company, with my encouragement, pleasures over the whole of which I could have kept watch, thus avoiding any fear of falsehood; I might perhaps not have been jealous either if she had removed to a place so unfamiliar and remote that I could not imagine nor find any possibility, feel any temptation to know the manner of her life. In either alternative, my uncertainty would have been killed by a knowledge or an ignorance equally complete.

The decline of day plunging me back by an act of memory in a cool atmosphere of long ago, I breathed it with the same delight with which Orpheus inhaled the subtle air, unknown upon this earth, of the Elysian Fields.

But already the day was ending and I was overpowered by the desolation of the evening. Looking mechanically at the clock to see how many hours must elapse before Albertine's return, I saw that I had still time to dress and go downstairs to ask my landlady, Mme. de Guermantes, for particulars of various becoming garments which I was anxious to procure for my mistress. Sometimes I met the Duchess in the courtyard, going out for a walk, even if the weather was bad, in a close-fitting hat and furs. I knew quite well that, to many people of intelligence, she was merely a lady like any other, the name Duchesse de Guermantes signifying nothing, now that there are no longer any sovereign Duchies or Principalities, but I had adopted a different point of view in my method of enjoying people and places. All the castles of the territories of which she was Duchess, Princess, Viscountess, this lady in furs defying the weather seemed to me to be carrying them on her person, as a figure carved over the lintel of a church door holds in his hand the cathedral that he has built or the city that he has defended. But these castles, these forests, my mind's eye alone could discern them in the left hand of the lady in furs, whom the King called cousin. My bodily eyes distinguished in it only, on days when the sky was threatening, an umbrella with which the Duchess was not afraid to arm herself. "One can never be certain, it is wiser, I may find myself miles from home, with a cabman demanding a fare *beyond my means*." The words "too dear" and "beyond my means" kept recurring all the time in the Duchess's conversation, as did also: "I am too poor"—without its being possible to decide whether she spoke thus because she thought it amusing to say that she was poor, being so rich, or because she thought it smart, being so aristocratic, in spite of her affectation of peasant ways, not to attach to riches the importance that people give them who are merely rich and nothing else, and who look down upon the poor. Perhaps it was, rather, a habit contracted at a time in her life when, already rich, but not rich enough to satisfy her needs, considering the expense of keeping up all those properties, she felt a certain shortage of money which she did not wish to appear to be concealing. The things about which we most often jest are generally, on the contrary, the things that embarrass us, but we do not wish to appear to be embarrassed by them, and feel perhaps a secret hope of the further advantage that the person to whom we are talking, hearing us treat the matter as a joke, will conclude that it is not true.

But upon most evenings, at this hour, I could count upon finding the Duchess at home, and I was glad of this, for it was more convenient for me to ask her in detail for the information that Albertine required. And down I went almost without thinking how extraordinary it was that I should be calling upon that mysterious Mme. de Guermantes of my boyhood, simply in order to make use of her for a practical purpose, as one makes use of the telephone, a supernatural instrument before whose miracles we used to stand amazed, and which we now employ without giving it a thought, to summon our tailor or to order ices for a party.

Albertine delighted in any sort of finery. I could not deny myself the pleasure of giving her some new trifle every day. And whenever she had spoken to me with rapture of a scarf, a stole, a sunshade which, from the window or as they passed one another in the courtyard, her eyes that so quickly distinguished anything smart, had seen round the throat, over the shoulders, in the hand of Mme. de Guermantes, knowing how the girl's naturally fastidious taste (refined still further by the lessons in elegance of attire which Elstir's conversation had been to her) would not be at all satisfied by any mere substitute, even of a pretty thing, such as fills its place in the eyes of the common herd, but differs from it entirely, I went in secret to make the Duchess explain to me where, how, from what model the article had been created that had taken Albertine's fancy, how I should set about to obtain one exactly similar, in what the creator's secret, the charm (what Albertine called the "*chic*," the "style") of his manner, the precise name—the beauty of the material being of importance also—and quality of the stuffs that I was to insist upon their using.

When I mentioned to Albertine, on our return from Balbec, that the Duchess de Guermantes lived opposite to us, in the same mansion, she had assumed, on hearing the proud title and great name, that air more than indifferent, hostile, contemptuous, which is the sign of an impotent desire in proud and passionate natures. Splendid as Albertine's nature might be, the fine qualities which it contained were free to develop only amid those hindrances which are our personal tastes, or that lamentation for those of our tastes which we have been obliged to relinquish—in Albertine's case snobbishness—which is called antipathy. Albertine's antipathy to people in society occupied, for that matter, but a very small part in her nature, and appealed to me as an aspect of the revolutionary spirit—that is to say an embittered love of the nobility—engraved upon the opposite side of the

French character to that which displays the aristocratic manner of Mme. de Guermantes. To this aristocratic manner Albertine, in view of the impossibility of her acquiring it, would perhaps not have given a thought, but remembering that Elstir had spoken to her of the Duchess as the best dressed woman in Paris, her republican contempt for a Duchess gave place in my mistress to a keen interest in a fashionable woman. She was always asking me to tell her about Mme. de Guermantes, and was glad that I should go to the Duchess to obtain advice as to her own attire. No doubt I might have got this from Mme. Swann and indeed I did once write to her with this intention. But Mme. de Guermantes seemed to me to carry to an even higher pitch the art of dressing. If, on going down for a moment to call upon her, after making sure that she had not gone out and leaving word that I was to be told as soon as Albertine returned, I found the Duchess swathed in the mist of a garment of grey crêpe de Chine, I accepted this aspect of her which I felt to be due to complex causes and to be quite inevitable, I let myself be overpowered by the atmosphere which it exhaled, like that of certain late afternoons cushioned in pearly grey by a vaporous fog; if, on the other hand, her indoor gown was Chinese with red and yellow flames, I gazed at it as at a glowing sunset; these garments were not a casual decoration alterable at her pleasure, but a definite and poetical reality like that of the weather, or the light peculiar to a certain hour of the day.

Of all the outdoor and indoor gowns that Mme. de Guermantes wore, those which seemed most to respond to a definite intention, to be endowed with a special significance, were the garments made by Fortuny from old Venetian models. Is it their historical character, is it rather the fact that each one of them is unique that gives them so special a significance that the pose of the woman who is wearing one while she waits for you to appear or while she talks to you assumes an exceptional importance, as though the costume had been the fruit of a long deliberation and your conversation was detached from the current of everyday life like a scene in a novel? In the novels of Balzac, we see his heroines purposely put on one or another dress on the day on which they are expecting some particular visitor. The dresses of to-day have less character, always excepting the creations of Fortuny. There is no room for vagueness in the novelist's description, since the gown does really exist, and the merest sketch of it is as naturally preordained as a copy of a work of art. Before putting on one or another of them, the woman has had to make a choice between two garments, not more or less alike but each one profoundly individual, and answering to its name. But the dress did not prevent me from thinking of the woman.

Indeed, Mme. de Guermantes seemed to me at this time more attractive than in the days when I was still in love with her. Expecting less of her (whom I no longer went to visit for her own sake), it was almost with the ease and comfort of a man in a room by himself, with his feet on the fender, that I listened to her as though I were reading a book written in the speech of long ago. My mind was sufficiently detached to enjoy in what she said that pure charm of the French language which we no longer find either in the speech or in the literature of the present day. I listened to her conversation as to a folk song deliciously and purely French, I realised that I would have allowed her to belittle Maeterlinck (whom for that matter she now admired, from a feminine weakness of intellect, influenced by those literary fashions whose rays spread slowly), as I realised that Mérimée had belittled Baudelaire, Stendhal Balzac, Paul-Louis Courier Victor Hugo, Meilhac Mallarmé. I realised that the critic had a far more restricted outlook than his victim, but also a purer vocabulary. That of Mme. de Guermantes, almost as much as that of Saint-Loup's mother, was purified to an enchanting degree. It is not in the bloodless formulas of the writers of to-day, who say: *au fait* (for "in reality"), *singulièrement* (for "in particular"), *étonné* (for "struck with amazement"), and the like, that we recapture the old speech and the true pronunciation of words, but in conversing with a Mme. de Guermantes or a Françoise; I had learned from the latter, when I was five years old, that one did not say "the Tarn" but "the Tar"; not "Béarn" but "Béar." The effect of which was that at twenty, when I began to go into society, I had no need to be taught there that one ought not to say, like Mme. Bontemps: "Madame de Béarn."

It would be untrue to pretend that of this territorial and semi-peasant quality which survived in her the Duchess was not fully conscious, indeed she displayed a certain affectation in emphasising it. But, on her part, this was not so much the false simplicity of a great lady aping the countrywoman or the pride of a Duchess bent upon snubbing the rich ladies who express contempt for the peasants whom they do not know as the almost artistic preference of a woman who knows the charm of what belongs to her, and is not going to spoil it with a coat of modern varnish. In the same way, everybody will remember at Dives a Norman innkeeper, landlord of the Guillaume le Conquérant, who carefully refrained— which is very rare—from giving his hostelry the modern comforts of an hotel, and, albeit a millionaire, retained the speech, the blouse of a Norman peasant and allowed you to enter his kitchen and watch him prepare with his own hands, as in a farmhouse, a dinner which was never-theless infinitely better and even more expensive than are the dinners in the most luxurious hotels.

All the local sap that survives in the old noble families is not enough, there must also be born of them a person of sufficient intelligence not to despise it, not to conceal it beneath the varnish of society. Mme. de Guermantes, unfortunately clever and Parisian, who, when I first knew her, retained nothing of her native soil but its accent, had at least, when she wished to describe her life as a girl, found for her speech one of those compromises (be-tween what would have seemed too spontaneously provin-cial on the one hand or artificially literary on the other), one of those compromises which form the attraction of George Sand's *La Petite Fadette* or of certain legends preserved by Chateaubriand in his *Mémoires d'Outre-Tombe*. My chief pleasure was in hearing her tell some anecdote which brought peasants into the picture with herself. The historic names, the old customs gave to these blendings of the castle with the village a distinctly attractive savour. Having remained in contact with the lands over which it once ruled, a certain class of the nobility has remained regional, with the result that the simplest remark unrolls before our eyes a political and physical map of the whole history of France.

If there was no affectation, no desire to fabricate a special language, then this manner of pronouncing words was a regular museum of French history displayed in conversation. "My great-uncle Fitt-jam" was not at all surprising, for we know that the Fitz-James family are proud to boast that they are French nobles, and do not like to hear their name pronounced in the English fashion. One must, incidentally, admire the touching docility of the people who had previously supposed themselves obliged to pronounce certain names phonetically, and who, all of a sudden, after hearing the Duchesse de Guermantes pronounce them otherwise, adopted the pronunciation which they could never have guessed. Thus the Duchess, who had had a great-grandfather in the suite of the Comte de Chambord, liked to tease her husband for having turned Orleanist by proclaiming: "We old Frochedorf people. . . ." The visitor, who had always imagined that he was correct in saying "Frohsdorf," at once turned his coat, and ever afterwards might be heard saying "Frochedorf."

On one occasion when I asked Mme. de Guermantes who a young blood was whom she had introduced to me as her nephew but whose name I had failed to catch, I was none the wiser when from the back of her throat the Duchess uttered in a very loud but quite inarticulate voice: "*C'est l'*... *i Eon*... *l*...*b*... *frère à Robert.* He makes out that he has the same shape of skull as the ancient Gauls." Then I realised that she had said: "*C'est le petit Léon,*" and that this was the Prince de Léon, who was indeed Robert de Saint-Loup's brother-in-law. "I know nothing about his skull," she went on, "but the way he dresses, and I must say he does dress quite well, is not at all in the style of those parts. Once when I was staying at Josselin, with the Rohans, we all went over to one of the pilgrimages, where there were peasants from every part of Brittany. A great hulking fellow from one of the Léon villages stood gaping open-mouthed at Robert's brother-in-law in his beige breeches! 'What are you staring at me like that for?' said Léon, 'I bet you don't know who I am?' The peasant admitted that he did not. 'Very well,' said Léon, 'I'm your Prince.' 'Oh!' said the peasant, taking off his cap and apologising. 'I thought you were an *Englische*.'"

And if, taking this opportunity, I led Mme. de Guermantes on to talk about the Rohans (with whom her own family had frequently intermarried), her conversation would become impregnated with a hint of the wistful charm of the Pardons, and (as that true poet Pampille would say) with "the harsh savour of pancakes of black grain fried over a fire of rushes."

Of the Marquis du Lau (whose tragic decline we all know, when, himself deaf, he used to be taken to call on Mme. H... who was blind), she would recall the less tragic years when, after the day's sport, at Guermantes, he would change into slippers before taking tea with the Prince of Wales, to whom he would not admit himself inferior, and with whom, as we see, he stood upon no ceremony. She described all this so picturesquely that she seemed to invest him with the plumed musketeer bonnet of the somewhat vainglorious gentlemen of the Périgord.

But even in the mere classification of different people, her care to distinguish and indicate their native provinces was in Mme. de Guermantes, when she was her natural self, a great charm which a Parisian-born woman could never have acquired, and those simple names Anjou, Poitou, the Périgord, filled her conversation with pictorial landscapes.

To revert to the pronunciation and vocabulary of Mme. de Guermantes, it is in this aspect that the nobility shews itself truly conservative, with everything that the word implies at once somewhat puerile and somewhat perilous, stubborn in its resistance to evolution but interesting also to an artist. I was anxious to know the original spelling of the name Jean. I learned it when I received a letter from a nephew of Mme. de Villeparisis who signs himself—as he was christened, as he figures in Gotha—Jehan de Villeparisis, with the same handsome, superfluous, heraldic H that we admire, illuminated in vermilion or ultramarine in a Book of Hours or in a window.

Unfortunately, I never had time to prolong these visits indefinitely, for I was anxious, if possible, not to return home after my mistress. But it was only in driblets that I was able to obtain from Mme. de Guermantes that information as to her garments which was of use in helping me to order garments similar in style, so far as it was possible for a young girl to wear them, for Albertine. "For instance, Madame, that evening when you dined with Mme. de Saint-Euverte, and then went on to the Princesse de Guermantes, you had a dress that was all red, with red shoes, you were marvellous, you reminded me of a sort of great blood-red blossom, a blazing ruby

—now, what was that dress? Is it the sort of thing that a girl can wear?"

The Duchess, imparting to her tired features the radiant expression that the Princesse des Laumes used to assume when Swann, in years past, paid her compliments, looked, with tears of merriment in her eyes, quizzingly, questioningly and delightedly at M. de Bréauté who was always there at that hour and who set beaming from behind his monocle a smile that seemed to pardon this outburst of intellectual trash for the sake of the physical excitement of youth which seemed to him to lie beneath it. The Duchess appeared to be saying: "What is the matter with him? He must be mad." Then turning to me with a coaxing air: "I wasn't aware that I looked like a blazing ruby or a blood-red blossom, but I do remember, as it happens, that I had on a red dress: it was red satin, which was being worn that season. Yes, a girl can wear that sort of thing at a pinch, but you told me that your friend never went out in the evening. That is a full evening dress, not a thing that she can put on to pay calls."

What is extraordinary is that of the evening in question, which after all was not so very remote, Mme. de Guermantes should remember nothing but what she had been wearing, and should have forgotten a certain incident which nevertheless, as we shall see presently, ought to have mattered to her greatly. It seems that among men and women of action (and people in society are men and women of action on a minute, a microscopic scale, but are nevertheless men and women of action), the mind, overcharged by the need of attending to what is going to happen in an hour's time, confides only a very few things to the memory. As often as not, for instance, it was not with the object of putting his questioner in the wrong and making himself appear not to have been mistaken that M. de Norpois, when you reminded him of the prophecies he had uttered with regard to an alliance with Germany of which nothing had ever come, would say: "You must be mistaken, I have no recollection of it whatever, it is not like me, for in that sort of conversation I am always most laconic, and I would never have predicted the success of one of those *coups d'éclat* which are often nothing more than *coups de tête* and almost always degenerate into *coups de force.* It is beyond question that in the remote future a Franco-German *rapprochement* might come into being and would be highly profitable to both countries, nor would France have the worse of the bargain, I dare say, but I have never spoken of it because the fruit is not yet ripe, and if you wish to know my opinion, in asking our late enemies to join with us in solemn wedlock, I consider that we should be setting out to meet a severe rebuff, and that the attempt could end only in disaster." In saying this M. de Norpois was not being untruthful, he had simply forgotten. We quickly forget what we have not deeply considered, what has been dictated to us by the spirit of imitation, by the passions of our neighbours. These change, and with them our memory undergoes alteration. Even more than diplomats, politicians are unable to remember the point of view which they adopted at a certain moment, and some of their palinodes are due less to a surfeit of ambition than to a shortage of memory. As for people in society, there are very few things that they remember.

Mme. de Guermantes assured me that, at the party to which she had gone in a red gown, she did not remember Mme. de Chaussepierre's being present, and that I must be mistaken. And yet, heaven knows, the Chaussepierres had been present enough in the minds of both Duke and Duchess since then. For the following reason. M. de Guermantes had been the senior vice-president of the Jockey, when the president died. Certain members of the club who were not popular in society and whose sole pleasure was to blackball the men who did not invite them to their houses started a campaign against the Duc de Guermantes who, certain of being elected, and relatively indifferent to the presidency which was a small matter for a man in his social position, paid no attention. It was urged against him that the Duchess was a Dreyfusard (the Dreyfus case had long been concluded, but twenty years later people were still talking about it, and so far only two years had elapsed), and entertained the Rothschilds, that too much consideration had been shewn of late to certain great international magnates like the Duc de Guermantes, who was half German. The campaign found its ground well prepared, clubs being always jealous of men who are in the public eye, and detesting great fortunes.

Chaussepierre's own fortune was no mere pittance, but nobody could take offence at it; he never spent a penny, the couple lived in a modest apartment, the wife went about dressed in black serge. A passionate music-lover, she did indeed give little afternoon parties to which many more singers were invited than to the Guermantes. But no one ever mentioned these parties, no refreshments were served, the husband did not put in an appearance even, and everything went off quite quietly in the obscurity of the Rue de la Chaise. At the Opera, Mme. de Chaussepierre passed unnoticed, always among people whose names recalled the most "die-hard" element of the intimate circle of Charles X, but people quite obsolete, who went nowhere. On the day of the election, to the general surprise, obscurity triumphed over renown: Chaussepierre, the second vice-president, was elected president of the Jockey, and the Duc de Guermantes was left sitting —that is to say, in the senior vice-president's chair. Of course, being president of the Jockey means little or nothing to Princes of the highest rank such as the Guermantes. But not to be it when it is your turn, to see preferred to you a Chaussepierre to whose wife Oriane, two years earlier, had not merely refused to bow but had taken offence that an unknown scarecrow like that should bow to her, this the Duke did find hard to endure. He pretended to be superior to this rebuff, asserting moreover that it was his long-standing friendship with Swann that was at the root of it. Actually, his anger never cooled.

One curious thing was that nobody had ever before heard the Duc de Guermantes make use of the quite commonplace expression "out and out," but ever since the Jockey election, whenever anybody referred to the Dreyfus case, pat would come "out and out." "Dreyfus case, Dreyfus case, that's soon said, and it's a misuse of the term. It is not a question of religion, it's *out and out* a political matter." Five years might go by without your hearing him say "out and out" again, if during that time nobody mentioned the Dreyfus case, but if, at the end of five years, the name Dreyfus cropped up, "out and

44

out" would at once follow automatically. The Duke could not, anyhow, bear to hear any mention of the case, "which has been responsible," he would say, "for so many disasters" albeit he was really conscious of one and one only; his own failure to become president of the Jockey. And so on the afternoon in question, when I reminded Madame de Guermantes of the red gown that she had worn at her cousin's party, M. de Bréauté was none too well received when, determined to say something, by an association of ideas which remained obscure and which he did not illuminate, he began, twisting his tongue about between his pursed lips: "Talking of the Dreyfus case—" (why in the world of the Dreyfus case, we were talking simply of a red dress, and certainly poor Bréauté, whose only desire was to make himself agreeable, can have had no malicious intention). But the mere name of Dreyfus made the Duc de Guermantes knit his Jupiterian brows. "I was told," Bréauté went on, "a jolly good thing, damned clever, 'pon my word, that was said by our friend Cartier" (we must warn the reader that this Cartier, Mme. de Villefranche's brother, was in no way related to the jeweller of that name) "not that I'm in the least surprised, for he's got plenty of brains to spare." "Oh!" broke in Oriane, "he can spare me his brains. I hardly like to tell you how much your friend Cartier has always bored me, and I have never been able to understand the boundless charm that Charles de La Trémoïlle and his wife seem to find in the creature, for I meet him there every time that I go to their house." "My dear Dutt-yess," replied Bréauté, who was unable to pronounce the soft *c*, "I think you are very hard upon Cartier. It is true that he has perhaps made himself rather too mutt-y-at home at the La Trémoïlles', but after all he does provide Tyarles with a sort of—what shall I say?—a sort of *fidus Achates,* which has become a very rare bird indeed in these days. Anyhow, this is the story as it was told to me. Cartier appears to have said that if M. Zola had gone out of his way to stand his trial and to be convicted, it was in order to enjoy the only sensation he had never yet tried, that of being in prison." " And so he ran away before they could arrest him," Oriane broke in. " Your story don't hold water. Besides, even if it was plausible, I think his remark absolutely idiotic. If that's what you call being witty! " " Good grate-ious, my dear Oriane," replied Bréauté who, finding himself contradicted, was beginning to lose confidence, " it's not my remark, I'm telling you it as it was told to me, take it for what it's worth. Anyhow, it earned M. Cartier a first rate blowing up from that excellent fellow La Trémoïlle who, and quite rightly, does not like people to discuss what one might call, so to speak, current events, in his drawing-room, and was all the more annoyed because Mme. Alphonse Rothschild was present. Cartier had to listen to a positive jobation from La Trémoïlle." " I should think so," said the Duke, in the worst of tempers, " the Alphonse Rothschilds, even if they have the tact never to speak of that abominable affair, are Dreyfusards at heart, like all the Jews. Indeed that is an argument *ad hominem* " (the Duke was a trifle vague in his use of the expression *ad hominem*) " which is not sufficiently made use of to prove the dishonesty of the Jews. If a Frenchman robs or murders somebody, I do not consider myself bound, because he is a Frenchman like myself, to find him innocent. But the Jews will never admit that one of their fellow-countrymen is a traitor, although they know it perfectly well, and never think of the terrible repercussions" (the Duke was thinking, naturally, of that accursed defeat by Chaussepierre) "which the crime of one of their people can bring even to . . . Come, Oriane, you're not going to pretend that it ain't damning to the Jews that they all support a traitor. You're not going to tell me that it ain't because they're Jews." "Of course not," retorted Oriane (feeling, with a trace of irritation, a certain desire to hold her own against Jupiter Tonans and also to set "intellect" above the Dreyfus case). "Perhaps it is just because they are Jews and know their own race that they realise that a person can be a Jew and not necessarily a traitor and anti-French, as M. Drumont seems to maintain. Certainly, if he'd been a Christian, the Jews wouldn't have taken any interest in him, but they did so because they knew quite well that if he hadn't been a Jew people wouldn't have been so ready to think him a traitor *a priori*, as my nephew Robert would say." "Women never understand a thing about politics," exclaimed the Duke, fastening his gaze upon the Duchess. "That shocking crime is not simply a Jewish cause, but *out and out* an affair of vast national importance which may lead to the most appalling consequences for France, which ought to have driven out all the Jews, whereas I am sorry to say that the measures taken up to the present have been directed (in an ignoble fashion, which will have to be overruled) not against them but against the most eminent of their adversaries, against men of the highest rank, who have been flung into the gutter, to the ruin of our unhappy country."

I felt that the conversation had taken a wrong turning and reverted hurriedly to the topic of clothes.

"Do you remember, Madame," I said, "the first time that you were friendly with me?" "The first time that I was friendly with him," she repeated, turning with a smile to M. de Bréauté, the tip of whose nose grew more pointed, his smile more tender out of politeness to Mme. de Guermantes, while his voice, like a knife on the grindstone, emitted various vague and rusty sounds. "You were wearing a yellow gown with big black flowers." "But, my dear boy, that's the same thing, those are evening dresses." "And your hat with the cornflowers that I liked so much! Still, those are all things of the past. I should like to order for the girl I mentioned to you a fur cloak like the one you had on yesterday morning. Would it be possible for me to see it?" "Of course; Hannibal has to be going in a moment. You shall come to my room and my maid will shew you anything you want to look at. Only, my dear boy, though I shall be delighted to lend you anything, I must warn you that if you have things from Callot's or Doucet's or Paquin's copied by some small dressmaker, the result is never the same." "But I never dreamed of going to a small dressmaker, I know quite well it wouldn't be the same thing, but I should be interested to hear you explain why." "You know quite well I can never explain anything, I am a perfect fool, I talk like a peasant. It is a question of handiwork, of style; as far as furs go, I can at least give you a line to my furrier, so that he shan't rob you. But you realise that even then it will cost you eight or nine thousand francs." "And that indoor gown that you were wearing the other evening, with such a curious smell, dark, fluffy, speckled, streaked with gold like a butterfly's wing?" "Ah! That is one of Fortuny's. Your young lady can quite well wear that in the house. I have heaps of them; you shall see them presently, in fact I can give you one or two if you like. But I should like you to see one that my cousin Talleyrand has. I must write to her for the loan of it." "But you had such charming shoes as well, are they Fortuny's too?" "No, I know the ones you mean, they are made of some gilded kid we came across in London, when I was shopping with Consuelo Manchester. It was amazing. I could never make out how they did it, it was just like a golden skin, simply that with a tiny diamond in front. The poor Duchess of Manchester is dead, but if it's any help to you I can write and ask Lady Warwick or the Duchess of Marlborough to try and get me some more. I wonder, now, if I haven't a piece of the stuff left. You might be able to have a pair made here. I shall look for it this evening, and let you know."

As I endeavoured as far as possible to leave the Duchess before Albertine had returned, it often happened that I met in the courtyard as I came away from her door M. de Charlus and Morel on their way to take tea at Jupien's, a supreme favour for the Baron. I did not encounter them every day but they went there every day. Here we may perhaps remark that the regularity of a habit is generally in proportion to its absurdity. The sensational things, we do as a rule only by fits and starts. But the senseless life, in which the maniac deprives himself of all pleasure and inflicts the greatest discomforts upon himself, is the type that alters least. Every ten years, if we had the curiosity to inquire, we should find the poor wretch still asleep at the hours when he might be living his life, going out at the hours when there is nothing to do but let oneself be murdered in the streets, sipping iced drinks when he is hot, still trying desperately to cure a cold. A slight impulse of energy, for a single day, would be sufficient to change these habits for good and all. But the fact is that this sort of life is almost always the appanage of a person devoid of energy. Vices are another aspect of these monotonous existences which the exercise of will power would suffice to render less painful. These two aspects might be observed simultaneously when M. de Charlus came every day with Morel to take tea at Jupien's. A single outburst had marred this daily custom. The tailor's niece having said one day to Morel: "That's all right then, come to-morrow and I'll stand you a tea," the Baron had quite justifiably considered this expression very vulgar on the lips of a person whom he regarded as almost a prospective daughter-in-law, but as he enjoyed being offensive and became carried away by his own anger, instead of simply saying to Morel that he begged him to give her a lesson in polite manners, the whole of their homeward walk was a succession of violent scenes. In the most insolent, the most arrogant tone: "So your 'touch' which, I can see, is not necessarily allied to 'tact,' has hindered the normal development of your sense of smell, since you could allow that fetid expression 'stand a tea'—at fifteen centimes, I suppose—to waft its stench of sewage to my regal nostrils? When you have come to the end of a violin solo, have you ever seen yourself in my house rewarded with a fart, instead of frenzied applause, or a silence more eloquent still, since it is due to exhaustion from the effort to restrain, not what your young woman lavishes upon you, but the sob that you have brought to my lips? "

When a public official has had similar reproaches heaped upon him by his chief, he invariably loses his post next day. Nothing, on the contrary, could have been more painful to M. de Charlus than to dismiss Morel, and, fearing indeed that he had gone a little too far, he began to sing the girl's praises in detailed terms, with an abundance of good taste mingled with impertinence. "She is charming; as you are a musician, I suppose that she seduced you by her voice, which is very beautiful in the high notes, where she seems to await the accompaniment of your B sharp. Her lower register appeals to me less, and that must bear some relation to the triple rise of her strange and slender throat, which when it seems to have come to an end begins again; but these are trivial details, it is her outline that I admire. And as she is a dressmaker and must be handy with her scissors, you must make her give me a charming silhouette of herself cut out in paper."

Charlie had paid but little attention to this eulogy, the charms which it extolled in his betrothed having completely escaped his notice. But he said, in reply to M. de Charlus: "That's all right, my boy, I shall tell her off properly, and she won't talk like that again." If Morel addressed M. de Charlus thus as his "boy," it was not that the good-looking violinist was unaware that his own years numbered barely a third of the Baron's. Nor did he use the expression as Jupien would have done, but with that simplicity which in certain relations postulates that a suppression of the difference in age has tacitly preceded affection. A feigned affection on Morel's part. In others, a sincere affection. Thus, about this time M. de Charlus received a letter worded as follows: "My dear Palamède, when am I going to see thee again? I am longing terribly for thee and always thinking of thee. PIERRE." M. de Charlus racked his brains to discover which of his relatives it could be that took the liberty of addressing him so familiarly, and must consequently know him intimately, although he failed to recognise the handwriting. All the Princes to whom the Almanach de Gotha accords a few lines passed in procession for days on end through his mind. And then, all of a sudden, an address written on the back of the letter enlightened him: the writer was the page at a gambling club to which M. de Charlus sometimes went. This page had not felt that he was being discourteous in writing in this tone to M. de Charlus, for whom on the contrary he felt the deepest respect. But he thought that it would not be civil not to address in the second person singular a gentleman who had many times kissed one, and thereby—he imagined in his simplicity—bestowed his affection. M. de Charlus was really delighted by this familiarity. He even brought M. de Vaugoubert away from an afternoon party in order to shew him the letter. And yet, heaven knows that M. de Charlus did not care to go about with M. de Vaugoubert. For the latter, his monocle in his eye, kept gazing in all directions at every passing youth. What was worse, emancipating himself when he was with M. de Charlus, he employed a form of speech which the Baron detested. He gave feminine endings to all the masculine words and, being intensely stupid, imagined this pleasantry to be extremely witty, and was continually in fits of laughter. As at the same time he attached enormous importance to his position in the diplomatic service, these deplorable outbursts of merriment in the street were perpetually interrupted by the shock caused him by the simultaneous appearance of somebody in society, or, worse still, of a civil servant. "That little telegraph messenger," he said, nudging the disgusted Baron with his elbow, "I used to know her, but she's turned respectable, the wretch! Oh, that messenger from the Galeries Lafayette, what a dream! Good God, there's the head of the Commercial Department. I hope he didn't notice anything. He's quite capable of mentioning it to the Minister, who would put me on the retired list, all the more as, it appears, he's so himself." M. de Charlus was speechless with rage. At length, to bring this infuriating walk to an end, he decided to produce the letter and give it to the Ambassador to read, but warned him to be discreet, for he liked to pretend that Charlie was jealous, in order to be able to make people think that he was enamoured. "And," he added with an indescribable air of benevolence, "we ought always to try to cause as little trouble as possible." Before we come back to Jupien's shop, the author would like to say how deeply he would regret it should any reader be offended by his portrayal of such unusual characters. On the one hand (and this is the less important aspect of the matter), it may be felt that the aristocracy is, in these pages, disproportionately accused of degeneracy in comparison with the other classes of society. Were this true, it would be in no way surprising. The oldest families end by displaying, in a red and bulbous nose, or a deformed chin, characteristic signs in which everyone admires "blood." But among these persistent and perpetually developing features, there are others that are not visible, to wit tendencies and tastes. It would be a more serious objection, were there any foundation for it, to say that all this is alien to us, and that we ought to extract truth from the poetry that is close at hand. Art extracted from the most familiar reality does indeed exist and its domain is perhaps the largest of any. But it is no less true that a strong interest, not to say beauty, may be found in actions inspired by a cast of mind so remote from anything that we feel, from anything that we believe, that we cannot ever succeed in understanding them, that they are displayed before our eyes like a spectacle without rhyme or reason. What could be more poetic than Xerxes, son of Darius, ordering the sea to be scourged with rods for having engulfed his fleet?

We may be certain that Morel, relying on the influence which his personal attractions gave him over the girl, communicated to her, as coming from himself, the Baron's criticism, for the expression " stand you a tea " disappeared as completely from the tailor's shop as disappears from a drawing-room some intimate friend who used to call daily, and with whom, for one reason or another, we have quarrelled, or whom we are trying to keep out of sight and meet only outside the house. M. de Charlus was satisfied by the cessation of " stand you a tea." He saw in it a proof of his own ascendancy over Morel and the removal of its one little blemish from the girl's perfection. In short, like everyone of his kind, while genuinely fond of Morel and of the girl who was all but engaged to him, an ardent advocate of their marriage, he thoroughly enjoyed his power to create at his pleasure more or less inoffensive little scenes, aloof from and above which he himself remained as Olympian as his brother.

Morel had told M. de Charlus that he was in love with Jupien's niece, and wished to marry her, and the Baron liked to accompany his young friend upon visits in which he played the part of father-in-law to be, indulgent and discreet. Nothing pleased him better.

My personal opinion is that "stand you a tea" had originated with Morel himself, and that in the blindness of her love the young seamstress had adopted an expression from her beloved which clashed horribly with her own pretty way of speaking. This way of speaking, the charming manners that went with it, the patronage of M. de Charlus brought it about that many customers for whom she had worked received her as a friend, invited her to dinner, introduced her to their friends, though the girl accepted their invitations only with the Baron's permission and on the evenings that suited him. "A young seamstress received in society?" the reader will exclaim, "how improbable!" If you come to think of it, it was no less improbable that at one time Albertine should have come to see me at midnight, and that she should now be living in my house. And yet this might perhaps have been improbable of anyone else, but not of Albertine, a fatherless and motherless orphan, leading so uncontrolled a life that at first I had taken her, at Balbec, for the mistress of a bicyclist, a girl whose next of kin was Mme. Bontemps who in the old days, at Mme. Swann's, had admired nothing about her niece but her bad manners and who now shut her eyes, especially if by doing so she might be able to get rid of her by securing for her a wealthy marriage from which a little of the wealth would trickle into the aunt's pocket (in the highest society, a mother who is very well-born and quite penniless, when she has succeeded in finding a rich bride for her son, allows the young couple to support her, accepts presents of furs, a motor-car, money from a daughter-in-law whom she does not like but whom she introduces to her friends).

The day may come when dressmakers—nor should I find it at all shocking—will move in society. Jupien's niece being an exception affords us no base for calculation, for one swallow does not make a summer. In any case, if the very modest advancement of Jupien's niece did scandalise some people, Morel was not among them, for, in certain respects, his stupidity was so intense that not only did he label "rather a fool" this girl a thousand times cleverer than himself, and foolish only perhaps in her love for himself, but he actually took to be adventuresses, dressmakers' assistants in disguise playing at being ladies, the persons of rank and position who invited her to their houses and whose invitations she accepted without a trace of vanity. Naturally these were not Guermantes, nor even people who knew the Guermantes, but rich and smart women of the middle-class, broad-minded enough to feel that it is no disgrace to invite a dressmaker to your house and at the same time servile enough to derive some satisfaction from patronising a girl whom His Highness the Baron de Charlus was in the habit—without any suggestion, of course, of impropriety—of visiting daily.

Nothing could have pleased the Baron more than the idea of this marriage, for he felt that in this way Morel would not be taken from him. It appears that Jupien's niece had been, when scarcely more than a child, " in trouble." And M. de Charlus, while he sang her praises to Morel, would have had no hesitation in revealing this secret to his friend, who would be furious, and thus sowing the seeds of discord. For M. de Charlus, although terribly malicious, resembled a great many good people who sing the praises of some man or woman, as a proof of their own generosity, but would avoid like poison the soothing words, so rarely uttered, that would be capable of putting an end to strife. Notwithstanding this, the Baron refrained from making any insinuation, and for two reasons. " If I tell him," he said to himself, " that his ladylove is not spotless, his vanity will be hurt, he will be angry with me. Besides, how am I to know that he is not in love with her? If I say nothing, this fire of straw will burn itself out before long, I shall be able to control their relations as I choose, he will love her only to the extent that I shall allow. If I tell him of his young lady's past transgression, who knows that my Charlie is not still sufficiently enamoured of her to become jealous. Then I shall by my own doing be converting a harmless and easily controlled flirtation into a serious passion, which is a difficult thing to manage." For these reasons, M. de Charlus preserved a silence which had only the outward appearance of discretion, but was in another respect meritorious, since it is almost impossible for men of his sort to hold their tongues.

Anyhow, the girl herself was charming, and M. de Charlus, who found that she satisfied all the aesthetic interest that he was capable of feeling in women, would have liked to have hundreds of photographs of her. Not such a fool as Morel, he was delighted to hear the names of the ladies who invited her to their houses, and whom his social instinct was able to place, but he took care (as he wished to retain his power) not to mention this to Charlie who, a regular idiot in this respect, continued to believe that, apart from the " violin class " and the Verdurins, there existed only the Guermantes, and the few almost royal houses enumerated by the Baron, all the rest being but " dregs " or " scum." Charlie interpreted these expressions of M. de Charlus literally.

Among the reasons which made M. de Charlus look forward to the marriage of the young couple was this, that Jupien's niece would then be in a sense an extension of Morel's personality, and so of the Baron's power over and knowledge of him. As for " betraying " in the conjugal sense the violinist's future wife, it would never for a moment have occurred to M. de Charlus to feel the slightest scruple about that. But to have a " young couple " to manage, to feel himself the redoubtable and all-powerful protector of Morel's wife, who if she regarded the Baron as a god would thereby prove that Morel had inculcated this idea into her, and would thus contain in herself something of Morel, added a new variety to the form of M. de Charlus's domination and brought to light in his " creature," Morel, a creature the more, that is to say gave the Baron something different, new, curious, to love in him. Perhaps even this domination would be stronger now than it had ever been. For whereas Morel by himself, naked so to speak, often resisted the Baron whom he felt certain of reconquering, once he was married, the thought of his home, his house, his future would alarm him more quickly, he would offer to M. de Charlus's desires a wider surface, an easier hold.

All this, and even, failing anything else, on evenings when he was bored, the prospect of stirring up trouble between husband and wife (the Baron had never objected to battle-pictures) was pleasing to him. Less pleasing, however, than the thought of the state of dependence upon himself in which the young people would live. M. de Charlus's love for Morel acquired a delicious novelty when he said to himself: "His wife too will be mine just as much as he is, they will always take care not to annoy me, they will obey my caprices, and thus she will be a sign (which hitherto I have failed to observe) of what I had almost forgotten, what is so very dear to my heart, that to all the world, to everyone who sees that I protect them, house them, to myself, Morel is mine." This testimony in the eyes of the world and in his own pleased M. de Charlus more than anything. For the possession of what we love is an even greater joy than love itself. Very often those people who conceal this possession from the world do so only from the fear that the beloved object may be taken from them. And their happiness is diminished by this prudent reticence.

The reader may remember that Morel had once told the Baron that his great ambition was to seduce some young girl, and this girl in particular, that to succeed in his enterprise he would promise to marry her, and, the outrage accomplished, would "cut his hook"; but this confession, what with the declarations of love for Jupien's niece which Morel had come and poured out to him, M. de Charlus had forgotten. What was more, Morel had quite possibly forgotten it himself. There was perhaps a real gap between Morel's nature—as he had cynically admitted, perhaps even artfully exaggerated it—and the moment at which it would regain control of him. As he became better acquainted with the girl, she had appealed to him, he began to like her. He knew himself so little that he doubtless imagined that he was in love with her, perhaps indeed that he would be in love with her always. To be sure his initial desire, his criminal intention remained, but glossed over by so many layers of sentiment that there is nothing to shew that the violinst would not have been sincere in saying that this vicious desire was not the true motive of his action. There was, moreover, a brief period during which, without his actually admitting it to himself, this marriage appeared to him to be necessary. Morel was suffering at the time from violent cramp in the hand, and found himself obliged to contemplate the possibility of his having to give up the violin. As, in everything but his art, he was astonishingly lazy, the question who was to maintain him loomed before him, and he preferred that it should be Jupien's niece rather than M. de Charlus, this arrangement offering him greater freedom and also a wider choice of several kinds of women, ranging from the apprentices, perpetually changing, whom he would make Jupien's niece debauch for him, to the rich and beautiful ladies to whom he would prostitute her. That his future wife might refuse to lend herself to these arrangements, that she could be so perverse never entered Morel's calculations for a moment. However, they passed into the background, their place being taken by pure love, now that his cramp had ceased. His violin would suffice, together with his allowance from M. de Charlus, whose claims upon him would certainly be reduced once he, Morel, was married to the girl. Marriage was the urgent

thing, because of his love, and in the interest of his freedom. He made a formal offer of marriage to Jupien,
who consulted his niece. This was wholly unnecessary.
The girl's passion for the violinist streamed round about
her, like her hair when she let it down, like the joy in her
beaming eyes. In Morel, almost everything that was
agreeable or advantageous to him awakened moral emotions and words to correspond, sometimes even melting
him to tears. It was therefore sincerely—if such a word
can be applied to him—that he addressed Jupien's niece
in speeches as steeped in sentimentality (sentimental too
are the speeches that so many young noblemen who look
forward to a life of complete idleness address to some
charming daughter of a middle-class millionaire) as had
been steeped in unredeemed vileness the speech he had
made to M. de Charlus about the seduction and de-
flowering of a virgin. Only there was another side to
this virtuous enthusiasm for a person who afforded him
pleasure and the solemn engagement that he made with
her. As soon as the person ceased to afford him pleasure,
or indeed if, for example, the obligation to fulfil the
promise that he had made caused him displeasure, she
at once became the object of an antipathy which he
justified in his own eyes and which, after some neuras-
thenic disturbance, enabled him to prove to himself, as
soon as the balance of his nervous system was restored,
that he was, even looking at the matter from a purely
virtuous point of view, released from any obligation.
Thus, towards the end of his stay at Balbec, he had
managed somehow to lose all his money and, not daring
to mention the matter to M. de Charlus, looked about
for some one to whom he might appeal. He had learned

from his father (who at the same time had forbidden him ever to become a " sponger ") that in such circumstances the correct thing is to write to the person whom you intend to ask for a loan, " that you have to speak to him on business," to " ask him for a business appointment." This magic formula had so enchanted Morel that he would, I believe, have been glad to lose his money, simply to have the pleasure of asking for an appointment " on business." In the course of his life he had found that the formula had not quite the virtue that he supposed. He had discovered that certain people, to whom otherwise he would never have written at all, did not reply within five minutes of receiving his letter asking to speak to them " on business." If the afternoon went by without his receiving an answer, it never occurred to him that, to put the best interpretation on the matter, it was quite possible that the gentleman addressed had not yet come home, or had had other letters to write, if indeed he had not gone away from home altogether, fallen ill, or something of that sort. If by an extraordinary stroke of fortune Morel was given an appointment for the following morning, he would accost his intended creditor with: " I was quite surprised not to get an answer, I was wondering if there was anything wrong with you, I'm glad to see you're quite well," and so forth. Well then, at Balbec, and without telling me that he wished to talk " business " to him, he had asked me to introduce him to that very Bloch to whom he had made himself so unpleasant a week earlier in the train. Bloch had not hesitated to lend him—or rather to secure a loan for him, from M. Nissim Bernard, of five thousand francs. From that moment Morel had worshipped Bloch. He asked himself with tears in his eyes how he could shew his indebtedness to a person who had saved his life. Finally, I undertook to ask on his behalf for a thousand francs monthly from M. de Charlus, a sum which he would at once forward to Bloch who would thus find himself repaid within quite a short time. The first month, Morel, still under the impression of Bloch's generosity, sent him the thousand francs immediately, but after this he doubtless found that a different application of the remaining four thousand francs might be more satisfactory to himself, for he began to say all sorts of unpleasant things about Bloch. The mere sight of Bloch was enough to fill his mind with dark thoughts, and Bloch himself having forgotten the exact amount that he had lent Morel, and having asked him for 3,500 francs instead of 4,000, which would have left the violinist 500 francs to the good, the latter took the line that, in view of so preposterous a fraud, not only would he not pay another centime but his creditor might think himself very fortunate if Morel did not bring an action against him for slander. As he said this his eyes blazed. He did not content himself with asserting that Bloch and M. Nissim Bernard had no cause for complaint against him, but was soon saying that they might consider themselves lucky that he made no complaint against them. Finally, M. Nissim Bernard having apparently stated that Thibaut played as well as Morel, the last-named decided that he ought to take the matter into court, such a remark being calculated to damage him in his profession, then, as there was no longer any justice in France, especially against the Jews (antisemitism being in Morel the natural effect of a loan of 5,000 francs from an Israelite), took to never going out without a loaded revolver. A similar nervous reaction, in the wake of keen affection, was soon to occur in Morel with regard to the tailor's niece. It is true that M. de Charlus may have been unconsciously responsible, to some extent, for this change, for he was in the habit of saying, without meaning what he said for an instant, and merely to tease them, that, once they were married, he would never set eyes on them again but would leave them to fly upon their own wings. This idea was, in itself, quite insufficient to detach Morel from the girl; but, lurking in his mind, it was ready when the time came to combine with other analogous ideas, capable, once the compound was formed, of becoming a powerful disruptive agent.

It was not very often, however, that I was fated to meet M. de Charlus and Morel. Often they had already passed into Jupien's shop when I came away from the Duchess, for the pleasure that I found in her society was such that I was led to forget not merely the anxious expectation that preceded Albertine's return, but even the hour of that return.

I shall set apart from the other days on which I lingered at Mme. de Guermantes's, one that was distinguished by a trivial incident the cruel significance of which entirely escaped me and did not enter my mind until long afterwards. On this particular afternoon, Mme. de Guermantes had given me, knowing that I was fond of them, some branches of syringa which had been sent to her from the South. When I left the Duchess and went upstairs to our flat, Albertine had already returned, and on the staircase I ran into Andrée who seemed to be dis-

tressed by the powerful fragrance of the flowers that I
was bringing home.

"What, are you back already?" I said. "Only this
moment, but Albertine had letters to write, so she sent
me away." "You don't think she's up to any mis-
chief?" "Not at all, she's writing to her aunt, I think,
but you know how she dislikes strong scents, she won't
be particularly pleased to see those syringas." "How
stupid of me! I shall tell Françoise to put them out on
the service stair." "Do you imagine Albertine won't
notice the scent of them on you? Next to tuberoses
they've the strongest scent of any flower, I always think;
anyhow, I believe Françoise has gone out shopping."
"But in that case, as I haven't got my latchkey, how am
I to get in?" "Oh, you've only got to ring the bell.
Albertine will let you in. Besides, Françoise may have
come back by this time."

I said good-bye to Andrée. I had no sooner pressed
the bell than Albertine came to open the door, which
required some doing, as Françoise had gone out and
Albertine did not know where to turn on the light. At
length she was able to let me in, but the scent of the
syringas put her to flight. I took them to the kitchen,
with the result that my mistress, leaving her letter un-
finished (why, I did not understand), had time to go to
my room, from which she called to me, and to lay herself down on my bed. Even then, at the actual moment,
I saw nothing in all this that was not perfectly natural, at
the most a little confused, but in any case unimportant.
She had nearly been caught out with Andrée and had
snatched a brief respite for herself by turning out the
lights, going to my room so that I should not see the

disordered state of her own bed, and pretending to be busy writing a letter. But we shall see all this later on, a situation the truth of which I never ascertained. In general, and apart from this isolated incident, everything was quite normal when I returned from my visit to the Duchess. Since Albertine never knew whether I might not wish to go out with her before dinner, I usually found in the hall her hat, cloak and umbrella, which she had left lying there in case they should be needed. As soon as, on opening the door, I caught sight of them, the atmosphere of the house became breathable once more. I felt that, instead of a rarefied air, it was happiness that filled it. I was rescued from my melancholy, the sight of these trifles gave me possession of Albertine, I ran to greet her.

On the days when I did not go down to Mme. de Guermantes, to pass the time somehow, during the hour that preceded the return of my mistress, I would take up an album of Elstir's work, one of Bergotte's books, Vinteuil's sonata.

Then, just as those works of art which seem to address themselves to the eye or ear alone require that, if we are to enjoy them, our awakened intelligence shall collaborate closely with those organs, I would unconsciously evoke from myself the dreams that Albertine had inspired in me long ago, before I knew her, dreams that had been stifled by the routine of everyday life. I cast them into the composer's phrase or the painter's image as into a crucible, or used them to enrich the book that I was reading. And no doubt the book appeared all the more vivid in consequence. But Albertine herself profited just as much by being thus transported out of one of the two worlds to which we have access, and in which we can place alternately the same object, by escaping thus from the crushing weight of matter to play freely in the fluid space of mind. I found myself suddenly and for the instant capable of feeling an ardent desire for this irritating girl. She had at that moment the appearance of a work by Elstir or Bergotte, I felt a momentary enthusiasm for her, seeing her in the perspective of imagination and art.

Presently some one came to tell me that she had returned; though there was a standing order that her name was not to be mentioned if I was not alone, if for instance I had in the room with me Bloch, whom I would compel to remain with me a little longer so that there should be no risk of his meeting my mistress in the hall. For I concealed the fact that she was staying in the house, and even that I ever saw her there, so afraid was I that one of my friends might fall in love with her, and wait for her outside, or that in a momentary encounter in the passage or the hall she might make a signal and fix an appointment. Then I heard the rustle of Albertine's petticoats on her way to her own room, for out of discretion and also no doubt in that spirit in which, when we used to go to dinner at la Raspelière, she took care that I should have no cause for jealousy, she did not come to my room, knowing that I was not alone. But it was not only for this reason, as I suddenly realised. I remembered; I had known a different Albertine, then all at once she had changed into another, the Albertine of today. And for this change I could hold no one responsible but myself. The admissions that she would have made to me, easily at first, then deliberately, when we were simply friends, had ceased to flow from her as soon as she had suspected that I was in love with her, or, without perhaps naming Love, had divined the existence in me of an inquisitorial sentiment that desires to know, is pained by the knowledge, and seeks to learn yet more. Ever since that day, she had concealed everything from me. She kept away from my room if she thought that my companion was (rarely as this happened) not male but female, she whose eyes used at one time to sparkle so brightly whenever I mentioned a girl: "You must try and get her to come here. I should like to meet her." "But she has what you call a bad style." "Of course, that makes it all the more fun." At that moment, I might perhaps have learned all that there was to know. And indeed when in the little Casino she had withdrawn her breast from Andrée's, I believe that this was due not to my presence but to that of Cottard, who was capable, she doubtless thought, of giving her a bad reputation. And yet, even then, she had already begun to "set," the confiding speeches no longer issued from her lips, her gestures became reserved. After this, she had stripped herself of everything that could stir my emotions. To those parts of her life of which I knew nothing she ascribed a character the inoffensiveness of which my ignorance made itself her accomplice in accentuating. And now, the transformation was completed, she went straight to her room if I was not alone, not merely from fear of disturbing me, but in order to shew me that she did not care who was with me. There was one thing alone which she would never again do for me, which she would have done only in the days when it would have left me cold, which she would then have done without hesitation for that very reason, namely make me a detailed admission. I should always be obliged, like a judge, to draw indefinite conclusions from imprudences of speech that were perhaps not really inexplicable without postulating criminality. And always she would feel that I was jealous, and judging her.

As I listened to Albertine's footsteps with the consoling pleasure of thinking that she would not be going out again that evening, I thought how wonderful it was that for this girl, whom at one time I had supposed that I could never possibly succeed in knowing, the act of returning home every day was nothing else than that of entering my home. The pleasure, a blend of mystery and sensuality, which I had felt, fugitive and fragmentary, at Balbec, on the night when she had come to sleep at the hotel, was completed, stabilised, filled my dwelling, hitherto void, with a permanent store of domestic, almost conjugal bliss (radiating even into the passages) upon which all my senses, either actively, or, when I was alone, in imagination as I waited for her to return, quietly battened. When I had heard the door of Albertine's room shut behind her, if I had a friend with me, I made haste to get rid of him, not leaving him until I was quite sure that he was on the staircase, down which I might even escort him for a few steps. He warned me that I would catch cold, informing me that our house was indeed icy, a cave of the winds, and that he would not live in it if he was paid to do so. This cold weather was a source of complaint because it had just begun, and people were not yet accustomed to it, but for that very reason it released in me a joy accompanied by an unconscious memory of the first evenings of winter when, in past years, returning from the country, in order to reestablish contact with the forgotten delights of Paris, I used to go to a café-concert. And so it was with a song on my lips that, after bidding my friend good-bye, I climbed the stair again and entered the flat. Summer had flown, carrying the birds with it. But other musicians, invisible, internal, had taken their place. And the icy blast against which Bloch had inveighed, which was whistling delightfully through the ill fitting doors of our apartment was (as the fine days of summer by the woodland birds) passionately greeted with snatches, irrepressibly hummed, from Fragson, Mayol or Paulus. In the passage, Albertine was coming towards me. "I say, while I'm taking off my things, I shall send you Andrée, she's looked in for a minute to say how d'ye do." And still swathed in the big grey veil, falling from her chinchilla toque, which I had given her at Balbec, she turned from me and went back to her room, as though she had guessed that Andrée, whom I had charged with the duty of watching over her, would presently, by relating their day's adventures in full detail, mentioning their meeting with some person of their acquaintance, impart a certain clarity of outline to the vague regions in which that excursion had been made which had taken the whole day and which I had been incapable of imagining. Andrée's defects had become more evident; she was no longer as pleasant a companion as when I first knew her. One noticed now, on the surface, a sort of bitter uneasiness, ready to gather like a swell on the sea, merely if I happened to mention something that gave pleasure to Albertine and myself. This did not prevent Andrée from being kinder to me, liking me better—and I have had frequent proof of this—than

other more sociable people. But the slightest look of
happiness on a person's face, if it was not caused by
herself, gave a shock to her nerves, as unpleasant as
that given by a banging door. She could allow the pains
in which she had no part, but not the pleasures; if she
saw that I was unwell, she was distressed, was sorry for
me, would have stayed to nurse me. But if I displayed a satisfaction as trifling as that of stretching myself with a blissful expression as I shut a book, saying:
" Ah! I have spent a really happy afternoon with this
entertaining book," these words, which would have given
pleasure to my mother, to Albertine, to Saint-Loup, provoked in Andrée a sort of disapprobation, perhaps simply
a sort of nervous irritation. My satisfactions caused her
an annoyance which she was unable to conceal. These
defects were supplemented by others of a more serious
nature; one day when I mentioned that young man so
learned in matters of racing and golf, so uneducated in
all other respects, Andrée said with a sneer: " You know
that his father is a swindler, he only just missed being
prosecuted. They're swaggering now more than ever,
but I tell everybody about it. I should love them to
bring an action for slander against me. I should be
wonderful in the witness-box!" Her eyes sparkled.
Well, I discovered that the father had done nothing
wrong, and that Andrée knew this as well as anybody.
But she had thought that the son looked down upon her,
had sought for something that would embarrass him,
put him to shame, had invented a long story of evidence
which she imagined herself called upon to give in court,
and, by dint of repeating the details to herself, was perhaps no longer aware that they were not true. And so,

in her present state (and even without her fleeting, foolish hatreds), I should not have wished to see her, were it merely on account of that malicious susceptibility which clasped with a harsh and frigid girdle her warmer and better nature. But the information which she alone could give me about my mistress was of too great interest for me to be able to neglect so rare an opportunity of acquiring it. Andrée came into my room, shutting the door behind her; they had met a girl they knew, whom Albertine had never mentioned to me. "What did they talk about?" "I can't tell you; I took the opportunity, as Albertine wasn't alone, to go and buy some worsted." "Buy some worsted?" "Yes, it was Albertine asked me to get it." "All the more reason not to have gone, it was perhaps a plot to get you out of the way." "But she asked me to go for it before we met her friend." "Ah!" I replied, drawing breath again. At once my suspicion revived; she might, for all I knew, have made an appointment beforehand with her friend and have provided herself with an excuse to be left alone when the time came. Besides, could I be certain that it was not my former hypothesis (according to which Andrée did not always tell me the truth) that was correct? Andrée was perhaps in the plot with Albertine. Love, I used to say to myself, at Balbec, is what we feel for a person whose actions seem rather to arouse our jealousy; we feel that if she were to tell us everything, we might perhaps easily be cured of our love for her. However skilfully jealousy is concealed by him who suffers from it, it is at once detected by her who has inspired it, and who when the time comes is no less skilful. She seeks to lead us off the trail of what might make us unhappy, and succeeds, for, to the man who is not forewarned, how should a casual utterance reveal the falsehoods that lie beneath it? We do not distinguish this utterance from the rest; spoken in terror, it is received without attention. Later on, when we are by ourself, we shall return to this speech, it will seem to us not altogether adequate to the facts of the case. But do we remember it correctly? It seems as though there arose spontaneously in us, with regard to it and to the accuracy of our memory, an uncertainty of the sort with which, in certain nervous disorders, we can never remember whether we have bolted the door, no better after the fiftieth time than after the first; it would seem that we can repeat the action indefinitely without its ever being accompanied by a precise and liberating memory. At any rate, we can shut the door again, for the fifty-first time. Whereas the disturbing speech exists in the past in an imperfect hearing of it which it does not lie in our power to repeat. Then we concentrate our attention upon other speeches which conceal nothing and the sole remedy which we do not seek is to be ignorant of everything, so as to have no desire for further knowledge.

As soon as jealousy is discovered, it is regarded by her who is its object as a challenge which authorises deception. Moreover, in our endeavour to learn something, it is we who have taken the initiative in lying and deceit. Andrée, Aimé may promise us that they will say nothing, but will they keep their promise? Bloch could promise nothing because he knew nothing, and Albertine has only to talk to any of the three in order to learn, with the help of what Saint Loup would have called cross-references, that we are lying to her when we pretend to be indifferent to her actions and morally incapable of having her watched. And so, replacing in this way my habitual boundless uncertainty as to what Albertine might be doing, an uncertainty too indeterminate not to remain painless, which was to jealousy what is to grief that beginning of forgetfulness in which relief is born of vagueness, the little fragment of response which Andrée had brought me at once began to raise fresh questions; the only result of my exploration of one sector of the great zone that extended round me had been to banish farther from me that unknowable thing which, when we seek to form a definite idea of it, another person's life invariably is to us. I continued to question Andrée, while Albertine, from discretion and in order to leave me free (was she conscious of this?) to question the other, prolonged her toilet in her own room. "I think that Albertine's uncle and aunt both like me," I stupidly said to Andrée, forgetting her peculiar nature.

At once I saw her gelatinous features change. Like a syrup that has turned, her face seemed permanently clouded. Her mouth became bitter. Nothing remained in Andrée of that juvenile gaiety which, like all the little band and notwithstanding her feeble health, she had displayed in the year of my first visit to Balbec and which now (it is true that Andrée was now several years older) was so speedily eclipsed in her. But I was to make it reappear involuntarily before Andrée left me that evening to go home to dinner. "Somebody was singing your praises to me to-day in the most glowing language," I said to her. Immediately a ray of joy beamed from her eyes, she looked as though she really loved me. She avoided my gaze but smiled at the empty air with a pair of eyes that suddenly became quite round. "Who was it?" she asked, with an artless, avid interest. I told her, and, whoever it was, she was delighted.

Then the time came for us to part, and she left me. Albertine came to my room; she had undressed, and was wearing one of the charming crêpe de Chine wrappers, or one of the Japanese gowns which I had asked Mme. de Guermantes to describe to me, and for some of which supplementary details had been furnished me by Mme. Swann, in a letter that began: "After your long eclipse, I felt as I read your letter about my tea-gowns that I was receiving a message from the other world."

Albertine had on her feet a pair of black shoes studded with brilliants which Françoise indignantly called "pattens," modelled upon the shoes which, from the drawing-room window, she had seen Mme. de Guermantes wearing in the evening, just as a little later Albertine took to wearing slippers, some of gilded kid, others of chinchilla, the sight of which was pleasant to me because they were all of them signs (which other shoes would not have been) that she was living under my roof. She had also certain things which had not come to her from me, including a fine gold ring. I admired upon it the outspread wings of an eagle. "It was my aunt gave me it," she explained. "She can be quite nice sometimes after all. It makes me feel terribly old, because she gave it to me on my twentieth birthday."

Albertine took a far keener interest in all these pretty things than the Duchess, because, like every obstacle in the way of possession (in my own case the ill health which made travel so difficult and so desirable), poverty, more generous than opulence, gives to women what is better than the garments that they cannot afford to buy, the desire for those garments which is the genuine, detailed, profound knowledge of them. She, because she had never been able to afford these things, I, because in ordering them for her I was seeking to give her pleasure, we were both of us like students who already know all about the pictures which they are longing to go to Dresden or Vienna to see. Whereas rich women, amid the multitude of their hats and gowns, are like those tourists to whom the visit to a gallery, being preceded by no desire, gives merely a sensation of bewilderment, boredom and exhaustion.

A particular toque, a particular sable cloak, a particular Doucet wrapper, its sleeves lined with pink, assumed for Albertine, who had observed them, coveted them and, thanks to the exclusiveness and minute nicety that are elements of desire, had at once isolated them from everything else in a void against which the lining or the scarf stood out to perfection, and learned them by heart in every detail—and for myself who had gone to Mme. de Guermantes in quest of an explanation of what constituted the peculiar merit, the superiority, the smartness of the garment and the inimitable style of the great designer—an importance, a charm which they certainly did not possess for the Duchess, surfeited before she had even acquired an appetite and would not, indeed, have possessed for myself had I beheld them a few years earlier while accompanying some lady of fashion on one of her wearisome tours of the dressmakers' shops.

To be sure, a lady of fashion was what Albertine was gradually becoming. For, even if each of the things that I ordered for her was the prettiest of its kind, with all the refinements that had been added to it by Mme. de Guermantes or Mme. Swann, she was beginning to possess these things in abundance. But no matter, so long as she admired them from the first, and each of them separately.

When we have been smitten by one painter, then by another, we may end by feeling for the whole gallery an admiration that is not frigid, for it is made up of successive enthusiasms, each one exclusive in its day, which finally have joined forces and become reconciled in one whole.

She was not, for that matter, frivolous, read a great deal when she was by herself, and used to read aloud when she was with me. She had become extremely intelligent. She would say, though she was quite wrong in saying: "I am appalled when I think that but for you I should still be quite ignorant. Don't contradict. You have opened up a world of ideas to me which I never suspected, and whatever I may have become I owe entirely to you."

It will be remembered that she had spoken in similar terms of my influence over Andrée. Had either of them a sentimental regard for me? And, in themselves, what were Albertine and Andrée? To learn the answer, I should have to immobilise you, to cease to live in that perpetual expectation, ending always in a different presentment of you, I should have to cease to love you, in order to fix you, to cease to know your interminable and ever disconcerting arrival, oh girls, oh recurrent ray in the swirl wherein we throb with emotion upon seeing you reappear while barely recognising you, in the dizzy velocity of light. That velocity, we should perhaps remain unaware of it and everything would seem to us motionless, did not a sexual attraction set us in pursuit of you, drops of gold always different, and always passing our expectation! On each occasion a girl so little resembles what she was the time before (shattering in fragments as soon as we catch sight of her the memory that we had retained of her and the desire that we were proposing to gratify), that the stability of nature which we ascribe to her is purely fictitious and a convenience of speech. We have been told that some pretty girl is tender, loving, full of the most delicate sentiments. Our imagination accepts this assurance, and when we behold for the first time, within the woven girdle of her golden hair, the rosy disc of her face, we are almost afraid that this too virtuous sister may chill our ardour by her very virtue, that she can never be to us the lover for whom we have been longing. What secrets, at least, we confide in her from the first moment, on the strength of that nobility of heart, what plans we discuss together. But a few days later, we regret that we were so confiding, for the rose-leaf girl, at our second meeting, addresses us in the language of a lascivious Fury. As for the successive portraits which after a pulsation lasting for some days the renewal of the rosy light presents to us, it is not even certain that a momentum external to these girls has not modified their aspect, and this might well have happened with my band of girls at Balbec.

People extol to us the gentleness, the purity of a virgin. But afterwards they feel that something more seasoned would please us better, and recommend her to shew more boldness. In herself was she one more than the other? Perhaps not, but capable of yielding to any number of different possibilities in the headlong current of life. With another girl, whose whole attraction lay in something implacable (which we counted upon subduing to our own will), as, for instance, with the terrible jumping girl at Balbec who grazed in her spring the bald pates of startled old gentlemen, what a disappointment when, in the fresh aspect of her, just as we were addressing her in affectionate speeches stimulated by our memory of all her cruelty to other people, we heard her, as her first move in the game, tell us that she was shy, that she could never say anything intelligent to anyone at a first introduction, so frightened was she, and that it was only after a fortnight or so that she would be able to talk to us at her ease. The steel had turned to cotton, there was nothing left for us to attempt to break, since she herself had lost all her consistency. Of her own accord, but by our fault perhaps, for the tender words which we had addressed to Severity had perhaps, even without any deliberate calculation on her part, suggested to her that she ought to be gentle.

Distressing as the change may have been to us, it was not altogether maladroit, for our gratitude for all her gentleness would exact more from us perhaps than our delight at overcoming her cruelty. I do not say that a day will not come when, even to these luminous maidens, we shall not assign sharply differentiated characters, but that will be because they have ceased to interest us, because their entry upon the scene will no longer be to our heart the apparition which it expected in a different form and which leaves it overwhelmed every time by fresh incarnations. Their immobility will spring from our indifference to them, which will hand them over to the judgment of our mind. This will not, for that matter, be expressed in any more categorical terms, for after it has decided that some defect which was prominent in one is fortunately absent from the other, it will see that this defect had as its counterpart some priceless merit. So that the false judgment of our intellect, which comes into play only when we have ceased to take any interest, will define permanent characters of girls, which will enlighten us no more than the surprising faces that used to appear every day when, in the dizzy speed of our expectation, our friends presented themselves daily, weekly, too different to allow us, as they never halted in their passage, to classify them, to award degrees of merit. As for our sentiments, we have spoken of them too often to repeat again now that as often as not love is nothing more than the association of the face of a girl (whom otherwise we should soon have found intolerable) with the heartbeats inseparable from an endless, vain expectation, and from some trick that she has played upon us. All this is true not merely of imaginative young men brought into contact with changeable girls. At the stage that our narrative has now reached, it appears, as I have since heard, that Jupien's niece had altered her opinion of Morel and M. de Charlus. My motorist, reinforcing the love that she felt for Morel, had extolled to her, as existing in the violinist, boundless refinements of delicacy in which she was all too ready to believe. And at the same time Morel never ceased to complain to her of the despotic treatment that he received from M. de Charlus, which she ascribed to malevolence, never imagining that it could be due to love. She was moreover bound to acknowledge that M. de Charlus was tyrannically present at all their meetings.

In corroboration of all this, she had heard women in society speak of the Baron's terrible spite. Now, quite recently, her judgment had been completely reversed. She had discovered in Morel (without ceasing for that reason to love him) depths of malevolence and perfidy, compensated it was true by frequent kindness and genuine feeling, and in M. de Charlus an unimaginable and immense generosity blended with asperities of which she knew nothing. And so she had been unable to arrive at any more definite judgment of what, each in himself, the violinist and his protector really were, than I was able to form of Andrée, whom nevertheless I saw every day, or of Albertine who was living with me. On the evenings when the latter did not read aloud to me, she would play to me or begin a game of draughts, or a conversation, either of which I would interrupt with kisses. The simplicity of our relations made them soothing. The very emptiness of her life gave Albertine a sort of eagerness to comply with the only requests that I made of her. Behind this girl, as behind the purple light that used to filter beneath the curtains of my room at Balbec, while outside the concert blared, were shining the blue-green undulations of the sea. Was she not, after all (she in whose heart of hearts there was now regularly installed an idea of myself so familiar that, next to her aunt, I was perhaps the person whom she distinguished least from herself), the girl whom I had seen the first time at Balbec, in her flat polo-cap, with her insistent laughing eyes, a stranger still, exiguous as a silhouette projected against the waves? These effigies preserved intact in our memory, when we recapture them, we are astonished at their unlikeness to the person whom we know, and we begin to realise what a task of remodelling is performed every day by habit. In the charm that Albertine had in Paris, by my fireside, there still survived the desire that had been aroused in me by that insolent and blossoming parade along the beach, and just as Rachel retained in Saint-Loup's eyes, even after he had made her abandon it, the prestige of her life on the stage, so in this Albertine cloistered in my house, far from Balbec, from which I had hurried her away, there persisted the emotion, the social confusion, the uneasy vanity, the roving desires of life by the seaside. She was so effectively caged that on certain evenings I did not even ask her to leave her room for mine, her to whom at one time all the world gave chase, whom I had found it so hard to overtake as she sped past on her bicycle, whom the liftboy himself was unable to capture for me, leaving me with scarcely a hope of her coming, although I sat up waiting for her all the night. Had not Albertine been—out there in front of the Hotel—like a great actress of the blazing beach, arousing jealousy when she advanced upon that natural stage, not speaking to anyone, thrusting past its regular frequenters, dominating the girls, her friends, and was not this so greatly coveted actress the same who, withdrawn by me from the stage, shut up in my house, was out of reach now of the desires of all the rest, who might hereafter seek for her in vain, sitting now in my room, now in her own, and engaged in tracing or cutting out some pattern?

No doubt, in the first days at Balbec, Albertine seemed to be on a parallel plane to that upon which I was living, but one that had drawn closer (after my visit to Elstir) and had finally become merged in it, as my relations with her, at Balbec, in Paris, then at Balbec again, grew more intimate. Besides, between the two pictures of Balbec, at my first visit and at my second, pictures composed of the same villas from which the same girls walked down to the same sea, what a difference! In Albertine's friends at the time of my second visit, whom I knew so well, whose good and bad qualities were so clearly engraved on their features, how was I to recapture those fresh, mysterious strangers who at first could not, without making my heart throb, thrust open the door of their bungalow over the grinding sand and set the tamarisks shivering as they came down the path! Their huge eyes had, in the interval, been absorbed into their faces, doubtless because they had ceased to be children, but also because those ravishing strangers, those ravishing actresses of the romantic first year, as to whom I had gone ceaselessly in quest of information, no longer held any mystery for me. They had become obedient to my caprices, a mere grove of budding girls, from among whom I was quite distinctly proud of having plucked, and carried off from them all, their fairest rose.

Between the two Balbec scenes, so different one from the other, there was the interval of several years in Paris, the long expanse of which was dotted with all the visits that Albertine had paid me. I saw her in successive years of my life occupying, with regard to myself, different positions, which made me feel the beauty of the interposed gaps, that long extent of time in which I never set eyes on her and against the diaphanous background of which the rosy person that I saw before me was modelled with mysterious shadows and in bold relief. This was due also to the superimposition not merely of the successive images which Albertine had been for me, but also of the great qualities of brain and heart, the defects of character, all alike unsuspected by me, which Albertine, in a germination, a multiplication of herself, a carnal efflorescence in sombre colours, had added to a nature that formerly could scarcely have been said to exist, but was now deep beyond plumbing. For other people, even those of whom we have so often dreamed that they have become nothing more than a picture, a figure by Benozzo Gozzoli standing out upon a background of verdure, as to whom we were prepared to believe that the only variations depended upon the point of view from which we looked at them, their distance from us, the effect of light and shade, these people, while they change in relation to ourself, change also in themselves, and there had been an enrichment, a solidification and an increase of volume in the figure once so simply outlined against the sea. Moreover, it was not only the sea at the close of day that came to life for me in Albertine, but sometimes the drowsy murmur of the sea upon the shore on moonlit nights.

Sometimes, indeed, when I rose to fetch a book from my father's study, and had given my mistress permission to lie down while I was out of the room, she was so tired after her long outing in the morning and afternoon in the open air that, even if I had been away for a moment only, when I returned I found Albertine asleep and did not rouse her.

Stretched out at full length upon my bed, in an attitude so natural that no art could have designed it, she reminded me of a long blossoming stem that had been laid there, and so indeed she was: the faculty of dreaming which I possessed only in her absence I recovered at such moments in her presence, as though by falling asleep she had become a plant. In this way her sleep did to a certain extent make love possible. When she was present, I spoke to her, but I was too far absent from myself to be able to think. When she was asleep, I no longer needed to talk to her, I knew that she was no longer looking at me, I had no longer any need to live upon my own outer surface.

By shutting her eyes, by losing consciousness, Albertine had stripped off, one after another, the different human characters with which she had deceived me ever since the day when I had first made her acquaintance. She was animated now only by the unconscious life of vegetation, of trees, a life more different from my own, more alien, and yet one that belonged more to me. Her personality did not escape at every moment, as when we were talking, by the channels of her unacknowledged thoughts and of her gaze. She had called back into herself everything of her that lay outside, had taken refuge, enclosed, reabsorbed, in her body. In keeping her before my eyes, in my hands, I had that impression of possessing her altogether, which I never had when she was awake. Her life was submitted to me, exhaled towards me its gentle breath.

I listened to this murmuring, mysterious emanation, soft as a breeze from the sea, fairylike as that moonlight which was her sleep. So long as it lasted, I was free to think about her and at the same time to look at her, and, when her sleep grew deeper, to touch, to kiss her. What I felt then was love in the presence of something as pure, as immaterial in its feelings, as mysterious, as if I had

85

been in the presence of those inanimate creatures which are the beauties of nature. And indeed, as soon as her sleep became at all heavy, she ceased to be merely the plant that she had been; her sleep, on the margin of which I remained musing, with a fresh delight of which I never tired, but could have gone on enjoying it indefinitely, was to me an undiscovered country. Her sleep brought within my reach something as calm, as sensually delicious as those nights of full moon on the bay of Balbec, turned quiet as a lake over which the branches barely stir, where stretched out upon the sand one could listen for hours on end to the waves breaking and receding.

When I entered the room, I remained standing in the doorway, not venturing to make a sound, and hearing none but that of her breath rising to expire upon her lips at regular intervals, like the reflux of the sea, but drowsier and more gentle. And at the moment when my ear absorbed that divine sound, I felt that there was, condensed in it, the whole person, the whole life of the charming captive, outstretched there before my eyes. Carriages went rattling past in the street, her features remained as motionless, as pure, her breath as light, reduced to the simplest expulsion of the necessary quantity of air. Then, seeing that her sleep would not be disturbed, I advanced cautiously, sat down upon the chair that stood by the bedside, then upon the bed itself.

I have spent charming evenings talking, playing games with Albertine, but never any so pleasant as when I was watching her sleep. Granted that she might have, as she chatted with me, or played cards, that spontaneity which no actress could have imitated, it was a spontaneity carried to the second degree that was offered me by her sleep. Her hair, falling all along her rosy face, was spread out beside her on the bed, and here and there a separate straight tress gave the same effect of perspective as those moonlit trees, lank and pale, which one sees standing erect and stiff in the backgrounds of Elstir's raphaelesque pictures. If Albertine's lips were closed, her eyelids, on the other hand, seen from the point at which I was standing, seemed so loosely joined that I might almost have questioned whether she really was asleep. At the same time those drooping lids introduced into her face that perfect continuity, unbroken by any intrusion of eyes. There are people whose faces assume a quite unusual beauty and majesty the moment they cease to look out of their eyes.

I measured with my own Albertine outstretched at my feet. Now and then a slight, unaccountable tremor ran through her body, as the leaves of a tree are shaken for a few moments by a sudden breath of wind. She would touch her hair, then, not having arranged it to her liking, would raise her hand to it again with motions so consecutive, so deliberate, that I was convinced that she was about to wake. Not at all, she grew calm again in the sleep from which she had not emerged. After this she lay without moving. She had laid her hand on her bosom with a sinking of the arm so artlessly childlike that I was obliged, as I gazed at her, to suppress the smile that is provoked in us by the solemnity, the innocence and the charm of little children.

I, who was acquainted with many Albertines in one person, seemed now to see many more again, reposing by my side. Her eyebrows arched as I had never seen them enclosed the globes of her eyelids like a halcyon's downy nest. Races, atavisms, vices reposed upon her face. Whenever she moved her head, she created a fresh woman, often one whose existence I had never suspected. I seemed to possess not one, but innumerable girls. Her breathing, as it became gradually deeper, was now regularly stirring her bosom and, through it, her folded hands, her pearls, displaced in a different way by the same movement, like the boats, the anchor chains that are set swaying by the movement of the tide. Then, feeling that the tide of her sleep was full, that I should not ground upon reefs of consciousness covered now by the high water of profound slumber, deliberately, I crept without a sound upon the bed, lay down by her side, clasped her waist in one arm, placed my lips upon her cheek and heart, then upon every part of her body in turn laid my free hand, which also was raised, like the pearls, by Albertine's breathing; I myself was gently rocked by its regular motion: I had embarked upon the tide of Albertine's sleep. Sometimes it made me taste a pleasure that was less pure. For this I had no need to make any movement, I allowed my leg to dangle against hers, like an oar which one allows to trail in the water, imparting to it now and again a gentle oscillation like the intermittent flap given to its wing by a bird asleep in the air. I chose, in gazing at her, this aspect of her face which no one ever saw and which was so pleasing.

It is I suppose comprehensible that the letters which we receive from a person are more or less similar and combine to trace an image of the writer so different from the person whom we know as to constitute a second personality. But how much stranger is it that a woman should be conjoined, like Rosita and Doodica, with another woman whose different beauty makes us infer another character, and that in order to behold one we must look at her in profile, the other in full face. The sound of her breathing as it grew louder might give the illusion of the breathless ecstasy of pleasure and, when mine was at its climax, I could kiss her without having interrupted her sleep. I felt at such moments that I had been possessing her more completely, like an unconscious and unresisting object of dumb nature. I was not affected by the words that she muttered occasionally in her sleep, their meaning escaped me, and besides, whoever the unknown person to whom they referred, it was upon my hand, upon my cheek that her hand, as an occasional tremor recalled it to life, stiffened for an instant. I relished her sleep with a disinterested, soothing love, just as I would remain for hours listening to the unfurling of the waves.

Perhaps it is laid down that people must be capable of making us suffer intensely before, in the hours of respite, they can procure for us the same soothing calm as Nature. I had not to answer her as when we were engaged in conversation, and even if I could have remained silent, as for that matter I did when it was she that was talking, still while listening to her voice I did not penetrate so far into herself. As I continued to hear, to gather from moment to moment the murmur, soothing as a barely perceptible breeze, of her breath, it was a whole physiological existence that was spread out before me, for me; as I used to remain for hours lying on the beach, in the moonlight, so long could I have remained there gazing at her, listening to her.

Sometimes one would have said that the sea was becoming rough, that the storm was making itself felt even inside the bay, and like the bay I lay listening to the gathering roar of her breath. Sometimes, when she was too warm, she would take off, already half asleep, her kimono which she flung over my armchair. While she was asleep I would tell myself that all her correspondence was in the inner pocket of this kimono, into which she always thrust her letters. A signature, a written appointment would have sufficed to prove a lie or to dispel a suspicion. When I could see that Albertine was sound asleep, leaving the foot of the bed where I had been standing motionless in contemplation of her, I took a step forward, seized by a burning curiosity, feeling that the secret of this other life lay offering itself to me, flaccid and defenceless, in that armchair. Perhaps I took this step forward also because to stand perfectly still and watch her sleeping became tiring after a while. And so, on tiptoe, constantly turning round to make sure that Albertine was not waking, I made my way to the armchair. There I stopped short, stood for a long time gazing at the kimono, as I had stood for a long time gazing at Albertine. But (and here perhaps I was wrong) never once did I touch the kimono, put my hand in the pocket, examine the letters. In the end, realising that I would never make up my mind, I started back, on tiptoe, returned to Albertine's bedside and began again to watch her sleeping, her who would tell me nothing, whereas I could see lying across an arm of the chair that kimono which would have told me much. And just as people pay a hundred francs a day for a room at the Hotel at Balbec in order to breathe the sea air, I felt it to be quite natural that I should spend more than that upon her since I had her breath upon my cheek, between her lips which I parted with my own, through which her life flowed against my tongue.

But this pleasure of seeing her sleep, which was as precious as that of feeling her live, was cut short by another pleasure, that of seeing her wake. It was, carried to a more profound and more mysterious degree, the same pleasure that I felt in having her under my roof. It was gratifying, of course, in the afternoon, when she alighted from the carriage, that it should be to my address that she was returning. It was even more so to me that when from the underworld of sleep she climbed the last steps of the stair of dreams, it was in my room that she was reborn to consciousness and life, that she asked herself for an instant: "Where am I?" and, seeing all the things in the room round about her, the lamp whose light scarcely made her blink her eyes, was able to assure herself that she was at home, as soon as she realised that she was waking in my home. In that first delicious moment of uncertainty, it seemed to me that once again I took a more complete possession of her since, whereas after an outing it was to her own room that she returned, it was now my room that, as soon as Albertine should have recognised it, was about to enclose, to contain her, without any sign of misgiving in the eyes of my mistress, which remained as calm as if she had never slept at all.

The uncertainty of awakening revealed by her silence was not at all revealed in her eyes. As soon as she was able to speak she said: "My ——" or "My dearest ——" followed by my Christian name, which if, we give the narrator the same name as the author of this book, would be "My Marcel," or "My dearest Marcel." After this I would never allow my relatives, by calling me "dearest," to rob of their priceless uniqueness the delicious words that Albertine uttered to me. As she uttered them, she pursed her lips in a little pout which she herself transformed into a kiss. As quickly as, earlier in the evening, she had fallen asleep, so quickly had she awoken.

No more than my own progression in time, no more than the act of gazing at a girl seated opposite to me beneath the lamp, which shed upon her a different light from that of the sun when I used to behold her striding along the seashore, was this material enrichment, this autonomous progress of Albertine the determining cause of the difference between my present view of her and my original impression of her at Balbec. A longer term of years might have separated the two images without effecting so complete a change; it had come to pass, essential and sudden, when I learned that my mistress had been virtually brought up by Mlle. Vinteuil's friend. If at one time I had been carried away by excitement when I thought that I saw a trace of mystery in Albertine's eyes, now I was happy only at the moments when from those eyes, from her cheeks even, as mirroring as her eyes, so gentle now but quickly turning sullen, I succeeded in expelling every trace of mystery.

The image for which I sought, upon which I reposed, against which I would have liked to lean and die, was no longer that of Albertine leading a hidden life, it was that of an Albertine as familiar to me as possible (and for this reason my love could not be lasting unless it was unhappy, for in its nature it did not satisfy my need of mystery), an Albertine who did not reflect a distant world, but desired nothing else—there were moments when this did indeed appear to be the case—than to be with me, a person like myself, an Albertine the embodiment of what belonged to me and not of the unknown. When it is in this way, from an hour of anguish caused by another person, when it is from uncertainty whether we shall be able to keep her or she will escape, that love is born, such love bears the mark of the revolution that has created it, it recalls very little of what we had previously seen when we thought of the person in question. And my first impressions at the sight of Albertine, against a background of sea, might to some small extent persist in my love of her: actually, these earlier impressions occupy but a tiny place in a love of this sort; in its strength, in its agony, in its need of comfort and its return to a calm and soothing memory with which we would prefer to abide and to learn nothing more of her whom we love, even if there be something horrible that we ought to know —would prefer still more to consult only these earlier memories—such a love is composed of very different material!

Sometimes I put out the light before she came in. It was in the darkness, barely guided by the glow of a smouldering log, that she lay down by my side. My hands, my cheeks alone identified her without my eyes' beholding her, my eyes that often were afraid of finding her altered. With the result that by virtue of this unseeing love she may have felt herself bathed in a warmer affection than usual. On other evenings, I undressed, I lay down, and, with Albertine perched on the side of my bed, we resumed our game or our conversation interrupted by kisses; and, in the desire that alone makes us take an interest in the existence and character of another person, we remain so true to our own nature (even if, at the same time, we abandon successively the different people whom we have loved in turn), that on one occasion, catching sight of myself in the glass at the moment when I was kissing Albertine and calling her my little girl, the sorrowful, passionate expression on my own face, similar to the expression it had assumed long ago with Gilberte whom I no longer remembered, and would perhaps assume one day with another girl, if I was fated ever to forget Albertine, made me think that over and above any personal considerations (instinct requiring that we consider the person of the moment as the only true person) I was performing the duties of an ardent and painful devotion dedicated as an oblation to the youth and beauty of Woman. And yet with this desire, honouring youth with an *ex voto*, with my memories also of Balbec, there was blended, in the need that I felt of keeping Albertine in this way every evening by my side, something that had hitherto been unknown, at least in my amorous existence, if it was not entirely novel in my life.

It was a soothing power the like of which I had not known since the evenings at Combray long ago when my mother, stooping over my bed, brought me repose in a kiss. To be sure, I should have been greatly astonished at that time, had anyone told me that I was not wholly virtuous, and more astonished still to be told that I would ever seek to deprive some one else of a pleasure. I must have known myself very slightly, for my pleasure in having Albertine to live with me was much less a positive pleasure than that of having withdrawn from the world, where everyone was free to enjoy her in turn, the blossoming damsel who, if she did not bring me any great joy, was at least withholding joy from others. Ambition, fame would have left me unmoved. Even more was I incapable of feeling hatred. And yet to me to love in a carnal sense was at any rate to enjoy a triumph over countless rivals. I can never repeat it often enough; it was first and foremost a sedative.

For all that I might, before Albertine returned, have doubted her loyalty, have imagined her in the room at Montjouvain, once she was in her dressing-gown and seated facing my chair, or (if, as was more frequent, I had remained in bed) at the foot of my bed, I would deposit my doubts in her, hand them over for her to relieve me of them, with the abnegation of a worshipper uttering his prayer. All the evening she might have been there, huddled in a provoking ball upon my bed, playing with me, like a great cat; her little pink nose, the tip of which she made even tinier with a coquettish glance which gave it that sharpness which we see in certain people who are inclined to be stout, might have given her a fiery and rebellious air; she might have allowed a tress of her long, dark hair to fall over a cheek of rosy wax and, half shutting her eyes, unfolding her arms, have seemed to be saying to me: " Do with me what you please!"; when, as the time came for her to leave me, she drew nearer to say goodnight, it was a meekness that had become almost a part of my family life that I kissed on either side of her firm throat which now never seemed to me brown or freckled enough, as though these solid qualities had been in keeping with some loyal generosity in Albertine.

When it was Albertine's turn to bid me good-night, kissing me on either side of my throat, her hair caressed me like a wing of softly bristling feathers. Incomparable as were those two kisses of peace, Albertine slipped into my mouth, making me the gift of her tongue, like a gift of the Holy Spirit, conveyed to me a viaticum, left me with a provision of tranquillity almost as precious as when my mother in the evening at Combray used to lay her lips upon my brow.

"Are you coming with us to-morrow, you naughty man?" she asked before leaving me. "Where are you going?" "That will depend on the weather and on yourself. But have you written anything to-day, my little darling? No? Then it was hardly worth your while, not coming with us. Tell me, by the way, when I came in, you knew my step, you guessed at once who it was?" "Of course. Could I possibly be mistaken, couldn't I tell my little sparrow's hop among a thousand? She must let me take her shoes off, before she goes to bed, it will be such a pleasure to me. You are so nice and pink in all that white lace."

Such was my answer; among the sensual expressions, we may recognise others that were peculiar to my grandmother and mother for, little by little, I was beginning to resemble all my relatives, my father who—in a very different fashion from myself, no doubt, for if things do repeat themselves, it is with great variations—took so keen an interest in the weather; and not my father only, I was becoming more and more like my aunt Léonie. Otherwise, Albertine could not but have been a reason for my going out of doors, so as not to leave her by herself, beyond my control. My aunt Léonie, wrapped up in her religious observances, with whom I could have sworn that I had not a single point in common, I so passionately keen on pleasure, apparently worlds apart from that maniac who had never known any pleasure in her life and lay mumbling her rosary all day long, I who suffered from my inability to embark upon a literary career whereas she had been the one person in the family who could never understand that reading was anything more than an amusing pastime, which made reading, even at the paschal season, lawful upon Sunday, when every serious occupation is forbidden, in order that the day may be hallowed by prayer alone. Now, albeit every day I found an excuse in some particular indisposition which made me so often remain in bed, a person (not Albertine, not any person that I loved, but a person with more power over me than any beloved) had migrated into me, despotic to the extent of silencing at times my jealous suspicions or at least of preventing me from going to find out whether they had any foundation, and this was my aunt Léonie. It was quite enough that I should bear an exaggerated resemblance to my father, to the extent of not being satisfied like him with consulting the barometer, but becoming an animated barometer myself; it was quite enough that I should allow myself to be ordered by my aunt Léonie to stay at home and watch the weather, from my bedroom window or even from my bed; yet here I was talking now to Albertine, at one moment as the child that I had been at Combray used to talk to my mother, at another as my grandmother used to talk to me.

When we have passed a certain age, the soul of the child that we were and the souls of the dead from whom we spring come and bestow upon us in handfuls their treasures and their calamities, asking to be allowed to cooperate in the new sentiments which we are feeling and in which, obliterating their former image, we recast them in an original creation. Thus my whole past from my earliest years, and earlier still the past of my parents and relatives, blended with my impure love for Albertine the charm of an affection at once filial and maternal. We have to give hospitality, at a certain stage in our life, to all our relatives who have journeyed so far and gathered round us.

Before Albertine obeyed and allowed me to take off her shoes, I opened her chemise. Her two little upstanding breasts were so round that they seemed not so much to be an integral part of her body as to have ripened there like fruit; and her belly (concealing the place where a man's is marred as though by an iron clamp left sticking in a statue that has been taken down from its niche) was closed, at the junction of her thighs, by two valves of a curve as hushed, as reposeful, as cloistral as that of the horizon after the sun has set. She took off her shoes, and lay down by my side.

O mighty attitudes of Man and Woman, in which there seeks to be reunited, in the innocence of the world's first age and with the humility of clay, what creation has cloven apart, in which Eve is astonished and submissive before the Man by whose side she has awoken, as he himself, alone still, before God Who has fashioned him. Albertine folded her arms behind her dark hair, her swelling hip, her leg falling with the inflexion of a swan's neck that stretches upwards and then curves over towards its starting point. It was only when she was lying right on her side that one saw a certain aspect of her face (so good and handsome when one looked at it from in front) which

I could not endure, hook-nosed as in some of Leonardo's caricatures, seeming to indicate the shiftiness, the greed for profit, the cunning of a spy whose presence in my house would have filled me with horror and whom that profile seemed to unmask. At once I took Albertine's face in my hands and altered its position.

"Be a good boy, promise me that if you don't come out to-morrow you will work," said my mistress as she slipped into her chemise. "Yes, but don't put on your dressing-gown yet." Sometimes I ended by falling asleep by her side. The room had grown cold, more wood was wanted. I tried to find the bell above my head, but failed to do so, after fingering all the copper rods in turn save those between which it hung, and said to Albertine who had sprung from the bed so that Françoise should not find us lying side by side: "No, come back for a moment, I can't find the bell."

Comforting moments, gay, innocent to all appearance, and yet moments in which there accumulates in us the never suspected possibility of disaster, which makes the amorous life the most precarious of all, that in which the incalculable rain of sulphur and brimstone falls after the most radiant moments, after which, without having the courage to derive its lesson from our mishap, we set to work immediately to rebuild upon the slopes of the crater from which nothing but catastrophe can emerge. I was as careless as everyone who imagines that his happiness will endure.

It is precisely because this comfort has been necessary to bring grief to birth—and will return moreover at intervals to calm it—that men can be sincere with each other, and even with themselves, when they pride themselves upon a woman's kindness to them, although, taking things all in all, at the heart of their intimacy there lurks continually in a secret fashion, unavowed to the rest of the world, or revealed unintentionally by questions, inquiries, a painful uncertainty. But as this could not have come to birth without the preliminary comfort, as even afterwards the intermittent comfort is necessary to make suffering endurable and to prevent ruptures, their concealment of the secret hell that life can be when shared with the woman in question, carried to the pitch of an ostentatious display of an intimacy which, they pretend, is precious, expresses a genuine point of view, a universal process of cause and effect, one of the modes in which the production of grief is rendered possible.

It no longer surprised me that Albertine should be in the house, and would not be going out to-morrow save with myself or in the custody of Andrée. These habits of a life shared in common, this broad outline which defined my existence and within which nobody might penetrate but Albertine, also (in the future plan, of which I was still unaware, of my life to come, like the plan traced by an architect for monumental structures which will not be erected until long afterwards) the remoter lines, parallel to the others but vaster, that sketched in me, like a lonely hermitage, the somewhat rigid and monotonous formula of my future loves, had in reality been traced that night at Balbec when, in the little tram, after Albertine had revealed to me who it was that had brought her up, I had decided at any cost to remove her from certain influences and to prevent her from straying out of my sight for some days to come. Day after day had gone by, these habits had become mechanical, but, like those primitive rites the meaning of which historians seek to discover,

I might (but would not) have said to anybody who asked me what I meant by this life of seclusion which I carried so far as not to go any more to the theatre, that its origin was the anxiety of a certain evening, and my need to prove to myself, during the days that followed, that the girl whose unfortunate childhood I had learned should not find it possible, if she wished, to expose herself to similar temptations. I no longer thought, save very rarely, of these possibilities, but they were nevertheless to remain vaguely present in my consciousness. The fact that I was destroying—or trying to destroy—them day by day was doubtless the reason why it comforted me to kiss those cheeks which were no more beautiful than many others; beneath any carnal attraction which is at all profound, there is the permanent possibility of danger.

I had promised Albertine that, if I did not go out with her, I would settle down to work, but in the morning, just as if, taking advantage of our being asleep, the house had miraculously flown, I awoke in different weather beneath another clime. We do not begin to work at the moment of landing in a strange country to the conditions of which we have to adapt ourself. But each day was for me a different country. Even my laziness itself, beneath the novel forms that it had assumed, how was I to recognise it?

Sometimes, on days when the weather was, according to everyone, past praying for, the mere act of staying in the house, situated in the midst of a steady and continuous rain, had all the gliding charm, the soothing silence, the interest of a sea voyage; at another time, on a bright day, to lie still in bed was to let the lights and shadows play around me as round a tree-trunk.

Or yet again, in the first strokes of the bell of a neighbouring convent, rare as the early morning worshippers, barely whitening the dark sky with their fluttering snow-fall, melted and scattered by the warm breeze, I had discerned one of those tempestuous, disordered, delightful days, when the roofs soaked by an occasional shower and dried by a breath of wind or a ray of sunshine let fall a cooing eavesdrop, and, as they wait for the wind to resume its turn, preen in the momentary sunlight that has burnished them their pigeon's-breast of slates, one of those days filled with so many changes of weather, atmospheric incidents, storms, that the idle man does not feel that he has wasted them, because he has been taking an interest in the activity which, in default of himself, the atmosphere, acting in a sense in his stead, has displayed; days similar to those times of revolution or war which do not seem empty to the schoolboy who has played truant from his classroom, because by loitering outside the Law Courts or by reading the newspapers, he has the illusion of finding, in the events that have occurred, failing the lesson which he has not learned, an intellectual profit and an excuse for his idleness; days to which we may compare those on which there occurs in our life some exceptional crisis from which the man who has never done anything imagines that he is going to acquire, if it comes to a happy issue, laborious habits; for instance, the morning on which he sets out for a duel which is to be fought under particularly dangerous conditions; then he is suddenly made aware, at the moment when it is perhaps about to be taken from him, of the value of a life of which he might have made use to begin some important work, or merely to enjoy pleasures, and of which he has failed to make any use at all. "If I can only not be killed," he says to himself, "how I shall settle down to work this very minute, and how I shall enjoy myself too."

Life has in fact suddenly acquired, in his eyes, a higher value, because he puts into life everything that it seems to him capable of giving, instead of the little that he normally makes it give. He sees it in the light of his desire, not as his experience has taught him that he was apt to make it, that is to say so tawdry! It has, at that moment, become filled with work, travel, mountain-climbing, all the pleasant things which, he tells himself, the fatal issue of the duel may render impossible, whereas they were already impossible before there was any question of a duel, owing to the bad habits which, even had there been no duel, would have persisted. He returns home without even a scratch, but he continues to find the same obstacles to pleasures, excursions, travel, to everything of which he had feared for a moment to be for ever deprived by death; to deprive him of them life has been sufficient. As for work—exceptional circumstances having the effect of intensifying what previously existed in the man, labour in the laborious, laziness in the lazy—he takes a holiday.

I followed his example, and did as I had always done since my first resolution to become a writer, which I had made long ago, but which seemed to me to date from yesterday, because I had regarded each intervening day as non-existent. I treated this day in a similar fashion, allowing its showers of rain and bursts of sunshine to pass without doing anything, and vowing that I would begin to work on the morrow. But then I was no longer the same man beneath a cloudless sky; the golden note of the bells did not contain merely (as honey contains) light, but the sensation of light and also the sickly savour of preserved fruits (because at Combray it had often loitered like a wasp over our cleared dinner-table). On this day of dazzling sunshine, to remain until nightfall with my eyes shut was a thing permitted, customary, healthgiving, pleasant, seasonable, like keeping the outside shutters closed against the heat.

It was in such weather as this that at the beginning of my second visit to Balbec I used to hear the violins of the orchestra amid the bluish flow of the rising tide. How much more fully did I possess Albertine to-day.

There were days when the sound of a bell striking the hour bore upon the sphere of its resonance a plate so cool, so richly loaded with moisture or with light that it was like a transcription for the blind, or if you prefer a musical interpretation of the charm of rain or of the charm of the sun. So much so that, at that moment, as I lay in bed, with my eyes shut, I said to myself that everything is capable of transposition and that a universe which was merely audible might be as full of variety as the other. Travelling lazily upstream from day to day, as in a boat, and seeing appear before my eyes an endlessly changing succession of enchanted memories, which I did not select, which a moment earlier had been invisible, and which my mind presented to me one after another, without my being free to choose them, I pursued idly over that continuous expanse my stroll in the sunshine.

Those morning concerts at Balbec were not remote in time. And yet, at that comparatively recent moment, I had given but little thought to Albertine. Indeed, on the very first mornings after my arrival, I had not known that she was at Balbec. From whom then had I learned it? Oh, yes, from Aimé. It was a fine sunny day like this. He was glad to see me again. But he does not like Albertine. Not everybody can be in love with her. Yes, it was he who told me that she was at Balbec. But how did he know? Ah! he had met her, had thought that she had a bad style. At that moment, as I regarded Aimé's story from another aspect than that in which he had told me it, my thoughts, which hitherto had been sailing blissfully over these untroubled waters, exploded suddenly, as though they had struck an invisible and perilous mine, treacherously moored at this point in my memory. He had told me that he had met her, that he had thought her style bad. What had he meant by a bad style? I had understood him to mean a vulgar manner, because, to contradict him in advance, I had declared that she was most refined. But no, perhaps he had meant the style of Gomorrah. She was with another girl, perhaps their arms were round one another's waist, they were staring at other women, they were indeed displaying a "style" which I had never seen Albertine adopt in my presence. Who was the other girl, where had Aimé met her, this odious Albertine?

I tried to recall exactly what Aimé had said to me, in order to see whether it could be made to refer to what I imagined, or he had meant nothing more than common manners. But in vain might I ask the question, the person who put it and the person who might supply the recollection were, alas, one and the same person, myself, who was momentarily duplicated but without adding anything to my stature... Question as I might, it was myself who answered, I learned nothing fresh. I no longer gave a thought to Mlle. Vinteuil. Born of a novel suspicion, the fit of jealousy from which I was suffering was novel also, or rather it was only the prolongation, the extension of that suspicion, it had the same theatre, which was no longer Montjouvain, but the road upon which Aimé had met Albertine, and for its object the various friends one or other of whom might be she who had been with Albertine that day. It was perhaps a certain Élisabeth, or else perhaps those two girls whom Albertine had watched in the mirror at the Casino, while appearing not to notice them. She had doubtless been having relations with them, and also with Esther, Bloch's cousin. Such relations, had they been revealed to me by a third person, would have been enough almost to kill me, but as it was myself that was imagining them, I took care to add sufficient uncertainty to deaden the pain.

We succeed in absorbing daily, under the guise of suspicions, in enormous doses, this same idea that we are being betrayed, a quite minute quantity of which might prove fatal, if injected by the needle of a stabbing word. It is no doubt for that reason, and by a survival of the instinct of self-preservation, that the same jealous man does not hesitate to form the most terrible suspicions upon a basis of innocuous details, provided that, whenever any proof is brought to him, he may decline to accept its evidence. Anyhow, love is an incurable malady, like those diathetic states in which rheumatism affords the sufferer a brief respite only to be replaced by epileptiform headaches. Was my jealous suspicion calmed, I then felt a grudge against Albertine for not having been gentle with me, perhaps for having made fun of me to Andrée. I thought with alarm of the idea that she must have formed if Andrée had repeated all our conversations; the future loomed black and menacing. This mood of depression left me only if a fresh jealous suspicion drove me upon another quest or if, on the other hand, Albertine's display of affection made the actual state of my fortunes seem to me immaterial. Whoever this girl might be, I should have to write to Aimé, to try to see him, and then I should check his statement by talking to Albertine, hearing her confession. In the mean time, convinced that it must be Bloch's cousin, I asked Bloch himself, who had not the remotest idea of my purpose, simply to let me see

her photograph, or, better still, to arrange if possible for
me to meet her.

How many persons, cities, roads does not jealousy
make us eager thus to know? It is a thirst for knowledge
thanks to which, with regard to various isolated points,
we end by acquiring every possible notion in turn except
those that we require. We can never tell whether a
suspicion will not arise, for, all of a sudden, we recall a
sentence that was not clear, an alibi that cannot have
been given us without a purpose. And yet, we have not
seen the person again, but there is such a thing as a posthumous jealousy, that is born only after we have left her,
a jealousy of the doorstep. Perhaps the habit that I had
formed of nursing in my bosom several simultaneous desires, a desire for a young girl of good family such as I
used to see pass beneath my window escorted by her
governess, and especially of the girl whom Saint Loup
had mentioned to me, the one who frequented houses of
ill fame, a desire for handsome lady's-maids, and especially for the maid of Mme. Putbus, a desire to go to the
country in early spring, to see once again hawthorns,
apple trees in blossom, storms at sea, a desire for Venice,
a desire to settle down to work, a desire to live like other
people—perhaps the habit of storing up, without assuag-
ing any of them, all these desires, contenting myself with
the promise, made to myself, that I would not forget
to satisfy them one day, perhaps this habit, so many years
old already, of perpetual postponement, of what M. de
Charlus used to castigate under the name of procrastina-
tion, had become so prevalent in me that it assumed control of my jealous suspicions also and, while it made me
take a mental note that I would not fail, some day, to

have an explanation from Albertine with regard to the girl, possibly the girls (this part of the story was confused, rubbed out, that is to say obliterated, in my memory) with whom Aimé had met her, made me also postpone this explanation. In any case, I would not mention it this evening to my mistress for fear of making her think me jealous and so offending her.

And yet when, on the following day, Bloch had sent me the photograph of his cousin Esther, I made haste to forward it to Aimé. And at the same moment I remembered that Albertine had that morning refused me a pleasure which might indeed have tired her. Was that in order to reserve it for some one else? This afternoon, perhaps? For whom?

Thus it is that jealousy is endless, for even if the beloved object, by dying for instance, can no longer provoke it by her actions, it so happens that posthumous memories, of later origin than any event, take shape suddenly in our minds as though they were events also, memories which hitherto we have never properly explored, which had seemed to us unimportant, and to which our own meditation upon them has been sufficient, without any external action, to give a new and terrible meaning. We have no need of her company, it is enough to be alone in our room, thinking, for fresh betrayals of us by our mistress to come to light, even though she be dead. And so we ought not to fear in love, as in everyday life, the future alone, but even the past which often we do not succeed in realising until the future has come and gone; and we are not speaking only of the past which we discover long afterwards, but of the past which we have long kept stored up in ourself and learn suddenly how to interpret.

No matter, I was very glad, now that afternoon was turning to evening, that the hour was not far off when I should be able to appeal to Albertine's company for the consolation of which I stood in need. Unfortunately, the evening that followed was one of those on which this consolation was not afforded me, on which the kiss that Albertine would give me when she left me for the night, very different from her ordinary kiss, would no more soothe me than my mother's kiss had soothed me long ago, on days when she was vexed with me and I dared not send for her, but at the same time knew that I should not be able to sleep. Such evenings were now those on which Albertine had formed for the morrow some plan of which she did not wish me to know. Had she confided in me, I would have employed, to assure its successful execution, an ardour which none but Albertine could have inspired in me. But she told me nothing, nor had she any need to tell me anything; as soon as she came in, before she had even crossed the threshold of my room, as she was still wearing her hat or toque, I had already detected the unknown, restive, desperate, indomitable desire. Now, these were often the evenings when I had awaited her return with the most loving thoughts, and looked forward to throwing my arms round her neck with the warmest affection.

Alas, those misunderstandings that I had often had with my parents, whom I found cold or cross at the moment when I was running to embrace them, overflowing with love, are nothing in comparison with these that occur between lovers! The anguish then is far less superficial, far harder to endure, it has its abode in a deeper stratum of the heart.

This evening, however, Albertine was obliged to mention the plan that she had in her mind; I gathered at once that she wished to go next day to pay a call on Mme. Verdurin, a call to which in itself I would have had no objection. But evidently her object was to meet some one there, to prepare some future pleasure. Otherwise she would not have attached so much importance to this call. That is to say, she would not have kept on assuring me that it was of no importance. I had in the course of my life developed in the opposite direction to those races which make use of phonetic writing only after regarding the letters of the alphabet as a set of symbols; I, who for so many years had sought for the real life and thought of other people only in the direct statements with which they furnished me of their own free will, failing these had come to attach importance, on the contrary, only to the evidence that is not a rational and analytical expression of the truth; the words themselves did not enlighten me unless they could be interpreted in the same way as a sudden rush of blood to the cheeks of a person who is embarrassed, or, what is even more telling, a sudden silence.

Some subsidiary word (such as that used by M. de Cambremer when he understood that I was " literary," and, not having spoken to me before, as he was describing a visit that he had paid to the Verdurins, turned to me with: " *Why*, Borelli was there! ") bursting into flames at the unintended, sometimes perilous contact of two ideas which the speaker has not expressed, but which, by applying the appropriate methods of analysis or electrolysis I was able to extract from it, told me more than a long speech.

Albertine sometimes allowed to appear in her conversation one or other of these precious amalgams which I made haste to "treat" so as to transform them into lucid ideas. It is by the way one of the most terrible calamities for the lover that if particular details—which only experiment, espionage, of all the possible realisations, would ever make him know—are so difficult to discover, the truth on the other hand is so easy to penetrate or merely to feel by instinct.

Often I had seen her, at Balbec, fasten upon some girls who came past us a sharp and lingering stare, like a physical contact, after which, if I knew the girls, she would say to me: "Suppose we asked them to join us? I should so love to be rude to them." And now, for some time past, doubtless since she had succeeded in reading my character, no request to me to invite anyone, not a word, never even a sidelong glance from her eyes, which had become objectless and mute, and as revealing, with the vague and vacant expression of the rest of her face, as had been their magnetic swerve before. Now it was impossible for me to reproach her, or to ply her with questions about things which she would have declared to be so petty, so trivial, things that I had stored up in my mind simply for the pleasure of making mountains out of molehills. It is hard enough to say: "Why did you stare at that girl who went past?" but a great deal harder to say: "Why did you not stare at her?" And yet I knew quite well, or at least I should have known, if I had not chosen to believe Albertine's assertions rather than all the trivialities contained in a glance, proved by it and by some contradiction or other in her speech, a contradiction which often I did not perceive until long after I had left her, which kept me on tenterhooks all the night long, which I never dared mention to her again, but which nevertheless continued to honour my memory from time to time with its periodical visits.

Often, in the case of these furtive or sidelong glances on the beach at Balbec or in the streets of Paris, I might ask myself whether the person who provoked them was not merely at the moment when she passed an object of desire but was an old acquaintance, or else some girl who had simply been mentioned to her, and of whom, when I heard about it, I was astonished that anybody could have spoken to her, so utterly unlike was she to anyone that Albertine could possibly wish to know. But the Gomorrah of to-day is a dissected puzzle made up of fragments which are picked up in the places where we least expected to find them. Thus I once saw at Rivebelle a big dinner-party of ten women, all of whom I happened to know—at least by name—women as unlike one another as possible, perfectly united nevertheless, so much so that I never saw a party so homogeneous, albeit so composite.

To return to the girls whom we passed in the street, never did Albertine gaze at an old person, man or woman, with such fixity, or on the other hand with such reserve, and as though she saw nothing. The cuckolded husbands who know nothing know everything all the same. But it requires more accurate and abundant evidence to create a scene of jealousy. Besides, if jealousy helps us to discover a certain tendency to falsehood in the woman whom we love, it multiplies this tendency an hundredfold when the woman has discovered that we are jealous. She lies (to an extent to which she has never lied to us before), whether from pity, or from fear, or because she instinctively withdraws by a methodical flight from our investigations. Certainly there are love affairs in which from the start a light woman has posed as virtue incarnate in the eyes of the man who is in love with her. But how many others consist of two diametrically opposite periods? In the first, the woman speaks almost spontaneously, with slight modifications, of her zest for sensual pleasure, of the gay life which it has made her lead, things all of which she will deny later on, with the last breath in her body, to the same man—when she has felt that he is jealous of and spying upon her. He begins to think with regret of the days of those first confidences, the memory of which torments him nevertheless. If the woman continued to make them, she would furnish him almost unaided with the secret of her conduct which he has been vainly pursuing day after day. And besides, what a surrender that would mean, what trust, what friendship. If she cannot live without betraying him, at least she would be betraying him as a friend, telling him of her pleasures, associating him with them. And he thinks with regret of the sort of life which the early stages of their love seemed to promise, which the sequel has rendered impossible, making of that love a thing exquisitely painful, which will render a final parting, according to circumstances, either inevitable or impossible.

Sometimes the script from which I deciphered Albertine's falsehoods, without being ideographic needed simply to be read backwards; so this evening she had flung at me in a careless tone the message, intended to pass almost unheeded: " It is possible that I may go to-morrow to the Verdurins', I don't in the least know whether I shall go, I don't really want to." A childish anagram of the admission: "I shall go to-morrow to the Verdurins', it is absolutely certain, for I attach the utmost importance to the visit." This apparent hesitation indicated a resolute decision and was intended to diminish the importance of the visit while warning me of it. Albertine always adopted a tone of uncertainty in speaking of her irrevocable decisions. Mine was no less irrevocable. I took steps to arrange that this visit to Mme. Verdurin should not take place. Jealousy is often only an uneasy need to be tyrannical, applied to matters of love. I had doubtless inherited from my father this abrupt, arbitrary desire to threaten the people whom I loved best in the hopes with which they were lulling themselves with a security that I determined to expose to them as false; when I saw that Albertine had planned without my knowledge, behind my back, an expedition which I would have done everything in the world to make easier and more pleasant for her, had she taken me into her confidence, I said carelessly, so as to make her tremble, that I intended to go out the next day myself.

I set to work to suggest to Albertine other expeditions in directions which would have made this visit to the Verdurins impossible, in words stamped with a feigned indifference beneath which I strove to conceal my excitement. But she had detected it. It encountered in her the electric shock of a contrary will which violently repulsed it; I could see the sparks flash from her eyes. Of what use, though, was it to pay attention to what her eyes were saying at that moment? How had I failed to observe long ago that Albertine's eyes belonged to the class which even in a quite ordinary person seem to be composed of a number of fragments, because of all the places which the person wishes to visit—and to conceal her desire to visit—that day. Those eyes which their falsehood keeps ever immobile and passive, but dynamic, measurable in the yards or miles to be traversed before they reach the determined, the implacably determined meeting-place, eyes that are not so much smiling at the pleasure which tempts them as they are shadowed with melancholy and discouragement because there may be a difficulty in their getting to the meeting-place. Even when you hold them in your hands, these people are fugitives. To understand the emotions which they arouse, and which other people, even better looking, do not arouse, we must take into account that they are not immobile but in motion, and add to their person a sign corresponding to what in physics is the sign that indicates velocity. If you upset their plans for the day, they confess to you the pleasure that they had hidden from you: " I did so want to go to tea at five o'clock with so and so, my dearest friend." Very well, if, six months later, you come to know the person in question, you will learn that the girl whose plans you upset, who, caught in the trap, in order that you might set her free, confessed to you that she was in the habit of taking tea like this with a dear friend, every day at the hour at which you did not see her,—has never once been inside this person's house, that they have never taken tea together, and that the girl used to explain that her whole time was taken up by none other than yourself. And so the person with whom she confessed that she had gone to tea, with whom she begged you to allow her to go to tea, that person, the excuse that necessity made her plead, was not the real person, there was somebody, something else! Something else, what? Some one, who?

Alas, the kaleidoscopic eyes starting off into the distance and shadowed with melancholy might enable us perhaps to measure distance, but do not indicate direction. The boundless field of possibilities extends before us, and if by any chance the reality presented itself to our gaze, it would be so far beyond the bounds of possibility that, dashing suddenly against the boundary wall, we should fall over backwards. It is not even essential that we should have proof of her movement and flight, it is enough that we should guess them. She had promised us a letter, we were calm, we were no longer in love. The letter has not come; no messenger appears with it; what can have happened? anxiety is born afresh, and love. It is such people more than any others who inspire love in us, for our destruction. For every fresh anxiety that we feel on their account strips them in our eyes of some of their personality. We were resigned to suffering, thinking that we loved outside ourself, and we perceive that our love is a function of our sorrow, that our love perhaps is our sorrow, and that its object is, to a very small extent only, the girl with the raven tresses. But, when all is said, it is these people more than any others who inspire love.

Generally speaking, love has not as its object a human body, except when an emotion, the fear of losing it, the uncertainty of finding it again have been infused into it. This sort of anxiety has a great affinity for bodies. It adds to them a quality which surpasses beauty even; which is one of the reasons why we see men who are indifferent to the most beautiful women fall passionately in love with others who appear to us ugly. To these people, these fugitives, their own nature, our anxiety fastens wings. And even when they are in our company the look in their eyes seems to warn us that they are about to take flight. The proof of this beauty, surpassing the beauty added by the wings, is that very often the same person is, in our eyes, alternately wingless and winged. Afraid of losing her, we forget all the others. Sure of keeping her, we compare her with those others whom at once we prefer to her. And as these emotions and these certainties may vary from week to week, a person may one week see sacrificed to her everything that gave us pleasure, in the following week be sacrificed herself, and so for weeks and months on end. All of which would be incomprehensible did we not know from the experience, which every man shares, of having at least once in a lifetime ceased to love, forgotten a woman, for how very little a person counts in herself when she is no longer—or is not yet—permeable by our emotions. And, be it understood, what we say of fugitives is equally true of those in prison, the captive women, we suppose that we are never to possess them. And so men detest procuresses, for these facilitate the flight, enhance the temptation, but if on the other hand they are in love with a cloistered woman, they willingly have recourse to a procuress to make her emerge from her prison and bring her to them. In so far as relations with women whom we abduct are less permanent than others, the reason is that the fear of not succeeding in procuring them or the dread of seeing them escape is the whole of our love for them and that once they have been carried off from their husbands, torn from their footlights, cured of the temptation to leave us, dissociated in short from our emotion whatever it may be, they are only themselves, that is to say almost nothing, and, so long desired, are soon forsaken by the very man who was so afraid of their forsaking him.

How, I have asked, did I not guess this? But had I not guessed it from the first day at Balbec? Had I not detected in Albertine one of those girls beneath whose envelope of flesh more hidden persons are stirring, than in . . . I do not say a pack of cards still in its box, a cathedral or a theatre before we enter it, but the whole, vast, ever changing crowd? Not only all these persons, but the desire, the voluptuous memory, the desperate quest of all these persons. At Balbec I had not been troubled because I had never even supposed that one day I should be following a trail, even a false trail. No matter! This had given Albertine, in my eyes, the plenitude of a person filled to the brim by the superimposition of all these persons, and desires and voluptuous memories of persons. And now that she had one day let fall the words "Mlle. Vinteuil," I would have wished not to tear off her garments so as to see her body but through her body to see and read that memorandum block of her memories and her future, passionate engagements.

How suddenly do the things that are probably the most insignificant assume an extraordinary value when a person whom we love (or who has lacked only this duplicity to make us love her) conceals them from us! In itself, suffering does not of necessity inspire in us sentiments of love or hatred towards the person who causes it: a surgeon can hurt our body without arousing any personal emotion. But a woman who has continued for some time to assure us that we are everything in the world to her, without being herself everything in the world to us, a woman whom we enjoy seeing, kissing, taking upon our knee, we are astonished if we merely feel from a sudden resistance that we are not free to dispose of her life. Disappointment may then revive in us the forgotten memory of an old anguish, which we know, all the same, to have been provoked not by this woman but by others whose betrayals are milestones in our past life; if it comes to that, how have we the courage to wish to live, how can we move a finger to preserve ourself from death, in a world in which love is provoked only by falsehood, and consists merely in our need to see our sufferings appeased by the person who has made us suffer? To restore us from the collapse which follows our discovery of her falsehood and her resistance, there is the drastic remedy of endeavouring to act against her will, with the help of people whom we feel to be more closely involved than we are in her life, upon her who is resisting us and lying to us, to play the cheat in turn, to make ourself loathed. But the suffering caused by such a love is of the sort which must inevitably lead the sufferer to seek in a change of posture an illusory comfort.

These means of action are not wanting, alas! And the horror of the kind of love which uneasiness alone has engendered lies in the fact that we turn over and over incessantly in our cage the most trivial utterances; not to mention that rarely do the people for whom we feel this love appeal to us physically in a complex fashion, since it is not our deliberate preference, but the chance of a minute of anguish, a minute indefinitely prolonged by our weakness of character, which repeats its experiments every evening until it yields to sedatives, that chooses for us.

No doubt my love for Albertine was not the most barren of those to which, through feebleness of will, a man may descend, for it was not entirely platonic; she did give me carnal satisfaction and, besides, she was intelligent. But all this was a superfluity. What occupied my mind was not the intelligent remark that she might have made, but some chance utterance that had aroused in me a doubt as to her actions; I tried to remember whether she had said this or that, in what tone, at what moment, in response to what speech of mine, to reconstruct the whole scene of her dialogue with me, to recall at what moment she had expressed a desire to call upon the Verdurins, what words of mine had brought that look of vexation to her face. The most important matter might have been in question, without my giving myself so much trouble to establish the truth, to restore the proper atmosphere and colour. No doubt, after these anxieties have intensified to a degree which we find insupportable, we do sometimes manage to soothe them altogether for an evening. The party to which the mistress whom we love is engaged to go, the true nature of which our mind has been toiling for days to discover, we are invited to it also, our mistress has neither looks nor words for anyone but ourself, we take her home and then we enjoy, all our anxieties dispelled, a repose as complete, as healing, as that which we enjoy at times in the profound sleep that comes after a long walk. And no doubt such repose deserves that we should pay a high price for it. But would it not have been more simple not to purchase for ourself, deliberately, the preceding anxiety, and at a higher price still? Besides, we know all too well that however profound these momentary relaxations may be, anxiety will still be the stronger. Sometimes indeed it is revived by the words that were intended to bring us repose. But as a rule, all that we do is to change our anxiety. One of the words of the sentence that was meant to calm us sets our suspicions running upon another trail. The demands of our jealousy and the blindness of our credulity are greater than the woman whom we love could ever suppose.

When, of her own accord, she swears to us that some man is nothing more to her than a friend, she appals us by informing us—a thing we never suspected—that he has been her friend. While she is telling us, in proof of her sincerity, how they took tea together, that very afternoon, at each word that she utters the invisible, the unsuspected takes shape before our eyes. She admits that he has asked her to be his mistress, and we suffer agonies at the thought that she can have listened to his overtures. She refused them, she says. But presently, when we recall what she told us, we shall ask ourself whether her story is really true, for there is wanting, between the different things that she said to us, that logical and necessary connexion which, more than the facts related, is a sign of the truth. Besides, there was that terrible note of scorn in her: "I said to him no, absolutely," which is to be found in every class of society, when a woman is lying. We must nevertheless thank her for having refused, encourage her by our kindness to repeat these cruel confidences in the future. At the most, we may remark: "But if he had already made advances to you, why did you accept his invitation to tea?" "So that he should not be angry with me and say that I hadn't been nice to him." And we dare not reply that by refusing she would perhaps have been nicer to us.

Albertine alarmed me further when she said that I was quite right to say, out of regard for her reputation, that I was not her lover, since "for that matter," she went on, "it's perfectly true that you aren't." I was not her lover perhaps in the full sense of the word, but then, was I to suppose that all the things that we did together she did also with all the other men whose mistress she swore to me that she had never been? The desire to know at all costs what Albertine was thinking, whom she was seeing, with whom she was in love, how strange it was that I should be sacrificing everything to this need, since I had felt the same need to know, in the case of Gilberte, names, facts, which now left me quite indifferent. I was perfectly well aware that in themselves Albertine's actions were of no greater interest. It is curious that a first love, if by the frail state in which it leaves our heart it opens the way to our subsequent loves, does not at least provide us, in view of the identity of symptoms and sufferings, with the means of curing them.

After all, is there any need to know a fact? Are we not aware beforehand, in a general fashion, of the mendacity and even the discretion of those women who have something to conceal? Is there any possibility of error? They make a virtue of their silence, when we would give anything to make them speak. And we feel certain that they have assured their accomplice: "I never tell anything. It won't be through me that anybody will hear about it, I never tell anything." A man may give his fortune, his life for a person, and yet know quite well that in ten years' time, more or less, he would refuse her the fortune, prefer to keep his life. For then the person would be detached from him, alone, that is to say null and void. What attaches us to people are those thousand roots, those innumerable threads which are our memories of last night, our hopes for to-morrow morning, those continuous trammels of habit from which we can never free ourself. Just as there are misers who hoard money from generosity, so we are spendthrifts who spend from avarice, and it is not so much to a person that we sacrifice our life as to all that the person has been able to attach to herself of our hours, our days, of the things compared with which the life not yet lived, the relatively future life, seems to us more remote, more detached, less practical, less our own. What we require is to disentangle ourself from those trammels which are so much more important than the person, but they have the effect of creating in us temporary obligations towards her, obligations which mean that we dare not leave her for fear of being misjudged by her, whereas later on we would so dare, for, detached from us, she would no longer be ourself, and because in reality we create for ourself obligations (even if, by an apparent contradiction, they should lead to suicide) towards ourself alone.

If I was not in love with Albertine (and of this I could not be sure) then there was nothing extraordinary in the place that she occupied in my life: we live only with what we do not love, with what we have brought to live with us only to kill the intolerable love, whether it be of a woman, of a place, or again of a woman embodying a place. Indeed we should be sorely afraid to begin to love again if a further separation were to occur. I had

not yet reached this stage with Albertine. Her falsehoods, her admissions, left me to complete the task of
elucidating the truth: her innumerable falsehoods because
she was not content with merely lying, like everyone who
imagines that he or she is loved, but was by nature, quite
apart from this, a liar, and so inconsistent moreover that,
even if she told me the truth every time, told me what,
for instance, she thought of other people, she would say
each time something different; her admissions, because,
being so rare, so quickly cut short, they left between them,
in so far as they concerned the past, huge intervals quite
blank over the whole expanse of which I was obliged to
retrace—and for that first of all to learn—her life.

As for the present, so far as I could interpret the sibyl-
line utterances of Françoise, it was not only in particular
details, it was as a whole that Albertine was lying to me,
and "one fine day" I would see what Françoise made a
pretence of knowing, what she refused to tell me, what I
dared not ask her. It was no doubt with the same jealousy that she had felt in the past with regard to Eulalie
that Françoise would speak of the most improbable
things, so vague that one could at the most suppose them
to convey the highly improbable insinuation that the poor
captive (who was a lover of women) preferred marriage
with somebody who did not appear altogether to be myself. If this were so, how, notwithstanding her power of
radiotelepathy, could Françoise have come to hear of it?
Certainly, Albertine's statements could give me no definite enlightenment, for they were as different day by day
as the colours of a spinning-top that has almost come to
a standstill. However, it seemed that it was hatred,
more than anything else, that impelled Françoise to

speak. Not a day went by but she said to me, and I in my mother's absence endured such speeches as:

"To be sure, you yourself are kind, and I shall never forget the debt of gratitude that I owe to you" (this probably so that I might establish fresh claims upon her gratitude) "but the house has become a plague-spot now that kindness has set up knavery in it, now that cleverness is protecting the stupidest person that ever was seen, now that refinement, good manners, wit, dignity in everything allow to lay down the law and rule the roast and put me to shame, who have been forty years in the family,—vice, everything that is most vulgar and abject."

What Françoise resented most about Albertine was having to take orders from somebody who was not one of ourselves, and also the strain of the additional housework which was affecting the health of our old servant, who would not, for all that, accept any help in the house, not being a "good for nothing." This in itself would have accounted for her nervous exhaustion, for her furious hatred. Certainly, she would have liked to see Albertine-Esther banished from the house. This was Françoise's dearest wish. And, by consoling her, its fulfilment alone would have given our old servant some repose. But to my mind there was more in it than this. So violent a hatred could have originated only in an overstrained body. And, more even than of consideration, Françoise was in need of sleep.

Albertine went to take off her things and, so as to lose no time in finding out what I wanted to know, I attempted to telephone to Andrée; I took hold of the receiver, invoked the implacable deities, but succeeded only in arous-

ing their fury which expressed itself in the single word
"Engaged!" Andrée was indeed engaged in talking to
some one else. As I waited for her to finish her conversation, I asked myself how it was—now that so many
of our painters are seeking to revive the feminine portraits
of the eighteenth century, in which the cleverly devised
setting is a pretext for portraying expressions of expectation, spleen, interest, distraction—how it was that none
of our modern Bouchers or Fragonards had yet painted,
instead of "The Letter" or "The Harpsichord," this
scene which might be entitled "At the Telephone," in
which there would come spontaneously to the lips of the
listener a smile all the more genuine in that it is conscious
of being unobserved. At length, Andrée was at the other
end: "You are coming to call for Albertine to-morrow?"
I asked, and as I uttered Albertine's name, thought of the
envy I had felt for Swann when he said to me on the day
of the Princesse de Guermantes's party: "Come and see
Odette," and I had thought how, when all was said, there
must be something in a Christian name which, in the eyes
of the whole world including Odette herself, had on
Swann's lips alone this entirely possessive sense.

Must not such an act of possession—summed up in a
single word—over the whole existence of another person
(I had felt whenever I was in love) be pleasant indeed!
But, as a matter of fact, when we are in a position to utter
it, either we no longer care, or else habit has not dulled
the force of affection, but has changed its pleasure into
pain. Falsehood is a very small matter, we live in the
midst of it without doing anything but smile at it, we
practise it without meaning to do any harm to anyone,
but our jealousy is wounded by it, and sees more than

the falsehood conceals (often our mistress refuses to spend the evening with us and goes to the theatre simply so that we shall not notice that she is not looking well). How blind it often remains to what the truth is concealing! But it can extract nothing, for those women who swear that they are not lying would refuse, on the scaffold, to confess their true character. I knew that I alone was in a position to say "Albertine" in that tone to Andrée. And yet, to Albertine, to Andrée, and to myself, I felt that I was nothing. And I realised the impossibility against which love is powerless.

We imagine that love has as its object a person whom we can see lying down before our eyes, enclosed in a human body. Alas, it is the extension of that person to all the points in space and time which the person has occupied and will occupy. If we do not possess its contact with this or that place, this or that hour, we do not possess it. But we cannot touch all these points. If only they were indicated to us, we might perhaps contrive to reach out to them. But we grope for them without finding them. Hence mistrust, jealousy, persecutions. We waste precious time upon absurd clues and pass by the truth without suspecting it.

But already one of the irascible deities, whose servants speed with the agility of lightning, was annoyed, not because I was speaking, but because I was saying nothing. "Come along, I've been holding the line for you all this time; I shall cut you off." However, she did nothing of the sort but, as she evoked Andrée's presence, enveloped it, like the great poet that a telephone girl always is, in the atmosphere peculiar to the home, the district, the very life itself of Albertine's friend. "Is that you?"

asked Andrée, whose voice was projected towards me with an instantaneous speed by the goddess whose privilege it is to make sound more swift than light. "Listen," I replied; "go wherever you like, anywhere, except to Mme. Verdurin's. Whatever happens, you simply must keep Albertine away from there to-morrow." "Why, that's where she promised to go to-morrow." "Ah!"

But I was obliged to break off the conversation for a moment and to make menacing gestures, for if Françoise continued—as though it had been something as unpleasant as vaccination or as dangerous as the aeroplane—to refuse to learn to telephone, whereby she would have spared us the trouble of conversations which she might intercept without any harm, on the other hand she would at once come into the room whenever I was engaged in a conversation so private that I was particularly anxious to keep it from her ears. When she had left the room, not without lingering to take away various things that had been lying there since the previous day and might perfectly well have been left there for an hour longer, and to place in the grate a log that was quite unnecessary in view of my burning fever at the intruder's presence and my fear of finding myself " cut off " by the operator: "I beg your pardon," I said to Andrée, "I was interrupted. Is it absolutely certain that she has to go to the Verdurins' to-morrow?" "Absolutely, but I can tell her that you don't like it." "No, not at all, but it is possible that I may come with you." "Ah!" said Andrée, in a tone of extreme annoyance and as though alarmed by my audacity, which was all the more encouraged by her opposition. "Then I shall say good night, and please forgive me for disturbing you for nothing." "Not at all," said

Andrée, and (since nowadays, the telephone having come into general use, a decorative ritual of polite speeches has grown up round it, as round the tea-tables of the past) added: " It has been a great pleasure to hear your voice."

I might have said the same, and with greater truth than Andrée, for I had been deeply touched by the sound of her voice, having never before noticed that it was so different from the voices of other people. Then I recalled other voices still, women's voices especially, some of them rendered slow by the precision of a question and by mental concentration, others made breathless, even silenced at moments, by the lyrical flow of what the speakers were relating; I recalled one by one the voices of all the girls whom I had known at Balbec, then Gilberte's voice, then my grandmother's, then that of Mme. de Guermantes, I found them all unlike, moulded in a language peculiar to each of the speakers, each playing upon a different instrument, and I said to myself how meagre must be the concert performed in paradise by the three or four angel musicians of the old painters, when I saw mount to the Throne of God, by tens, by hundreds, by thousands, the harmonious and multisonant salutation of all the Voices. I did not leave the telephone without thanking, in a few propitiatory words, her who reigns over the swiftness of sounds for having kindly employed on behalf of my humble words a power which made them a hundred times more rapid than thunder, but my thanksgiving received no other response than that of being cut off.

When Albertine returned to my room, she was wearing a garment of black satin which had the effect of making her seem paler, of turning her into the pallid, ardent Parisian, etiolated by want of fresh air, by the atmosphere of crowds and perhaps by vicious habits, whose eyes seemed more restless because they were not brightened by any colour in her cheeks.

"Guess," I said to her, "to whom I've just been talking on the telephone. Andrée!" "Andrée?" exclaimed Albertine in a harsh tone of astonishment and emotion, which so simple a piece of intelligence seemed hardly to require. "I hope she remembered to tell you that we met Mme. Verdurin the other day." "Mme. Verdurin? I don't remember," I replied, as though I were thinking of something else, so as to appear indifferent to this meeting and not to betray Andrée who had told me where Albertine was going on the morrow.

But how could I tell that Andrée was not herself betraying me, and would not tell Albertine to-morrow that I had asked her to prevent her at all costs from going to the Verdurins', and had not already revealed to her that I had many times made similar appeals. She had assured me that she had never repeated anything, but the value of this assertion was counterbalanced in my mind by the impression that for some time past Albertine's face had ceased to shew that confidence which she had for so long reposed in me.

What is remarkable is that, a few days before this dispute with Albertine, I had already had a dispute with her, but in Andrée's presence. Now Andrée, while she gave Albertine good advice, had always appeared to be insinuating bad. "Come, don't talk like that, hold your tongue," she said, as though she were at the acme of happiness. Her face assumed the dry raspberry hue of those pious housekeepers who make us dismiss each of our servants in turn. While I was heaping reproaches upon Albertine which I ought never to have uttered, Andrée looked as though she were sucking a lump of barley sugar with keen enjoyment. At length she was unable to restrain an affectionate laugh. "Come, Titine, with me. You know, I'm your dear little sister." I was not merely exasperated by this rather sickly exhibition, I asked myself whether Andrée really felt the affection for Albertine that she pretended to feel. Seeing that Albertine, who knew Andrée far better than I did, had always shrugged her shoulders when I asked her whether she was quite certain of Andrée's affection, and had always answered that nobody in the world cared for her more, I was still convinced that Andrée's affection was sincere. Possibly, in her wealthy but provincial family, one might find its equivalent in some of the shops in the Cathedral square, where certain sweetmeats are declared to be "the best going." But I do know that, for my own part, even if I had invariably come to the opposite conclusion, I had so strong an impression that Andrée was trying to rap Albertine's knuckles that my mistress at once regained my affection and my anger subsided.

Suffering, when we are in love, ceases now and then for a moment, but only to recur in a different form. We weep to see her whom we love no longer respond to us with those outbursts of sympathy, the amorous advances of former days, we suffer more keenly still when, having lost them with us, she recovers them for the benefit of others; then, from this suffering, we are distracted by a new and still more piercing grief, the suspicion that she was lying to us about how she spent the previous evening, when she doubtless played us false; this suspicion in turn is dispelled, the kindness that our mistress is

shewing us soothes us, but then a word that we had forgotten comes back to our mind; some one has told us
that she was ardent in moments of pleasure, whereas we
have always found her calm; we try to picture to ourself
what can have been these frenzies with other people, we
feel how very little we are to her, we observe an air of
boredom, longing, melancholy, while we are talking, we
observe like a black sky the unpretentious clothes which
she puts on when she is with us, keeping for other people
the garments with which she used to flatter us at first.
If on the contrary she is affectionate, what joy for a
moment; but when we see that little tongue outstretched
as though in invitation, we think of those people to
whom that invitation has so often been addressed, and
that perhaps even here at home, even although Albertine
was not thinking of them, it has remained, by force of
long habit, an automatic signal. Then the feeling that
we are bored with each other returns. But suddenly this
pain is reduced to nothing when we think of the unknown
evil element in her life, of the places impossible to identify
where she has been, where she still goes perhaps at the
hours when we are not with her, if indeed she is not planning to live there altogether, those places in which she
is parted from us, does not belong to us, is happier than
when she is with us. Such are the revolving searchlights
of jealousy.

Jealousy is moreover a demon that cannot be exorcised,
but always returns to assume a fresh incarnation. Even
if we could succeed in exterminating them all, in keeping
for ever her whom we love, the Spirit of Evil would then
adopt another form, more pathetic still, despair at having
obtained fidelity only by force, despair at not being loved.

Between Albertine and myself there was often the obstacle of a silence based no doubt upon grievances which she kept to herself, because she supposed them to be irremediable. Charming as Albertine was on some evenings, she no longer shewed those spontaneous impulses which I remembered at Balbec when she used to say: "How good you are to me all the same!" and her whole heart seemed to spring towards me without the reservation of any of those grievances which she now felt and kept to herself because she supposed them no doubt to be irremediable, impossible to forget, unconfessed, but which set up nevertheless between her and myself the significant prudence of her speech or the interval of an impassable silence.

"And may one be allowed to know why you telephoned to Andrée?" "To ask whether she had any objection to my joining you to-morrow, so that I may pay the Verdurins the call I promised them at la Raspelière." "Just as you like. But I warn you, there is an appalling mist this evening, and it's sure to last over to-morrow. I mention it, because I shouldn't like you to make yourself ill. Personally, you can imagine I would far rather you came with us. However," she added with a thoughtful air: "I'm not at all sure that I shall go to the Verdurins. They've been so kind to me that I ought, really. . . . Next to yourself, they have been nicer to me than anybody, but there are some things about them that I don't quite like. I simply must go to the Bon Marché and the Trois-Quartiers and get a white scarf to wear with this dress which is really too black."

Allow Albertine to go by herself into a big shop crowded with people perpetually rubbing against one, furnished

with so many doors that a woman can always say that
when she came out she could not find the carriage which
was waiting farther along the street; I was quite determined never to consent to such a thing, but the thought
of it made me extremely unhappy. And yet I did not
take into account that I ought long ago to have ceased to
see Albertine, for she had entered, in my life, upon that
lamentable period in which a person disseminated over
space and time is no longer a woman, but a series of
events upon which we can throw no light, a series of
insoluble problems, a sea which we absurdly attempt,
Xerxes-like, to scourge, in order to punish it for what it
has engulfed. Once this period has begun, we are per-
force vanquished. Happy are they who understand this
in time not to prolong unduly a futile, exhausting struggle
hemmed in on every side by the limits of the imagination,
a struggle in which jealousy plays so sorry a part that
the same man who once upon a time, if the eyes of the
woman who was always by his side rested for an instant
upon another man, imagined an intrigue, suffered endless
torments, resigns himself in time to allowing her to go
out by herself, sometimes with the man whom he knows
to be her lover, preferring to the unknown this torture
which at least he does know! It is a question of the
rhythm to be adopted, which afterwards one follows
from force of habit. Neurotics who could never stay
away from a dinner-party will afterwards take rest cures
which never seem to them to last long enough; women
who recently were still of easy virtue live for and by acts
of penitence. Jealous lovers who, in order to keep a
watch upon her whom they loved, cut short their own
hours of sleep, deprived themselves of rest, feeling that

her own personal desires, the world, so vast and so secret, time are stronger than they, allow her to go out without them, then to travel, and finally separate from her. Jealousy thus perishes for want of nourishment and has survived so long only by clamouring incessantly for fresh food. I was still a long way from this state.

I was now at liberty to go out with Albertine as often as I chose. As there had recently sprung up all round Paris a number of aerodromes, which are to aeroplanes what harbours are to ships, and as ever since the day when, on the way to la Raspelière, that almost mythological encounter with an airman, at whose passage overhead my horse had shied, had been to me like a symbol of liberty, I often chose to end our day's excursion—with the ready approval of Albertine, a passionate lover of every form of sport—at one of these aerodromes. We went there, she and I, attracted by that incessant stir of departure and arrival which gives so much charm to a stroll along the pier, or merely upon the beach, to those who love the sea, and to loitering about an " aviation centre " to those who love the sky. At any moment, amid the repose of the machines that lay inert and as though at anchor, we would see one, laboriously pushed by a number of mechanics, as a boat is pushed down over the sand at the bidding of a tourist who wishes to go for an hour upon the sea. Then the engine was started, the machine ran along the ground, gathered speed, until finally, all of a sudden, at right angles, it rose slowly, in the awkward, as it were paralysed ecstasy of a horizontal speed suddenly transformed into a majestic, vertical ascent. Albertine could not contain her joy, and demanded explanations of the mechanics who, now that the machine was in the air, were strolling back to the sheds. The passenger, meanwhile, was covering mile after mile; the huge skiff, upon which our eyes remained fixed, was nothing more now in the azure than a barely visible spot, which, however, would gradually recover its solidity, size, volume, when, as the time allowed for the excursion drew to an end, the moment came for landing. And we watched with envy, Albertine and I, as he sprang to earth, the passenger who had gone up like that to enjoy at large in those solitary expanses the calm and limpidity of evening. Then, whether from the aerodrome or from some museum, some church that we had been visiting, we would return home together for dinner. And yet, I did not return home calmed, as I used to be at Balbec by less frequent excursions which I rejoiced to see extend over a whole afternoon, used afterwards to contemplate standing out like clustering flowers from the rest of Albertine's life, as against an empty sky, before which we muse pleasantly, without thinking. Albertine's time did not belong to me then in such ample quantities as to-day. And yet, it had seemed to me then to be much more my own, because I took into account only—my love rejoicing in them as in the bestowal of a favour—the hours that she spent with me; now—my jealousy searching anxiously among them for the possibility of a betrayal—only those hours that she spent apart from me.

Well, on the morrow she was looking forward to some such hours. I must choose, either to cease from suffering, or to cease from loving. For, just as in the beginning it is formed by desire, so afterwards love is kept in existence only by painful anxiety. I felt that part of Albertine's life was escaping me. Love, in the painful anxiety as in the blissful desire, is the insistence upon a whole. It is born, it survives only if some part remains for it to conquer. We love only what we do not wholly possess. Albertine was lying when she told me that she probably would not go to the Verdurins', as I was lying when I said that I wished to go there. She was seeking merely to dissuade me from accompanying her, and I, by my abrupt announcement of this plan, which I had no intention of putting into practice, to touch what I felt to be her most sensitive spot, to track down the desire that she was concealing and to force her to admit that my company on the morrow would prevent her from gratifying it. She had virtually made this admission by ceasing at once to wish to go to see the Verdurins.

"If you don't want to go to the Verdurins'," I told her, "there is a splendid charity show at the Trocadéro." She listened to my urging her to attend it with a sorrowful air. I began to be harsh with her as at Balbec, at the time of my first jealousy. Her face reflected a disappointment, and I employed, to reproach my mistress, the same arguments that had been so often advanced against myself by my parents when I was little, and had appeared unintelligent and cruel to my misunderstood childhood. "No, for all your melancholy air," I said to Albertine, "I cannot feel any pity for you; I should feel sorry for you if you were ill, if you were in trouble, if you had suffered some bereavement; not that you would mind that in the least, I dare say, since you pour out false sentiment over every trifle. Anyhow, I have no opinion of the feelings of people who pretend to be so fond of us and are quite incapable of doing us the slightest service, and whose minds wander so that they forget to deliver the letter we have entrusted to them, on which our whole future depends."

These words—a great part of what we say being no more than a recitation from memory—I had heard spoken, all of them, by my mother, who was ever ready to explain to me that we ought not to confuse true feeling, what (she said) the Germans, whose language she greatly admired notwithstanding my father's horror of their nation, called *Empfindung,* and affectation or *Empfindelei.* She had gone so far, once when I was in tears, as to tell me that Nero probably suffered from his nerves and was none the better for that. Indeed, like those plants which bifurcate as they grow, side by side with the sensitive boy which was all that I had been, there was now a man of the opposite sort, full of common sense, of severity towards the morbid sensibility of others, a man resembling what my parents had been to me. No doubt, as each of us is obliged to continue in himself the life of his forebears, the balanced, cynical man who did not exist in me at the start had joined forces with the sensitive one, and it was natural that I should become in my turn what my parents had been to me.

What is more, at the moment when this new personality took shape in me, he found his language ready made in the memory of the speeches, ironical and scolding, that had been addressed to me, that I must now address to other people, and which came so naturally to my lips, whether I evoked them by mimicry and association of memories, or because the delicate and mysterious enchantments of the reproductive power had traced in me unawares, as upon the leaf of a plant, the same intonations, the same gestures, the same attitudes as had been

adopted by the people from whom I sprang. For sometimes, as I was playing the wise counsellor in conversation
with Albertine, I seemed to be listening to my grandmother; had it not, moreover, occurred to my mother (so
many obscure unconscious currents inflected everything
in me down to the tiniest movements of my fingers even,
to follow the same cycles as those of my parents) to
imagine that it was my father at the door, so similar was
my knock to his.

On the other hand the coupling of contrary elements is
the law of life, the principle of fertilisation, and, as we
shall see, the cause of many disasters. As a general rule,
we detest what resembles ourself, and our own faults
when observed in another person infuriate us. How
much the more does a man who has passed the age at
which we instinctively display them, a man who, for
instance, has gone through the most burning moments
with an icy countenance, execrate those same faults, if it
is another man, younger or simpler or stupider, that is
displaying them. There are sensitive people to whom
merely to see in other people's eyes the tears which they
themselves have repressed is infuriating. It is because
the similarity is too great that, in spite of family affection,
and sometimes all the more the greater the affection is,
families are divided.

Possibly in myself, and in many others, the second
man that I had become was simply another aspect of the
former man, excitable and sensitive in his own affairs, a
sage mentor to other people. Perhaps it was so also with
my parents according to whether they were regarded in
relation to myself or in themselves. In the case of my
grandmother and mother it was as clear as daylight that

their severity towards myself was deliberate on their part and indeed cost them a serious effort, but perhaps in my father himself his coldness was but an external aspect of his sensibility. For it was perhaps the human truth of this twofold aspect: the side of private life, the side of social relations, that was expressed in a sentence which seemed to me at the time as false in its matter as it was commonplace in form, when some one remarked, speaking of my father: "Beneath his icy chill, he conceals an extraordinary sensibility; what is really wrong with him is that he is ashamed of his own feelings."

Did it not, after all, conceal incessant secret storms, that calm (interspersed if need be with sententious reflexions, irony at the maladroit exhibitions of sensibility) which was his, but which now I too was affecting in my relations with everybody and never laid aside in certain circumstances of my relations with Albertine?

I really believe that I came near that day to making up my mind to break with her and to start for Venice. What bound me afresh in my chains had to do with Normandy, not that she shewed any inclination to go to that region where I had been jealous of her (for it was my good fortune that her plans never impinged upon the painful spots in my memory), but because when I had said to her: "It is just as though I were to speak to you of your aunt's friend who lived at Infreville," she replied angrily, delighted—like everyone in a discussion, who is anxious to muster as many arguments as possible on his side—to shew me that I was in the wrong and herself in the right: "But my aunt never knew anybody at Infreville, and I have never been near the place."

She had forgotten the lie that she had told me one

afternoon about the susceptible lady with whom she simply must take tea, even if by going to visit this lady she were to forfeit my friendship and shorten her own life. I did not remind her of her lie. But it appalled me. And once again I postponed our rupture to another day. A person has no need of sincerity, nor even of skill in lying, in order to be loved. I here give the name of love to a mutual torment. I saw nothing reprehensible this evening in speaking to her as my grandmother—that mirror of perfection—used to speak to me, nor, when I told her that I would escort her to the Verdurins', in having adopted my father's abrupt manner, who would never inform us of any decision except in the manner calculated to cause us the maximum of agitation, out of all proportion to the decision itself. So that it was easy for him to call us absurd for appearing so distressed by so small a matter, our distress corresponding in reality to the emotion that he had aroused in us. Since—like the inflexible wisdom of my grandmother—these arbitrary moods of my father had been passed on to myself to complete the sensitive nature to which they had so long remained alien, and, throughout my whole childhood, had caused so much suffering, that sensitive nature informed them very exactly as to the points at which they must take careful aim: there is no better informer than a reformed thief, or a subject of the nation we are fighting. In certain untruthful families, a brother who has come to call upon his brother without any apparent reason and asks him, quite casually, on the doorstep, as he is going away, for some information to which he does not even appear to listen, indicates thereby to his brother that this information was the main object of his visit, for the brother is quite familiar with that air of detachment, those words uttered as though in parentheses and at the last moment, having frequently had recourse to them himself. Well, there are also pathological families, kindred sensibilities, fraternal temperaments, initiated into that mute language which enables people in the family circle to make themselves understood without speaking. And who can be more nerve-wracking than a neurotic? Besides, my conduct, in these cases, may have had a more general, a more profound cause. I mean that in those brief but inevitable moments, when we detest some one whom we love—moments which last sometimes for a whole lifetime in the case of people whom we do not love—we do not wish to appear good, so as not to be pitied, but at once as wicked and as happy as possible so that our happiness may be truly hateful and may ulcerate the soul of the occasional or permanent enemy. To how many people have I not untruthfully slandered myself, simply in order that my "successes" might seem to them immoral and make them all the more angry! The proper thing to do would be to take the opposite course, to shew without arrogance that I have generous feelings, instead of taking such pains to hide them. And it would be easy if we were able never to hate, to love all the time. For then we should be so glad to say only the things that can make other people happy, melt their hearts, make them love us.

To be sure, I felt some remorse at being so irritating to Albertine, and said to myself: "If I did not love her, she would be more grateful to me, for I should not be nasty to her; but no, it would be the same in the end, for I should also be less nice." And I might, in order to justify myself, have told her that I loved her. But the confession of that love, apart from the fact that it could not have told Albertine anything new, would perhaps have made her colder to myself than the harshness and deceit for which love was the sole excuse. To be harsh and deceitful to the person whom we love is so natural! If the interest that we shew in other people does not prevent us from being kind to them and complying with their wishes, then our interest is not sincere. A stranger leaves us indifferent, and indifference does not prompt us to unkind actions.

The evening passed. Before Albertine went to bed, there was no time to lose if we wished to make peace, to renew our embraces. Neither of us had yet taken the initiative. Feeling that, anyhow, she was angry with me already, I took advantage of her anger to mention Esther Lévy. "Bloch tells me" (this was untrue) "that you are a great friend of his cousin Esther." "I shouldn't know her if I saw her," said Albertine with a vague air. "I have seen her photograph," I continued angrily. I did not look at Albertine as I said this, so that I did not see her expression, which would have been her sole reply, for she said nothing.

It was no longer the peace of my mother's kiss at Combray that I felt when I was with Albertine on these evenings, but, on the contrary, the anguish of those on which my mother scarcely bade me good night, or even did not come up at all to my room, whether because she was vexed with me or was kept downstairs by guests. This anguish—not merely its transposition in terms of love—no, this anguish itself which had at one time been specialised in love, which had been allocated to love alone when the division, the distribution of the passions took effect, seemed now to be extending again to them all, become indivisible again as in my childhood, as though all my sentiments which trembled at the thought of my not being able to keep Albertine by my bedside, at once as a mistress, a sister, a daughter; as a mother too, of whose regular good-night kiss I was beginning again to feel the childish need, had begun to coalesce, to unify in the premature evening of my life which seemed fated to be as short as a day in winter. But if I felt the anguish of my childhood, the change of person that made me feel it, the difference of the sentiment that it inspired in me, the very transformation in my character, made it impossible for me to demand the soothing of that anguish from Albertine as in the old days from my mother.

I could no longer say: " I am unhappy." I confined myself, with death at my heart, to speaking of unimportant things which afforded me no progress towards a happy solution. I waded knee-deep in painful platitudes. And with that intellectual egoism which, if only some insignificant fact has a bearing upon our love, makes us pay great respect to the person who has discovered it, as fortuitously perhaps as the fortune-teller who has foretold some trivial event which has afterwards come to pass, I came near to regarding Françoise as more inspired than Bergotte and Elstir because she had said to me at Balbec: " That girl will only land you in trouble."

Every minute brought me nearer to Albertine's good night, which at length she said. But this evening her kiss, from which she herself was absent, and which did not encounter myself, left me so anxious that, with a throbbing heart, I watched her make her way to the door, thinking: "If I am to find a pretext for calling her back, keeping her here, making peace with her, I must make haste; only a few steps and she will be out of the room, only two, now one, she is turning the handle; she is opening the door, it is too late, she has shut it behind her!" Perhaps it was not too late, all the same. As in the old days at Combray when my mother had left me without soothing me with her kiss, I wanted to dart in pursuit of Albertine, I felt that there would be no peace for me until I had seen her again, that this next meeting was to be something immense which no such meeting had ever yet been, and that—if I did not succeed by my own efforts in ridding myself of this melancholy—I might perhaps acquire the shameful habit of going to beg from Albertine. I sprang out of bed when she was already in her room, I paced up and down the corridor, hoping that she would come out of her room and call me; I stood without breathing outside her door for fear of failing to hear some faint summons, I returned for a moment to my own room to see whether my mistress had not by some lucky chance forgotten her handkerchief, her bag, something which I might have appeared to be afraid of her wanting during the night, and which would have given me an excuse for going to her room. No, there was nothing. I returned to my station outside her door, but the crack beneath it no longer shewed any light. Albertine had put out the light, she was in bed, I remained there motionless, hoping for some lucky accident but none occurred; and long afterwards, frozen, I returned to bestow myself between my own sheets and cried all night long.

But there were certain evenings also when I had recourse to a ruse which won me Albertine's kiss. Knowing how quickly sleep came to her as soon as she lay down (she knew it also, for, instinctively, before lying down, she would take off her slippers, which I had given her, and her ring which she placed by the bedside, as she did in her own room when she went to bed), knowing how heavy her sleep was, how affectionate her awakening, I would plead the excuse of going to look for something and make her lie down upon my bed. When I returned to the room she was asleep and I saw before me the other woman that she became whenever one saw her full face. But she very soon changed her identity, for I lay down by her side and recaptured her profile. I could place my hand in her hand, on her shoulder, on her cheek. Albertine continued to sleep.

I might take her head, turn it round, press it to my lips, encircle my neck in her arms, she continued to sleep like a watch that does not stop, like an animal that goes on living whatever position you assign to it, like a climbing plant, a convolvulus which continues to thrust out its tendrils whatever support you give it. Only her breathing was altered by every touch of my fingers, as though she had been an instrument on which I was playing and from which I extracted modulations by drawing from first one, then another of its strings different notes. My jealousy grew calm, for I felt that Albertine had become a creature that breathes, that is nothing else besides, as was indicated by that regular breathing in which is expressed that pure physiological function which, wholly fluid, has not the solidity either of speech or of silence; and, in its ignorance of all evil, her breath, drawn (it seemed) rather from a hollowed reed than from a human being, was truly paradisal, was the pure song of the angels to me who, at these moments, felt Albertine to be withdrawn from everything, not only materially but morally. And yet in that breathing, I said to myself of a sudden that perhaps many names of people borne on the stream of memory must be playing. Sometimes indeed to that music the human voice was added. Albertine uttered a few words. How I longed to catch their meaning! It happened that the name of a person of whom we had been speaking and who had aroused my jealousy came to her lips, but without making me unhappy, for the memory that it brought with it seemed to be only that of the conversations that she had had with me upon the subject. This evening, however, when with her eyes still shut she was half awake, she said, addressing myself: "Andrée." I concealed my emotion. "You are dreaming, I am not Andrée," I said to her, smiling. She smiled also. "Of course not, I wanted to ask you what Andrée was saying to you." "I should have supposed that you were used to lying like this by her side." "Oh no, never," she said. Only, before making this reply, she had hidden her face for a moment in her hands. So her silences were merely screens, her surface affection merely kept beneath the surface a thousand memories which would have rent my heart, her life was full of those incidents the derisive account, the comic history of which form our daily gossip at the expense of other people, people who do not matter, but which, so long as a person remains lost in the dark forest of our heart, seem to us so precious a revelation of her life that, for the privilege of exploring that subterranean world, we would gladly sacrifice our own. Then her sleep appeared to me a marvellous and magic world in which at certain moments there rises from the depths of the barely translucent element the confession of a secret which we shall not understand. But as a rule, when Albertine was asleep, she seemed to have recovered her innocence. In the attitude which I had imposed upon her, but which in her sleep she had speedily made her own, she looked as though she were trusting herself to me! Her face had lost any expression of cunning or vulgarity, and between herself and me, towards whom she was raising her arm, upon whom her hand was resting, there seemed to be an absolute surrender, an indissoluble attachment. Her sleep moreover did not separate her from me and allowed her to retain her consciousness of our affection; its effect was rather to abolish everything else; I embraced her, told her that I was going to take a turn outside, she half-opened her eyes, said to me with an air of astonishment—indeed the hour was late: "But where are you off to, my darling —— " calling me by my Christian name, and at once fell asleep again. Her sleep was only a sort of obliteration of the rest of her life, a continuous silence over which from time to time would pass in their flight words of intimate affection. By putting these words together, you would have arrived at the unalloyed conversation, the secret intimacy of a pure love. This calm slumber delighted me, as a mother is delighted, reckoning it among his virtues, by the sound sleep of her child. And her sleep was indeed that of a child. Her waking also, and so natural, so loving, before she even knew where she was, that I sometimes asked myself with terror whether she had been in the habit, before coming to live with me, of not sleeping by herself but of finding, when she opened her eyes, some one lying by her side. But her childish charm was more striking. Like a mother again, I marvelled that she should always awake in so good a humour. After a few moments she recovered consciousness, uttered charming words, unconnected with one another, mere bird-pipings. By a sort of " general post " her throat, which as a rule passed unnoticed, now almost startlingly beautiful, had acquired the immense importance which her eyes, by being closed in sleep, had forfeited, her eyes, my regular informants to which I could no longer address myself after the lids had closed over them. Just as the closed lids impart an innocent, grave beauty to the face by suppressing all that the eyes express only too plainly, there was in the words, not devoid of meaning, but interrupted by moments of silence, which Albertine uttered as she awoke, a pure beauty that is not at every moment polluted, as is conversation, by habits of speech, commonplaces, traces of blemish. Anyhow, when I had decided to wake Albertine, I had been able to do so without fear, I knew that her awakening would bear no relation to the evening that we had passed together, but would emerge from her sleep as morning emerges from night. As soon as she had begun to open her eyes with a smile, she had offered me her lips, and before she had even uttered a word, I had tasted their fresh savour, as soothing as that of a garden still silent before the break of day.

On the morrow of that evening when Albertine had told me that she would perhaps be going, then that she would not be going to see the Verdurins, I awoke early, and, while I was still half asleep, my joy informed me that there was, interpolated in the winter, a day of spring. Outside, popular themes skilfully transposed for various instruments, from the horn of the mender of porcelain, or the trumpet of the chair weaver to the flute of the goat driver who seemed, on a fine morning, to be a Sicilian goatherd, were lightly orchestrating the matutinal air, with an "Overture for a Public Holiday." Our hearing, that delicious sense, brings us the company of the street, every line of which it traces for us, sketches all the figures that pass along it, shewing us their colours. The iron shutters of the baker's shop, of the dairy, which had been lowered last night over every possibility of feminine bliss, were rising now like the canvas of a ship which is setting sail and about to proceed, crossing the transparent sea, over a vision of young female assistants. This sound of the iron curtain being raised would perhaps have been my sole pleasure in a different part of the town. In this quarter a hundred other sounds contributed to my joy, of which I would not have lost a single one by remaining too long asleep. It is the magic charm of the old aristocratic quarters that they are at the same time plebeian. Just as, sometimes, cathedrals used to have them within a stone's throw of their porches (which have even preserved the name, like the porch of Rouen styled the Booksellers', because these latter used to expose their merchandise in the open air against its walls), so various minor trades, but peripatetic, used to pass in front of the noble Hôtel de Guermantes, and made one think at times of the ecclesiastical France of long ago. For the appeal which they launched at the little houses on either side had, with rare exceptions, nothing of a song. It differed from song as much as the declamation—barely coloured by imperceptible modulations—of *Boris Godounov* and *Pelléas;* but on the other hand recalled the psalmody of a priest chanting his office of which these street scenes are but the good-humoured, secular, and yet half liturgical counterpart. Never had I so delighted in them as since Albertine had come to live with me; they seemed to me a joyous signal of her awakening, and by interesting me in the life of the world outside made me all the more conscious of the soothing virtue of a beloved presence, as constant as I could wish. Several of the foodstuffs cried in the street, which personally I detested, were greatly to Albertine's liking, so much so that Françoise used to send her young footman out to buy them, slightly humiliated perhaps at finding himself mingled with the plebeian crowd. Very distinct in this peaceful quarter (where the noise was no longer a cause of lamentation to Françoise and had become a source of pleasure to myself), there came to me, each with its different modulation, recitatives declaimed by those humble folk as they would be in the music—so entirely popular—of *Boris,* where an initial intonation is barely altered by the inflexion of one note which rests upon another, the music of the crowd which is more a language than a music. It was " ah! le bigorneau, deux sous le bigorneau," which brought people running to the cornets in which were sold those horrid little shellfish, which, if Albertine had not been there, would have disgusted me, just as the snails disgusted me which I heard cried for sale at the same hour. Here again it was of the barely lyrical declamation of Moussorgsky that the vendor reminded me, but not of it alone. For after having almost " spoken ": " Les escargots, ils sont frais, ils sont beaux," it was with the vague melancholy of Maeterlinck, transposed into music by Debussy, that the snail vendor, in one of those pathetic finales in which the composer of

Pelléas shews his kinship with Rameau: "If vanquished I must be, is it for thee to be my vanquisher?" added with a singsong melancholy: "On les vend six sous la douzaine. . . ."

I have always found it difficult to understand why these perfectly simple words were sighed in a tone so far from appropriate, mysterious, like the secret which makes everyone look sad in the old palace to which Mélisande has not succeeded in bringing joy, and profound as one of the thoughts of the aged Arkel who seeks to utter, in the simplest words, the whole lore of wisdom and destiny. The very notes upon which rises with an increasing sweetness the voice of the old King of Allemonde or that of Goland, to say: "We know not what is happening here, it may seem strange, maybe nought that happens is in vain," or else: "No cause here for alarm, 'twas a poor little mysterious creature, like all the world," were those which served the snail vendor to resume, in an endless cadenza: "On les vend six sous la douzaine. . . ." But this metaphysical lamentation had not time to expire upon the shore of the infinite, it was interrupted by a shrill trumpet. This time, it was no question of victuals, the words of the libretto were: "Tond les chiens, coupe les chats, les queues et les oreilles."

It was true that the fantasy, the spirit of each vendor or vendress frequently introduced variations into the words of all these chants that I used to hear from my bed. And yet a ritual suspension interposing a silence in the middle of a word, especially when it was repeated a second time, constantly reminded me of some old church. In his little cart drawn by a she-ass which he stopped in front of each house before entering the courtyard, the old-clothes man, brandishing a whip, intoned: "Habits, marchand d'habits, ha...bits" with the same pause between the final syllables as if he had been intoning in plainchant: "Per omnia saecula saeculo...rum" or "requiescat in pa...ce" albeit he had no reason to believe in the immortality of his clothes, nor did he offer them as cerements for the supreme repose in peace. And similarly, as the motives were beginning, even at this early hour, to become confused, a vegetable woman, pushing her little hand-cart, was using for her litany the Gregorian division:

> A la tendresse, à la verduresse,
> Artichauts tendres et beaux,
> Arti...chauts.

although she had probably never heard of the antiphonal, or of the seven tones that symbolise four the sciences of the quadrivium and three those of the trivium.

Drawing from a penny whistle, from a bagpipe, airs of his own southern country whose sunlight harmonised well with these fine days, a man in a blouse, wielding a bull's pizzle in his hand and wearing a basque *béret* on his head, stopped before each house in turn. It was the goatherd with two dogs driving before him his string of goats. As he came from a distance, he arrived fairly late in our quarter; and the women came running out with bowls to receive the milk that was to give strength to their little ones. But with the Pyrenean airs of this good shepherd was now blended the bell of the grinder, who cried: "Couteaux, ciseaux, rasoirs." With him the saw-setter was unable to compete, for, lacking an instrument, he had to be content with calling: "Avez-vous des scies à

repasser, v'là le repasseur," while in a gayer mood the
tinker, after enumerating the pots, pans and everything
else that he repaired, intoned the refrain:

> Tam, tam, tam,
> C'est moi qui rétame
> Même le macadam,
> C'est moi qui mets des fonds partout,
> Qui bouche tous les trous, trou, trou;

and young Italians carrying big iron boxes painted red,
upon which the numbers—winning and losing—were
marked, and springing their rattles, gave the invitation:
"Amusez-vous, mesdames, v'là le plaisir."

Françoise brought in the *Figaro*. A glance was sufficient to shew me that my article had not yet appeared.
She told me that Albertine had asked whether she might
come to my room and sent word that she had quite given
up the idea of calling upon the Verdurins, and had decided to go, as I had advised her, to the " special " matinée
at the Trocadéro—what nowadays would be called,
though with considerably less significance, a " gala "
matinée—after a short ride which she had promised to
take with Andrée. Now that I knew that she had re-
nounced her desire, possibly evil, to go and see Mme.
Verdurin, I said with a laugh: " Tell her to come in," and
told myself that she might go where she chose and that
it was all the same to me. I knew that by the end of the
afternoon, when dusk began to fall, I should probably be
a different man, moping, attaching to every one of Albertine's movements an importance that they did not
possess at this morning hour when the weather was so
fine. For my indifference was accompanied by a clear
notion of its cause, but was in no way modified by it.

"Françoise assured me that you were awake and that I should not be disturbing you," said Albertine as she entered the room. And since next to making me catch cold by opening the window at the wrong moment, what Albertine most dreaded was to come into my room when I was asleep: "I hope I have not done anything wrong," she went on. "I was afraid you would say to me: What insolent mortal comes here to meet his doom?" and she laughed that laugh which I always found so disturbing. I replied in the same vein of pleasantry: "Was it for you this stern decree was made?"—and, lest she should ever venture to break it, added: "Although I should be furious if you did wake me." "I know, I know, don't be frightened," said Albertine. And, to relieve the situation, I went on, still enacting the scene from *Esther* with her, while in the street below the cries continued, drowned by our conversation: "I find in you alone a certain grace That charms me and of which I never tire" (and to myself I thought: "yes, she does tire me very often"). And remembering what she had said to me overnight, as I thanked her extravagantly for having given up the Verdurins, so that another time she would obey me similarly with regard to something else, I said: "Albertine, you distrust me who love you and you place your trust in other people who do not love you" (as though it were not natural to distrust the people who love us and who alone have an interest in lying to us in order to find out things, to hinder us), and added these lying words: "You don't really believe that I love you, which is amusing. As a matter of fact, I don't *adore* you." She lied in her turn when she told me that she trusted nobody but myself and then became sincere when she assured me that she knew very well that I loved her. But this affirmation did not seem to imply that she did not believe me to be a liar and a spy. And she seemed to pardon me as though she had seen these defects to be the agonising consequence of a strong passion or as though she herself had felt herself to be less good: "I beg of you, my dearest girl, no more of that *haute voltige* you were practising the other day. Just think, Albertine, if you were to meet with an accident!" Of course I did not wish her any harm. But what a pleasure it would be if, with her horses, she should take it into her head to ride off somewhere, wherever she chose, and never to return again to my house. How it would simplify everything, that she should go and live happily somewhere else, I did not even wish to know where. "Oh! I know you wouldn't survive me for more than a day; you would commit suicide."

So we exchanged lying speeches. But a truth more profound than that which we would utter were we sincere may sometimes be expressed and announced by another channel than that of sincerity: "You don't mind all that noise outside," she asked me; "I love it. But you're such a light sleeper anyhow." I was on the contrary an extremely heavy sleeper (as I have already said, but I am obliged to repeat it in view of what follows), especially when I did not begin to sleep until the morning. As this kind of sleep is—on an average—four times as refreshing, it seems to the awakened sleeper to have lasted four times as long, when it has really been four times as short. A splendid, sixteenfold error in multiplication which gives so much beauty to our awakening and makes life begin again on a different scale, like those great changes of rhythm which, in music, mean that in an andante a quaver has the same duration as a minim in a prestissimo, and which are unknown in our waking state. There life is almost always the same, whence the disappointments of travel. It may seem indeed that our dreams are composed of the coarsest stuff of life, but that stuff is treated, kneaded so thoroughly, with a protraction due to the fact that none of the temporal limitations of the waking state is there to prevent it from spinning itself out to heights so vast that we fail to recognise it. On the mornings after this good fortune had befallen me, after the sponge of sleep had obliterated from my brain the signs of everyday occupations that are traced upon it as upon a blackboard, I was obliged to bring my memory back to life; by the exercise of our will we can recapture what the amnesia of sleep or of a stroke has made us forget, what gradually returns to us as our eyes open or our paralysis disappears. I had lived through so many hours in a few minutes that, wishing to address Françoise, for whom I had rung, in language that corresponded to the facts of real life and was regulated by the clock, I was obliged to exert all my power of internal repression in order not to say: "Well, Françoise, here we are at five o'clock in the evening and I haven't set eyes on you since yesterday afternoon." And seeking to dispel my dreams, giving them the lie and lying to myself as well, I said boldly, compelling myself with all my might to silence, the direct opposite: "Françoise, it must be at least ten!" I did not even say ten o'clock in the morning, but simply ten, so that this incredible hour might appear to be uttered in a more natural tone. And yet to say these words, instead of those that continued to run in the mind of the half-awakened sleeper that I still was, demanded the same effort of equilibrium that a man requires when he jumps out of a moving train and runs for some yards along the platform, if he is to avoid falling. He runs for a moment because the environment that he has just left was one animated by great velocity, and utterly unlike the inert soil upon which his feet find it difficult to keep their balance.

Because the dream world is not the waking world, it does not follow that the waking world is less genuine, far from it. In the world of sleep, our perceptions are so overcharged, each of them increased by a counterpart which doubles its bulk and blinds it to no purpose, that we are not able even to distinguish what is happening in the bewilderment of awakening; was it Françoise that had come to me, or I that, tired of waiting, went to her? Silence at that moment was the only way not to reveal anything, as at the moment when we are brought before a magistrate cognisant of all the charges against us, when **we have not been informed** of them ourself. Was it Françoise that had come, was it I that had summoned her? Was it not, indeed, Françoise that had been asleep and I that had just awoken her; nay more, was not Françoise enclosed in my breast, for the distinction between persons and their reaction upon one another barely exists in that murky obscurity in which reality is as little translucent as in the body of a porcupine, and our all but non-existent perception may perhaps furnish an idea of the perception of certain animals. Besides, in the limpid state of unreason that precedes these heavy slumbers, if fragments of wisdom float there luminously, if the names of Taine and George Eliot are not unknown, the waking life does still retain the superiority, inasmuch as it is possible to continue it every morning, whereas it is not possible to continue the dream life every night. But are there perhaps other worlds more real than the waking world? Even it we have seen transformed by every revolution in the arts, and still more, at the same time, by the degree of proficiency and culture that distinguishes an artist from an ignorant fool.

And often an extra hour of sleep is a paralytic stroke after which we must recover the use of our limbs, learn to speak. Our will would not be adequate for this task. We have slept too long, we no longer exist. Our waking is barely felt, mechanically and without consciousness, as a water pipe might feel the turning off of a tap. A life more inanimate than that of the jellyfish follows, in which we could equally well believe that we had been drawn up from the depths of the sea or released from prison, were we but capable of thinking anything at all. But then from the highest heaven the goddess Mnemotechnia bends down and holds out to us in the formula "the habit of ringing for our coffee" the hope of resurrection. However, the instantaneous gift of memory is not always so simple. Often we have before us, in those first minutes in which we allow ourself to slip into the waking state, a truth composed of different realities among which we imagine that we can choose, as among a pack of cards.

It is Friday morning and we have just returned from our walk, or else it is teatime by the sea. The idea of sleep and that we are lying in bed and in our nightshirt is often the last that occurs to us.

Our resurrection is not effected at once; we think that we have rung the bell, we have not done so, we utter senseless remarks. Movement alone restores our thought, and when we have actually pressed the electric button we are able to say slowly but distinctly: " It must be at least ten o'clock, Françoise, bring me my coffee." Oh, the miracle! Françoise could have had no suspicion of the sea of unreality in which I was still wholly immersed and through which I had had the energy to make my strange question pass. Her answer was: " It is ten past ten." Which made my remark appear quite reasonable, and enabled me not to let her perceive the fantastic conversations by which I had been interminably beguiled, on days when it was not a mountain of non-existence that had crushed all life out of me. By strength of will, I had reinstated myself in life. I was still enjoying the last shreds of sleep, that is to say of the only inventiveness, the only novelty that exists in story-telling, since none of our narrations in the waking state, even though they be adorned with literary graces, admit those mysterious differences from which beauty derives. It is easy to speak of the beauty created by opium. But to a man who is accustomed to sleeping only with the aid of drugs, an unexpected hour of natural sleep will reveal the vast, matutinal expanse of a country as mysterious and more refreshing. By varying the hour, the place at which we go to sleep, by wooing sleep in an artificial manner, or on the contrary by returning for once to natural sleep— the strangest kind of all to whoever is in the habit of putting himself to sleep with soporifics—we succeed in producing a thousand times as many varieties of sleep as a gardener could produce of carnations or roses. Gardeners produce flowers that are delicious dreams, and others too that are like nightmares. When I fell asleep in a certain way I used to wake up shivering, thinking that I had caught the measles, or, what was far more painful, that my grandmother (to whom I never gave a thought now) was hurt because I had laughed at her that day when, at Balbec, in the belief that she was about to die, she had wished me to have a photograph of herself. At once, albeit I was awake, I felt that I must go and explain to her that she had misunderstood me. But, already, my bodily warmth was returning. The diagnosis of measles was set aside, and my grandmother became so remote that she no longer made my heart throb. Sometimes over these different kinds of sleep there fell a sudden darkness. I was afraid to continue my walk along an entirely unlighted avenue, where I could hear prowling footsteps. Suddenly a dispute broke out between a policeman and one of those women whom one often saw driving hackney carriages, and mistook at a distance for young men. Upon her box among the shadows I could not see her, but she spoke, and in her voice I could read the perfections of her face and the youthfulness of her body. I strode towards her, in the darkness, to get into her carriage before she drove off. It was a long way. Fortunately, her dispute with the policeman continued. I overtook the carriage which was still drawn up. This part of the avenue was lighted by street lamps. The driver became visible. She was indeed a woman, but old and corpulent, with white hair tumbling beneath her hat, and a red birthmark on her face. I walked past her, thinking: Is this what happens to the youth of women? Those whom we have met in the past, if suddenly we desire to see them again, have they become old? Is the young woman whom we desire like a character on the stage, when, unable to secure the actress who created the part, the management is obliged to entrust it to a new star? But then it is no longer the same.

With this a feeling of melancholy invaded me. We have thus in our sleep a number of Pities, like the "Pietà" of the Renaissance, but not, like them, wrought in marble, being, rather, unsubstantial. They have their purpose, however, which is to make us remember a certain outlook upon things, more tender, more human, which we are too apt to forget in the common sense, frigid, sometimes full of hostility, of the waking state. Thus I was reminded of the vow that I had made at Balbec that I would always treat Françoise with compassion. And for the whole of that morning at least I would manage to compel myself not to be irritated by Françoise's quarrels with the butler, to be gentle with Françoise to whom the others shewed so little kindness. For that morning only, and I would have to try to frame a code that was a little more permanent; for, just as nations are not governed for any length of time by a policy of pure sentiment, so men are not governed by the memory of their dreams. Already this dream was beginning to fade away. In attempting to recall it in order to portray it I made it fade all the faster. My eyelids were no longer so firmly sealed over my eyes. If I tried to reconstruct my dream, they opened completely. At every moment we must choose between health and sanity on the one hand, and spiritual pleasures on the other. I have always taken the cowardly part of choosing the former. Moreover, the perilous power that I was renouncing was even more perilous than we suppose. Pities, dreams, do not fly away unaccompanied. When we alter thus the conditions in which we go to sleep, it is not our dreams alone that fade, but, for days on end, for years it may be, the faculty not merely of dreaming but of going to sleep. Sleep is divine but by no means stable; the slightest shock makes it volatile. A lover of habits, they retain it every night, being more fixed than itself, in the place set apart for it, they preserve it from all injury, but if we displace it, if it is no longer subordinated, it melts away like a vapour. It is like youth and love, never to be recaptured.

In these various forms of sleep, as likewise in music, it was the lengthening or shortening of the interval that created beauty. I enjoyed this beauty, but, on the other hand, I had lost in my sleep, however brief, a good number of the cries which render perceptible to us the peripatetic life of the tradesmen, the victuallers of Paris. And so, as a habit (without, alas, foreseeing the drama in which these late awakenings and the Draconian, Medo-Persian laws of a Racinian Assuérus were presently to involve me) I made an effort to awaken early so as to lose none of these cries.

And, more than the pleasure of knowing how fond Albertine was of them and of being out of doors myself without leaving my bed, I heard in them as it were the symbol of the atmosphere of the world outside, of the dangerous stirring life through the veins of which I did not allow her to move save under my tutelage, from which I withdrew her at the hour of my choosing to make her return home to my side. And so it was with the most perfect sincerity that I was able to say in answer to Albertine: "On the contrary, they give me pleasure because I know that you like them." "A la barque, les huitres,

164

à la barque." "Oh, oysters! I've been simply longing for some!" Fortunately Albertine, partly from inconsistency, partly from docility, quickly forgot the things for which she had been longing, and before I had time to tell her that she would find better oysters at Prunier's, she wanted in succession all the things that she heard cried by the fish hawker: "A la crevette, à la bonne crevette, j'ai de la raie toute en vie, toute en vie." "Merlans à frire, à frire." "Il arrive le maquereau, maquereau frais, maquereau nouveau." "Voilà le maquereau, mesdames, il est beau le maquereau." "A la moule fraîche et bonne, à la moule!" In spite of myself, the warning: "Il arrive le maquereau" made me shudder. But as this warning could not, I felt, apply to our chauffeur, I thought only of the fish of that name, which I detested, and my uneasiness did not last. "Ah! Mussels," said Albertine, "I should so like some mussels." "My darling! They were all very well at Balbec, here they're not worth eating; besides, I implore you, remember what Cottard told you about mussels." But my remark was all the more ill-chosen in that the vegetable woman who came next announced a thing that Cottard had forbidden even more strictly:

A la romaine, à la romaine!
On ne le vend pas, on la promène.

Albertine consented, however, to sacrifice her lettuces, on the condition that I would promise to buy for her in a few days' time from the woman who cried: "J'ai de la belle asperge d'Argenteuil, j'ai de la belle asperge." A mysterious voice, from which one would have expected some stranger utterance, insinuated: "Tonneaux, tonneaux!" We were obliged to remain under the disappointment that nothing more was being offered us than barrels, for the word was almost entirely drowned by the appeal: "Vitri, vitri-er, carreaux cassés, voilà le vitrier, vitri-er," a Gregorian division which reminded me less, however, of the liturgy than did the appeal of the rag vendor, reproducing unconsciously one of those abrupt interruptions of sound, in the middle of a prayer, which are common enough in the ritual of the church: "Praeceptis salutaribus moniti et divina institutione formati audemus dicere," says the priest, ending sharply upon "dicere." Without irreverence, as the populace of the middle ages used to perform plays and farces within the consecrated ground of the church, it is of that "dicere" that this rag vendor makes one think when, after drawling the other words, he utters the final syllable with a sharpness befitting the accentuation laid down by the great Pope of the seventh century: "Chiffons, ferrailles à vendre" (all this chanted slowly, as are the two syllables that follow, whereas the last concludes more briskly than "dicere") "peaux d'la-pins." "La Valence, la belle Valence, la fraîche orange." The humble leeks even: "Voilà d'beaux poireaux," the onions: "Huit sous mon oignon," sounded for me as it were an echo of the rolling waves in which, left to herself, Albertine might have perished, and thus assumed the sweetness of a "Suave mari magno." "Voilà des carrottes à deux ronds la botte." "Oh!" exclaimed Albertine, "cabbages, carrots, oranges. All the things I want to eat. Do make Françoise go out and buy some. She shall cook us a dish of creamed carrots. Besides, it will be so nice to eat all these things together. It will be all the sounds that we hear, trans-

formed into a good dinner. . . . Oh, please, ask Françoise to give us instead a ray with black butter. It is so
good!" "My dear child, of course I will, but don't wait;
if you do, you'll be asking for all the things on the
vegetable-barrows." "Very well, I'm off, but I never
want anything again for our dinners except what we've
heard cried in the street. It is such fun. And to think
that we shall have to wait two whole months before we
hear: 'Haricots verts et tendres, haricots, v'là l'haricot
vert.' How true that is: tender haricots; you know I like
them as soft as soft, dripping with vinegar sauce, you
wouldn't think you were eating, they melt in the mouth
like drops of dew. Oh dear, it's the same with the little
hearts of cream cheese, such a long time to wait: 'Bon
fromage à la cré, à la cré, bon fromage.' And the water-
grapes from Fontainebleau: 'J'ai du bon chasselas.'"
And I thought with dismay of all the time that I should
have to spend with her before the water-grapes were in
season. "Listen, I said that I wanted only the things
that we had heard cried, but of course I make exceptions.
And so it's by no means impossible that I may look in at
Rebattet's and order an ice for the two of us. You will
tell me that it's not the season for them, but I do so
want one!" I was disturbed by this plan of going to
Rebattet's, rendered more certain and more suspicious
in my eyes by the words "it's by no means impossible."
It was the day on which the Verdurins were at home,
and, ever since Swann had informed them that Rebattet's
was the best place, it was there that they ordered their
ices and pastry. "I have no objection to an ice, my
darling Albertine, but let me order it for you, I don't
know myself whether it will be from Poiré-Blanche's, or

Rebattet's, or the Ritz, anyhow I shall see." "Then you're going out?" she said with an air of distrust. She always maintained that she would be delighted if I went out more often, but if anything that I said could make her suppose that I would not be staying indoors, her uneasy air made me think that the joy that she would feel in seeing me go out every day was perhaps not altogether sincere. "I may perhaps go out, perhaps not, you know quite well that I never make plans beforehand. In any case ices are not a thing that is cried, that people hawk in the streets, why do you want one?" And then she replied in words which shewed me what a fund of intelligence and latent taste had developed in her since Balbec, in words akin to those which, she pretended, were due entirely to my influence, to living continually in my company, words which, however, I should never have uttered, as though I had been in some way forbidden by some unknown authority ever to decorate my conversation with literary forms. Perhaps the future was not destined to be the same for Albertine as for myself. I had almost a presentiment of this when I saw her eagerness to employ in speech images so "written," which seemed to me to be reserved for another, more sacred use, of which I was still ignorant. She said to me (and I was, in spite of everything, deeply touched, for I thought to myself: Certainly I would not speak as she does, and yet, all the same, but for me she would not be speaking like this, she has come profoundly under my influence, she cannot therefore help loving me, she is my handiwork): "What I like about these foodstuffs that are cried is that a thing which we hear like a rhapsody changes its nature when it comes to our table and addresses itself to

my palate. As for ices (for I hope that you won't order
me one that isn't cast in one of those old-fashioned moulds
which have every architectural shape imaginable), whenever I take one, temples, churches, obelisks, rocks, it
is like an illustrated geography-book which I look at
first of all and then convert its raspberry or vanilla monuments into coolness in my throat." I thought that this
was a little too well expressed, but she felt that I thought
that it was well expressed, and went on, pausing for a
moment when she had brought off her comparison to
laugh that beautiful laugh of hers which was so painful
to me because it was so voluptuous. "Oh dear, at the
Ritz I'm afraid you'll find Vendôme Columns of ice,
chocolate ice or raspberry, and then you will need a lot
of them so that they may look like votive pillars or
pylons erected along an avenue to the glory of Coolness.
They make raspberry obelisks too, which will rise up
here and there in the burning desert of my thirst, and I
shall make their pink granite crumble and melt deep
down in my throat which they will refresh better than
any oasis" (and here the deep laugh broke out, whether
from satisfaction at talking so well, or in derision of
herself for using such hackneyed images, or, alas, from a
physical pleasure at feeling inside herself something so
good, so cool, which was tantamount to a sensual satisfaction). "Those mountains of ice at the Ritz sometimes
suggest Monte Rosa, and indeed, if it is a lemon ice, I do
not object to its not having a monumental shape, its being irregular, abrupt, like one of Elstir's mountains. It
ought not to be too white then, but slightly yellowish, with
that look of dull, dirty snow that Elstir's mountains have.
The ice need not be at all big, only half an ice if you like,

those lemon ices are still mountains, reduced to a tiny scale, but our imagination restores their dimensions, like those little Japanese dwarf trees which, one knows quite well, are still cedars, oaks, manchineels; so much so that if I arranged a few of them beside a little trickle of water in my room I should have a vast forest stretching down to a river, in which children would be lost. In the same way, at the foot of my yellowish lemon ice, I can see quite clearly postilions, travellers, post-chaises over which my tongue sets to work to roll down freezing avalanches that will swallow them up " (the cruel delight with which she said this excited my jealousy); " just as," she went on, " I set my lips to work to destroy, pillar after pillar, those Venetian churches of a porphyry that is made with strawberries, and send what I spare of them crashing down upon the worshippers. Yes, all those monuments will pass from their stony state into my inside which throbs already with their melting coolness. But, you know, even without ices, nothing is so exciting or makes one so thirsty as the advertisements of mineral springs. At Montjouvain, at Mlle. Vinteuil's, there was no good confectioner who made ices in the neighbourhood, but we used to make our own tour of France in the garden by drinking a different sparkling water every day, like Vichy water which, as soon as you pour it out, sends up from the bottom of the glass a white cloud which fades and dissolves if you don't drink it at once." But to hear her speak of Montjouvain was too painful, I cut her short. "I am boring you, good-bye, my dear boy." What a change from Balbec, where I would defy Elstir himself to have been able to divine in Albertine this wealth of poetry, a poetry less strange, less personal than that of

Céleste Albaret, for instance. Albertine would never have thought of the things that Céleste used to say to me, but love, even when it seems to be nearing its end, is partial. I preferred the illustrated geography-book of her ices, the somewhat facile charm of which seemed to me a reason for loving Albertine and a proof that I had an influence over her, that she was in love with me.

As soon as Albertine had gone out, I felt how tiring it was to me, this perpetual presence, insatiable of movement and life, which disturbed my sleep with its movements, made me live in a perpetual chill by that habit of leaving doors open, forced me—in order to find pretexts that would justify me in not accompanying her, without, however, appearing too unwell, and at the same time to see that she was not unaccompanied—to display every day greater ingenuity than Scheherazade. Unfortunately, if by a similar ingenuity the Persian storyteller postponed her own death, I was hastening mine. There are thus in life certain situations which are not all created, as was this, by amorous jealousy and a precarious state of health which does not permit us to share the life of a young and active person, situations in which nevertheless the problem of whether to continue a life shared with that person or to return to the separate existence of the past sets itself almost in medical terms: to which of the two sorts of repose ought we to sacrifice ourself (by continuing the daily strain, or by returning to the agonies of separation) to that of the head or of the heart?

In any event, I was very glad that Andrée was to accompany Albertine to the Trocadéro, for certain recent and for that matter entirely trivial incidents had brought it about that while I had still, of course, the same confidence in the chauffeur's honesty, his vigilance, or at least the perspicacity of his vigilance did not seem to be quite what it had once been. It so happened that, only a short while since, I had sent Albertine alone in his charge to Versailles, and she told me that she had taken her luncheon at the Réservoirs; as the chauffeur had mentioned the restaurant Vatel, the day on which I noticed this contradiction, I found an excuse to go downstairs and speak to him (it was still the same man, whose acquaintance we had made at Balbec) while Albertine was dressing. "You told me that you had had your luncheon at the Vatel, Mlle. Albertine mentions the Réservoirs. What is the meaning of that?" The driver replied: "Oh, I said that I had had my luncheon at the Vatel, but I cannot tell where Mademoiselle took hers. She left me as soon as we reached Versailles to take a horse cab, which she prefers when it is not a question of time." Already I was furious at the thought that she had been alone; still, it was only during the time that she spent at her luncheon. "You might surely," I suggested mildly (for I did not wish to appear to be keeping Albertine actually under surveillance, which would have been humiliating to myself, and doubly so, for it would have shewn that she concealed her activities from me), "have had your luncheon, I do not say at her table, but in the same restaurant?" "But all she told me was to meet her at six o'clock at the Place d'Armes. I had no orders to call for her after luncheon." "Ah!" I said, making an effort to conceal my dismay. And I returned upstairs. And so it was for more than seven hours on end that Albertine had been alone, left to her own devices.

I might assure myself, it is true, that the cab had not been merely an expedient whereby to escape from the chauffeur's supervision. In town, Albertine preferred driving in a cab, saying that one had a better view, that the air was more pleasant. Nevertheless, she had spent seven hours, as to which I should never know anything. And I dared not think of the manner in which she must have employed them. I felt that the driver had been extremely clumsy, but my confidence in him was now absolute. For if he had been to the slightest extent in league with Albertine, he would never have acknowledged that he had left her unguarded from eleven o'clock in the morning to six in the afternoon. There could be but one other explanation, and it was absurd, of the chauffeur's admission. This was that some quarrel between Albertine and himself had prompted him, by making a minor disclosure to me, to shew my mistress that he was not the sort of man who could be hushed, and that if, after this first gentle warning, she did not do exactly as he told her, he would take the law into his own hands. But this explanation was absurd; I should have had first of all to assume a non-existent quarrel between him and Albertine, and then to label as a consummate blackmailer this good-looking motorist who had always shewn himself so affable and obliging. Only two days later, as it happened, I saw that he was more capable than I had for a moment supposed in my frenzy of suspicion of exercising over Albertine a discreet and far-seeing vigilance. For, having managed to take him aside and talk to him of what he had told me about Versailles, I said to him in a careless, friendly tone: "That drive to Versailles that you told me about the other day was everything that it should be, you behaved perfectly as you always do. But, if I may give you just a little hint, I have so much responsibility now that Mme. Bontemps has placed her niece under my charge, I am so afraid of accidents, I reproach myself so for not going with her, that I prefer that it should be yourself, you who are so safe, so wonderfully skilful, to whom no accident can ever happen, that shall take Mlle. Albertine everywhere. Then I need fear nothing." The charming apostolic motorist smiled a subtle smile, his hand resting upon the consecration-cross of his wheel. Then he uttered these words which (banishing all the anxiety from my heart where its place was at once filled by joy) made me want to fling my arms round his neck: "Don't be afraid," he said to me. "Nothing can happen to her, for, when my wheel is not guiding her, my eye follows her everywhere. At Versailles, I went quietly along and visited the town with her, as you might say. From the Réservoirs she went to the Château, from the Château to the Trianons, and I following her all the time without appearing to see her, and the astonishing thing is that she never saw me. Oh, if she had seen me, the fat would have been in the fire. It was only natural, as I had the whole day before me with nothing to do that I should visit the castle too. All the more as Mademoiselle certainly hasn't failed to notice that I've read a bit myself and take an interest in all those old curiosities" (this was true, indeed I should have been surprised if I had learned that he was a friend of Morel, so far more refined was his taste than the violinist's). "Anyhow, she didn't see me." "She must have met some of her own friends, of course, for she knows a great many ladies at Versailles." "No, she was alone all the time." "Then people must have stared at her, a girl of such striking appearance, all by herself." "Why, of course they stared at her, but she knew nothing about it; she went all the time with her eyes glued to her guide-book, or gazing up at the pictures." The chauffeur's story seemed to me all the more accurate in that it was indeed a "card" with a picture of the Château, and another of the Trianons, that Albertine had sent me on the day of her visit. The care with which the obliging chauffeur had followed every step of her course touched me deeply. How was I to suppose that this correction—in the form of a generous amplification—of his account given two days earlier was due to the fact that in those two days Albertine, alarmed that the chauffeur should have spoken to me, had surrendered, and made her peace with him. This suspicion never even occurred to me. It is beyond question that this version of the driver's story, as it rid me of all fear that Albertine might have deceived me, quite naturally cooled me towards my mistress and made me take less interest in the day that she had spent at Versailles. I think, however, that the chauffeur's explanations, which, by absolving Albertine, made her even more tedious than before, would not perhaps have been sufficient to calm me so quickly. Two little pimples which for some days past my mistress had had upon her brow were perhaps even more effective in modifying the sentiments of my heart. Finally these were diverted farther still from her (so far that I was conscious of her existence only when I set eyes upon her) by the strange confidence volunteered me by Gilberte's maid, whom I happened to meet. I learned that, when I used to go every day to see Gilberte, she was in love with a young man of whom she saw a great deal more than of myself. I had had an inkling of this for a moment at the time, indeed I had questioned this very maid. But, as she knew that I was in love with Gilberte, she had denied, sworn that never had Mlle. Swann set eyes on the young man. Now, however, knowing that my love had long since died, that for years past I had left all her letters unanswered—and also perhaps because she was no longer in Gilberte's service—of her own accord she gave me a full account of the amorous episode of which I had known nothing. This seemed to her quite natural. I supposed, remembering her oaths at the time, that she had not been aware of what was going on. Far from it, it was she herself who used to go, at Mme. Swann's orders, to inform the young man whenever the object of my love was alone. The object then of my love. . . . But I asked myself whether my love of those days was as dead as I thought, for this story pained me. As I do not believe that jealousy can revive a dead love, I supposed that my painful impression was due, in part at least, to the injury to my self-esteem, for a number of people whom I did not like and who at that time and even a little later—their attitude has since altered—affected a contemptuous attitude towards myself, knew perfectly well, while I was in love with Gilberte, that I was her dupe. And this made me ask myself retrospectively whether in my love for Gilberte there had not been an element of self-love, since it so pained me now to discover that all the hours of affectionate intercourse, which had made me so happy, were known to be nothing more than a deliberate hoodwinking of me by my mistress, by people whom I did not like. In any case, love or self-love, Gilberte was almost dead in me but not entirely, and the result of this annoyance was to prevent me from worrying myself beyond measure about Albertine, who occupied so small a place in my heart. Nevertheless, to return to her (after so long a parenthesis) and to her expedition to Versailles, the postcards of Versailles (is it possible, then, to have one's heart caught in a noose like this by two simultaneous and interwoven jealousies, each inspired by a different person?) gave me a slightly disagreeable impression whenever, as I tidied my papers, my eye fell upon them. And I thought that if the driver had not been such a worthy fellow, the harmony of his second narrative with Albertine's " cards " would not have amounted to much, for what are the first things that people send you from Versailles but the Château and the Trianons, unless that is to say the card has been chosen by some person of refined taste who adores a certain statue, or by some idiot who selects as a " view " of Versailles the station of the horse tramway or the goods depot. Even then I am wrong in saying an idiot, such postcards not having always been bought by a person of that sort at random, for their interest as coming from Versailles. For two whole years men of intelligence, artists, used to find Siena, Venice, Granada a " bore," and would say of the humblest omnibus, of every railway-carriage: " There you have true beauty." Then this fancy passed like the rest. Indeed, I cannot be certain that people did not revert to the " sacrilege of destroying the noble relics of the past." Anyhow, a first class railway carriage ceased to be regarded as *a priori* more beautiful than St. Mark's at Venice. People continued to say: " Here you have real life, the return to the past is artificial," but without drawing any definite conclusion. To make quite certain, without forfeiting any of my confidence in the chauffeur, in order that Albertine might not be able to send him away without his venturing to refuse for fear of her taking him for a spy, I never allowed her to go out after this without the reinforcement of Andrée, whereas for some time past I had found the chauffeur sufficient. I had even allowed her then (a thing I would never dare do now) to stay away for three whole days by herself with the chauffeur and to go almost as far as Balbec, so great was her longing to travel at high speed in an open car. Three days during which my mind had been quite at rest, although the rain of postcards that she had showered upon me did not reach me, owing to the appalling state of the Breton postal system (good in summer, but disorganised, no doubt, in winter), until a week after the return of Albertine and the chauffeur, in such health and vigour that on the very morning of their return they resumed, as though nothing had happened, their daily outings. I was delighted that Albertine should be going this afternoon to the Trocadéro, to this "special" matinée, but still more reassured that she would have a companion there in the shape of Andrée.

Dismissing these reflexions, now that Albertine had gone out, I went and took my stand for a moment at the window. There was at first a silence, amid which the whistle of the tripe vendor and the horn of the tramcar made the air ring in different octaves, like a blind piano-tuner. Then gradually the interwoven motives became distinct, and others were combined with them. There was also a new whistle, the call of a vendor the nature of whose wares I have never discovered, a whistle that was itself exactly like the scream of the tramway, and, as it was not carried out of earshot by its own velocity, one thought of a single car, not endowed with motion, or broken down, immobilised, screaming at short intervals like a dying animal. And I felt that, should I ever have to leave this aristocratic quarter—unless it were to move to one that was entirely plebeian—the streets and boulevards of central Paris (where the fruit, fish and other trades, stabilised in huge stores, rendered superfluous the cries of the street hawkers, who for that matter would not have been able to make themselves heard) would seem to me very dreary, quite uninhabitable, stripped, drained of all these litanies of the small trades and peripatetic victuals, deprived of the orchestra that returned every morning to charm me. On the pavement a woman with no pretence to fashion (or else obedient to an ugly fashion) came past, too brightly dressed in a sack overcoat of goatskin; but no, it was not a woman, it was a chauffeur who, enveloped in his ponyskin, was proceeding on foot to his garage. Escaped from the big hotels, their winged messengers, of variegated hue, were speeding towards the termini, bent over their handlebars, to meet the arrivals by the morning trains. The throb of a violin was due at one time to the passing of a motor-car, at another to my not having put enough water in my electric kettle. In the middle of the symphony there rang out an old-fashioned " air "; replacing the sweet seller, who generally accompanied her song with a rattle, the toy seller, to whose pipe was attached a jumping jack which he sent flying in all directions, paraded similar puppets for sale, and without heeding the ritual declamation of Gregory the Great, the reformed declamation of Palestrina or the lyrical declamation of the modern composers, entoned at the top of his voice, a belated adherent of pure melody: "Allons les papas, allons les mamans, contentez vos petits enfants, c'est moi qui les fais, c'est moi qui les vends, et c'est moi qui boulotte l'argent. Tra la la la. Tra la la la laire, tra la la la la la la. Allons les petits!" Some Italian boys in felt bérets made no attempt to compete with this lively aria, and it was without a word that they offered their little statuettes. Soon, however, a young fifer compelled the toy merchant to move on and to chant more inaudibly, though in brisk time: "Allons les papas, allons les mamans." This young fifer, was he one of the dragoons whom I used to hear in the mornings at Doncières? No, for what followed was: "Voilà le réparateur de faïence et de porcelaine. Je répare le verre, le marbre, le cristal, l'os, l'ivoire et objets d'antiquité. Voilà le réparateur." In a butcher's shop, between an aureole of sunshine on the left and a whole ox suspended from a hook on the right, an assistant, very tall and slender, with fair hair and a throat that escaped above his sky-blue collar, was displaying a lightning speed and a religious conscientiousness in putting on one side the most exquisite fillets of beef, on the other the coarsest parts of the rump, placed them upon glittering scales surmounted by a cross, from which hung down a number of beautiful chains, and—albeit he did nothing afterwards but arrange in the window a display of kidneys, steaks, ribs—was really far more suggestive of a handsome angel who, on the day of the Last Judgment, will prepare for God, according to their quality, the separation of the good and the evil and the weighing of souls. And once again the thin crawling music of the fife rose in the air, herald no longer of the destruction that Françoise used to dread whenever a regiment of cavalry filed past, but of " repairs " promised by an " antiquary," simpleton or rogue, who, in either case highly eclectic, instead of specialising, applied his art to the most diverse materials. The young bread carriers hastened to stuff into their baskets the long rolls ordered for some luncheon party, while the milk girls attached the bottles of milk to their yokes. The sense of longing with which my eyes followed these young damsels, ought I to consider it quite justified? Would it not have been different if I had been able to detain for a few moments at close quarters one of those whom from the height of my window I saw only inside her shop or in motion. To estimate the loss that I suffered by my seclusion, that is to say the wealth that the day held in store for me, I should have had to intercept in the long unrolling of the animated frieze some girl carrying her linen or her milk, make her pass for a moment, like a silhouette from some mobile scheme of decoration, from the wings to the stage, within the proscenium of my bedroom door, and keep her there under my eye, not without eliciting some information about her which would enable me to find her again some day, like the inscribed ring which ornithologists or ichthyologists attach before setting them free to the legs or bellies of the birds or fishes whose migrations they are anxious to trace.

And so I asked Françoise, since I had a message that I wished taken, to be good enough to send up to my room, should any of them call, one or other of those girls who were always coming to take away the dirty or bring back the clean linen, or with bread, or bottles of milk, and whom she herself used often to send on errands. In doing so I was like Elstir, who, obliged to remain closeted in his studio, on certain days in spring when the knowledge that the woods were full of violets gave him a hunger to gaze at them, used to send his porter's wife out to buy him a bunch; then it was not the table upon which he had posed the little vegetable model, but the whole carpet of the underwoods where he had seen in other years, in their thousands, the serpentine stems, bowed beneath the weight of their blue beaks, that Elstir would fancy that he had before his eyes, like an imaginary zone defined in his studio by the limpid odour of the sweet, familiar flower.

Of a laundry girl, on a Sunday, there was not the slightest prospect. As for the girl who brought the bread, as ill luck would have it, she had rung the bell when Françoise was not about, had left her rolls in their basket on the landing, and had made off. The fruit girl would not call until much later. Once I had gone to order a cheese at the dairy, and, among the various young assistants, had remarked one girl, extravagantly fair, tall in stature though still little more than a child, who, among the other errand girls, seemed to be dreaming, in a distinctly haughty attitude. I had seen her in the distance only, and for so brief an instant that I could not have described her appearance, except to say that she must have grown too fast and that her head supported a fleece that gave the impression far less of capillary details than of a sculptor's conventional rendering of the separate channels of parallel drifts of snow upon a glacier. This was all that I had been able to make out, apart from a nose sharply outlined (a rare thing in a child) upon a thin face which recalled the beaks of baby vultures.

Besides, this clustering of her comrades round about her had not been the only thing that prevented me from seeing her distinctly, there was also my uncertainty whether the sentiments which I might, at first sight and subsequently, inspire in her would be those of injured pride, or of irony, or of a scorn which she would express later on to her friends. These alternative suppositions which I had formed, in an instant, with regard to her, had condensed round about her the troubled atmosphere in which she disappeared, like a goddess in the cloud that is shaken by thunder. For moral uncertainty is a greater obstacle to an exact visual perception than any defect of vision would be. In this too skinny young person, who moreover attracted undue attention, the excess of what another person would perhaps have called her charms was precisely what was calculated to repel me, but had nevertheless had the effect of preventing me from perceiving even, far more from remembering anything about the other young dairymaids, whom the hooked nose of this one and her gaze—how unattractive it was!—pensive, personal, with an air of passing judgment, had plunged in perpetual night, as a white streak of lightning darkens the landscape on either side of it. And so, of my call to order a cheese, at the dairy, I had remembered (if we can say " remember " in speaking of a face so carelessly observed that we adapt to the nullity of the face ten different noses in succession), I had remembered only this girl who had not attracted me. This is sufficient to engender love. And yet I should have forgotten the extravagantly fair girl and should never have wished to see her again, had not Françoise told me that, child as she was, she had all her wits about her and would shortly be leaving her employer, since she had been going too fast and owed money among the neighbours. It has been said that beauty is a promise of happiness. Inversely, the possibility of pleasure may be a beginning of beauty.

I began to read Mamma's letter. Beneath her quotations from Madame de Sévigné: "If my thoughts are not entirely black at Combray, they are at least dark grey, I think of you at every moment; I long for you; your health, your affairs, your absence, what sort of cloud do you suppose they make in my sky?" I felt that my mother was vexed to find Albertine's stay in the house prolonged, and my intention of marriage, although not yet announced to my mistress, confirmed. She did not express her annoyance more directly because she was afraid that I might leave her letters lying about. Even then, veiled as her letters were, she reproached me with not informing her immediately, after each of them, that I had received it: "You remember how Mme. de Sévigné said: 'When we are far apart, we no longer laugh at letters which begin with *I have received yours.*'" Without referring to what distressed her most, she said that she was annoyed by my lavish expenditure: "Where on earth does all your money go? It is distressing enough that, like Charles de Sévigné, you do not know what you want and are 'two or three people at once,' but do try at least not to be like him in spending money so that I may never have to say of you: 'he has discovered how to spend and have nothing to shew, how to lose without staking and how to pay without clearing himself of debt.'" I had just finished Mamma's letter when Françoise returned to tell me that she had in the house that very same slightly overbold young dairymaid of whom she had spoken to me. "She can quite well take Monsieur's note and bring back the answer, if it's not too far. Monsieur shall see her, she's just like a Little Red Ridinghood." Françoise withdrew to fetch the girl, and I could hear her leading the way and saying: "Come along now, you're frightened because there's a passage, stuff and nonsense, I never thought you would be such a goose. Have I got to lead you by the hand?" And Françoise, like a good and honest servant who means to see that her master is respected as she respects him herself, had draped herself in that majesty which ennobles the matchmaker in a picture by an old master where, in comparison with her, the lover and his mistress fade into insignificance. But Elstir when he gazed at them had no need to bother about what the violets were doing. The entry of the young dairymaid at once robbed me of my contemplative calm; I could think only of how to give plausibility to the fable of the letter that she was to deliver and I began to write quickly without venturing to cast more than a furtive glance at her, so that I might not seem to have brought her into my room to be scrutinised. She was invested for me with that charm of the unknown which I should not discover in a pretty girl whom I had found in one of those houses where they come to meet one. She was neither naked nor in disguise, but a genuine dairymaid, one of those whom we imagine to be so pretty, when we have not time to approach them; she possessed something of what constitutes the eternal desire, the eternal regret of life, the twofold current of which is at length diverted, directed towards us. Twofold, for if it is a question of the unknown, of a person who must, we guess, be divine, from her stature, her proportions, her indifferent glance, her haughty calm, on the other hand we wish this woman to be thoroughly specialised in her profession, allowing us to escape from ourself into that world which a peculiar costume makes us romantically believe different. If for that matter we seek to comprise in a formula the law of our amorous curiosities, we should have to seek it in the maximum of difference between a woman of whom we have caught sight and one whom we have approached and caressed. If the women of what used at one time to be called the closed houses, if prostitutes themselves (provided that we know them to be prostitutes) attract us so little, it is not because they are less beautiful than other women, it is because they are ready and waiting; the very object that we are seeking to attain they offer us already; it is because they are not conquests. The difference there is at a minimum. A harlot smiles at us already in the street as she will smile when she is in our room. We are sculptors. We are anxious to obtain of a woman a statue entirely different from that which she has presented to us. We have seen a girl strolling, indifferent, insolent, along the seashore, we have seen a shop-assistant, serious and active, behind her counter, who will answer us stiffly, if only so as to escape the sarcasm of her comrades, a fruit seller who barely answers us at all. Well, we know no rest until we can discover by experiment whether the proud girl on the seashore, the shop-assistant on her high horse of " What will people say? ", the preoccupied fruit seller cannot be made, by skilful handling on our part, to relax their rectangular attitude, to throw about our neck their fruit-laden arms, to direct towards our lips, with a smile of consent, eyes hitherto frozen or absent—oh, the beauty of stern eyes—in working hours when the worker was so afraid of the gossip of her companions, eyes that avoided our beleaguering stare and, now that we have seen her alone and face to face, make their pupils yield beneath the sunlit burden of laughter when we speak of making love. Between the shopgirl, the laundress busy with her iron, the fruit seller, the dairymaid on the one hand, and the same girl when she is about to become our mistress, the maximum of difference is attained, stretched indeed to its extreme limits, and varied by those habitual gestures of her profession which make a pair of arms, during the hours of toil, something as different as possible (regarded as an arabesque pattern) from those supple bonds that already every evening are fastened about our throat while the mouth shapes itself for a kiss. And so we pass our whole life in uneasy advances, incessantly renewed, to respectable girls whom their calling seems to separate from us. Once they are in our arms, they are no longer anything more than they originally were, the gulf that we dreamed of crossing has been bridged. But we begin afresh with other women, we devote to these enterprises all our time, all our money, all our strength, our blood boils at the too cautious driver who is perhaps going to make us miss our first assignation, we work ourself into a fever. That first meeting, we know all the same that it will mean the vanishing of an illusion. It does not so much matter that the illusion still persists; we wish to see whether we can convert it into reality, and then we think of the laundress whose coldness we remarked. Amorous curiosity is like that which is aroused in us by the names of places; perpetually disappointed, it revives and remains for ever insatiable.

Alas! As soon as she stood before me, the fair dairymaid with the ribbed tresses, stripped of all that I had imagined and of the desire that had been aroused in me, was reduced to her own proportions. The throbbing cloud of my suppositions no longer enveloped her in a shimmering haze. She acquired an almost beggarly air from having (in place of the ten, the score that I recalled in turn without being able to fix any of them in my memory) but a single nose, rounder than I had thought, which made her appear rather a fool and had in any case lost the faculty of multiplying itself. This flyaway caught on the wing, inert, crushed, incapable of adding anything to its own paltry appearance, had no longer my imagination to collaborate with it. Fallen into the inertia of reality, I sought to rebound; her cheeks, which I had not seen in the shop, appeared to me so pretty that I became alarmed, and, to put myself in countenance, said to the young dairymaid: "Would you be so kind as to pass me the *Figaro* which is lying there, I must make sure of the address to which I am going to send you." Thereupon, as she picked up the newspaper, she disclosed as far as her elbow the red sleeve of her jersey and handed me the conservative sheet with a neat and courteous gesture which pleased me by its intimate rapidity, its pliable contour and its scarlet hue. While I was opening the *Figaro,* in order to say something and without raising my eyes, I asked the girl: "What do you call that red knitted thing you're wearing? It is very becoming." She replied: "It's my golf." For, by a slight downward tendency common to all fashions, the garments and styles which, a few years earlier, seemed to belong to the relatively smart world of Albertine's friends, were now the portion of working girls. "Are you quite sure it won't be giving you too much trouble," I said, while I pretended to be searching the columns of the *Figaro*, "if I send you rather a long way?" As soon as I myself appeared to find the service at all arduous that she would be performing by taking a message for me, she began to feel that it would be a trouble to her, "The only thing is, I have to be going out presently on my bike. Good lord, you know, Sunday's the only day we've got." "But won't you catch cold, going bare-headed like that?" "Oh, I shan't be bare-headed, I shall have my polo, and I could get on without it with all the hair I have." I raised my eyes to the blaze of curling tresses and felt myself caught in their swirl and swept away, with a throbbing heart, amid the lightning and the blasts of a hurricane of beauty. I continued to study the newspaper, but albeit this was only to keep myself in countenance and to gain time, while I merely pretended to read, I took in nevertheless the meaning of the words that were before my eyes, and my attention was caught by the following: "To the programme already announced for this afternoon in the great hall of the Trocadéro must be added the name of Mlle. Léa who has consented to appear in *Les Fourberies de Nérine*. She will of course sustain the part of Nérine, in which she is astounding in her display of spirit and bewitching gaiety." It was as though a hand had brutally torn from my heart the bandage beneath which its wound had begun since my return from Balbec to heal. The flood of my anguish escaped in torrents, Léa, that was the actress friend of the two girls at Balbec whom Albertine, without appearing to see them, had, one afternoon at the Casino, watched in the mirror. It was true that at Balbec Albertine, at the name of Léa, had adopted a special tone of compunction in order to say to me, almost shocked that anyone could suspect such a pattern of virtue: "Oh no, she is not in the least that sort of woman, she is a very respectable person." Unfortunately for me, when Albertine made a statement of this sort, it was never anything but the first stage towards other, divergent statements. Shortly after the first, came this second: "I don't know her." In the third phase, after Albertine had spoken to me of somebody who was "above suspicion" and whom (in the second place) she did not know, she first of all forgot that she had said that she did not know her and then, in a speech in which she contradicted herself unawares, informed me that she did know her. This first act of oblivion completed, and the fresh statement made, a second oblivion began, to wit that the person was above suspicion. "Isn't so and so," I would ask, "one of those women?" "Why, of course, everybody knows that!" Immediately the note of compunction was sounded afresh to utter a statement which was a vague echo, greatly reduced, of the first statement of all. "I'm bound to say that she has always behaved perfectly properly with me. Of course, she knows that I would send her about her business if she tried it on. Still, that makes no difference. I am obliged to give her credit for the genuine respect she has always shewn for me. It is easy to see she knew the sort of person she had to deal with." We remember the truth because it has a name, is rooted in the past, but a makeshift lie is quickly forgotten. Albertine forgot this latest lie, her fourth, and, one day when she was anxious to gain my confidence by confiding in me, went so far as to tell me, with regard to the same person who at the outset had been so respectable and whom she did not know: " She took quite a fancy to me at one time. She asked me, three or four times, to go home with her and to come upstairs to her room. I saw no harm in going home with her, where everybody could see us, in broad daylight, in the open air. But when we reached her front door I always made some excuse and I never went upstairs." Shortly after this, Albertine made an illusion to the beautiful things that this lady had in her room. By proceeding from one approximation to another, I should no doubt have arrived at making her tell me the truth which was perhaps less serious than I had been led to believe, for, although perhaps easy going with women, she preferred a male lover, and now that she had myself would not have given a thought to Léa. In any case, with regard to this person, I was still at the first stage of revelation and was not aware whether Albertine knew her. Already, in the case of many women at any rate, it would have been enough for me to collect and present to my mistress, in a synthesis, her contradictory statements, in order to convict her of her misdeeds (misdeeds which, like astronomical laws, it is a great deal easier to deduce by a process of reasoning than to observe, to surprise in the act). But then she would have preferred to say that one of her statements had been a lie, the withdrawal of which would thus bring about the collapse of my whole system of evidence, rather than admit that everything which she had told me from the start was simply a tissue of falsehood. There are similar tissues in the Thousand and One Nights, which we find charming. They pain us, coming from a person whom we love, and thereby enable us to penetrate a little deeper in our knowledge of human nature instead of being content to play upon the surface. Grief penetrates into us and forces us out of painful curiosity to penetrate other people. Whence emerge truths which we feel that we have no right to keep hidden, so much so that a dying atheist who has discovered them, certain of his own extinction, indifferent to fame, will nevertheless devote his last hours on earth to an attempt to make them known.

Of course, I was still at the first stage of enlightenment with regard to Léa. I was not even aware whether Albertine knew her. No matter, it all came to the same thing. I must at all costs prevent her from—at the Trocadéro—renewing this acquaintance or making the acquaintance of this stranger. I have said that I did not know whether she knew Léa; I ought, however, to have learned it at Balbec, from Albertine herself. For defective memory obliterated from my mind as well as from Albertine's a great many of the statements that she had made to me. Memory, instead of being a duplicate always present before our eyes of the various events of our life, is rather an abyss from which at odd moments a chance resemblance enables us to draw up, restored to life, dead impressions; but even then there are innumerable little details which have not fallen into that potential reservoir of memory, and which will remain for ever beyond our control. To anything that we do not know to be related to the real life of the person whom we love we pay but scant attention, we forget immediately what she has said to us about some incident or people that we do not know, and her expression while she was saying it. And so when, in due course, our jealousy is aroused by these same people, and seeks to make sure that it is not mistaken, that it is they who are responsible for the haste which our mistress shews in leaving the house, her annoyance when we have prevented her from going out by returning earlier than usual; our jealousy ransacking the past in search of a clue can find nothing; always retrospective, it is like a historian who has to write the history of a period for which he has no documents; always belated, it dashes like a mad bull to the spot where it will not find the proud and brilliant creature who is infuriating it with his darts and whom the crowd admire for his splendour and his cunning. Jealousy fights the empty air, uncertain as we are in those dreams in which we are distressed because we cannot find in his empty house a person whom we have known well in life, but who here perhaps is really another person and has merely borrowed the features of our friend, uncertain as we are even more after we awake when we seek to identify this or that detail of our dream. What was our mistress's expression when she told us this; did she not look happy, was she not actually whistling, a thing that she never does unless there is some amorous thought in her mind? In the time of our love, if our presence teased her and irritated her a little, has she not told us something that is contradicted by what she now affirms, that she knows or does not know such and such a person? We do not know, we shall never find out; we strain after the unsubstantial fragments of a dream, and all the time our life with our mistress continues, our life indifferent to what we do not know to be important to us, attentive to what is perhaps of no importance, hagridden by people who have no real connexion with us, full of lapses of memory, gaps, vain anxieties, our life as fantastic as a dream.

I realised that the young dairymaid was still in the room. I told her that the place was certainly a long way off, that I did not need her. Whereupon she also decided that it would be too much trouble: "There's a fine match coming off, I don't want to miss it." I felt that she must already be devoted to sport and that in a few years' time she would be talking about "living her own life." I told her that I certainly did not need her any longer, and gave her five francs. Immediately, having little expected this largesse, and telling herself that if she earned five francs for doing nothing she would have a great deal more for taking my message, she began to find that her match was of no importance. "I could easily have taken your message. I can always find time." But I thrust her from the room, I needed to be alone, I must at all costs prevent Albertine from any risk of meeting Léa's girl friends at the Trocadéro. I must try, and I must succeed; to tell the truth I did not yet see how, and during these first moments I opened my hands, gazed at them, cracked my knuckles, whether because the mind which cannot find what it is seeking, in a fit of laziness allows itself to halt for an instant at a spot where the most unimportant things are distinctly visible to it, like the blades of grass on the embankment which we see from the carriage window trembling in the wind, when the train halts in the open country—an immobility that is not always more fertile than that of the captured animal which, paralysed by fear or fascinated, gazes without moving a muscle—or that I might hold my body in readiness—with my mind at work inside it and, in my mind, the means of action against this or that person—as though it were no more than a weapon from which would be fired the shot that was to separate Albertine from Léa and her two friends. It is true that earlier in the morning, when Françoise had come in to tell me that Albertine was going to the Trocadéro, I had said to myself: "Albertine is at liberty to do as she pleases" and had supposed that until evening came, in this radiant weather, her actions would remain without any perceptible importance to myself; but it was not only the morning sun, as I had thought, that had made me so careless; it was because, having obliged Albertine to abandon the plans that she might perhaps have initiated or even completed at the Verdurins', and having restricted her to attending a performance which I myself had chosen, so that she could not have made any preparations, I knew that whatever she did would of necessity be innocent. Just as, if Albertine had said a few moments later: "If I kill myself, it's all the same to me," it would have been because she was certain that she would not kill herself. Surrounding myself and Albertine there had been this morning (far more than the sunlight in the air) that atmosphere which we do not see, but by the translucent and changing medium of which we do see, I her actions, she the importance of her own life, that is to say those beliefs which we do not perceive but which are no more assimilable to a pure vacuum than is the air that surrounds us; composing round about us a variable atmosphere, sometimes excellent, often unbreathable, they deserve to be studied and recorded as carefully as the temperature, the barometric pressure, the weather, for our days have their own singularity, physical and moral. My belief, which I had failed to remark this morning, and yet in which I had been joyously enveloped until the moment when I had looked a second time at the *Figaro,* that Albertine would do nothing that was not harmless, this belief had vanished. I was living no longer in the fine sunny day, but in a day carved out of the other by my anxiety lest Albertine might renew her acquaintance with Léa and more easily still with the two girls, should they go, as seemed to me probable, to applaud the actress at the Trocadéro where it would not be difficult for them, in one of the intervals, to come upon Albertine. I no longer thought of Mlle. Vinteuil, the name of Léa had brought back to my mind, to make me jealous, the image of Albertine in the Casino watching the two girls. For I possessed in my memory only series of Albertines, separate from one another, incomplete, outlines, snapshots; and so my jealousy was restricted to an intermittent expression, at once fugitive and fixed, and to the people who had caused that expression to appear upon Albertine's face. I remembered her when, at Balbec, she received undue attention from the two girls or from women of that sort; I remembered the distress that I used to feel when I saw her face subjected to an active scrutiny, like that of a painter preparing to make a sketch, entirely covered by them, and, doubtless on account of my presence, submitting to this contact without appearing to notice it, with a passivity that was perhaps clandestinely voluptuous. And before she recovered herself and spoke to me there was an instant during which Albertine did not move, smiled into the empty air, with the same air of feigned spontaneity and concealed pleasure as if she were posing for somebody to take her photograph; or even seeking to assume before the camera a more dashing pose—that which she had adopted at Doncières when we were walking with Saint-Loup, and, laughing and passing her tongue over her lips, she pretended to be teasing a dog. Certainly at such moments she was not at all the same as when it was she that was interested in little girls who passed us. Then, on the contrary, her narrow velvety gaze fastened itself upon, glued itself to the passer-by, so adherent, so corrosive, that you felt that when she removed it it must tear away the skin. But at that moment this other expression, which did at least give her a serious air, almost as though she were in pain, had seemed to me a pleasant relief after the toneless blissful expression she had worn in the presence of the two girls, and I should have preferred the sombre expression of the desire that she did perhaps feel at times to the laughing expression caused by the desire which she aroused. However she might attempt to conceal her consciousness of it, it bathed her, enveloped her, vaporous, voluptuous, made her whole face appear rosy. But everything that Albertine held at such moments suspended in herself, that radiated round her and hurt me so acutely, how could I tell whether, once my back was turned, she would continue to keep it to herself, whether to the advances of the two girls, now that I was no longer with her, she would not make some audacious response. Indeed, these memories caused me intense grief, they were like a complete admission of Albertine's failings, a general confession of her infidelity against which were powerless the various oaths that she swore to me and I wished to believe, the negative results of my incomplete researches, the assurances, made perhaps in connivance with her, of Andrée. Albertine might deny specified betrayals; by words that she let fall,. more emphatic than her declarations to the contrary, by that searching gaze alone, she had made confession of what she would fain have concealed, far more than any specified incident, what she would have let herself be killed sooner than admit: her natural tendency. For there is no one who will willingly deliver up his soul. Notwithstanding the grief that these memories were causing me, could I have denied that it was the programme of the matinée at the Trocadéro that had revived my need of Albertine? She was one of those women in whom their misdeeds may at a pinch take the place of absent charms, and no less than their misdeeds the kindness that follows them and restores to us that sense of comfort which in their company, like an invalid who is never well for two days in succession, we are incessantly obliged to recapture. And then, even more than their misdeeds while we are in love with them, there are.their misdeeds before we made their acquaintance, and first and foremost: their nature. What makes this sort of love painful is, in fact, that there preexists a sort of original sin of Woman, a sin which makes us love them, so that, when we forget it, we feel less need of them, and to begin to love afresh we must begin to suffer afresh. At this moment, the thought that she must not meet the two girls again and the question whether or not she knew Léa were what was chiefly occupying my mind, in spite of the rule that we ought not to take an interest in particular facts except in relation to their general significance, and notwithstanding the childishness, as great as that of longing to travel or to make friends with women, of shattering our curiosity against such elements of the invisible torrent of painful realities which will always remain unknown to us as have happened to crystallise in our mind. But, even if we should succeed in destroying that crystallisation, it would at once be replaced by another. Yesterday I was afraid lest Albertine should go to see Mme. Verdurin. Now my only thought was of Léa. Jealousy, which wears a bandage over its eyes, is not merely powerless to discover anything in the darkness that enshrouds it, it is also one of those torments where the task must be incessantly repeated, like that of the Danaids, or of Ixion. Even if her friends were not there, what impression might she not form of Léa, beautified by her stage attire, haloed with success, what thoughts would she leave in Albertine's mind, what desires which, even if she repressed them, would in my house disgust her with a life in which she was unable to gratify them.

Besides, how could I tell that she was not acquainted with Léa, and would not pay her a visit in her dressing-room; and, even if Léa did not know her, who could assure me that, having certainly seen her at Balbec, she would not recognise her and make a signal to her from the stage that would entitle Albertine to seek admission behind the scenes? A danger seems easy to avoid after it has been conjured away. This one was not yet conjured, I was afraid that it might never be, and it seemed to me all the more terrible. And yet this love for Albertine which I felt almost vanish when I attempted to realise it, seemed in a measure to acquire a proof of its existence from the intensity of my grief at this moment. I no longer cared about anything else, I thought only of

how I was to prevent her from remaining at the Trocadéro, I would have offered any sum in the world to
Léa to persuade her not to go there. If then we prove
our choice by the action that we perform rather than by
the idea that we form, I must have been in love with
Albertine. But this renewal of my suffering gave no
further consistency to the image that I beheld of Albertine. She caused my calamities, like a deity that
remains invisible. Making endless conjectures, I sought
to shield myself from suffering without thereby realising
my love. First of all, I must make certain that Léa was
really going to perform at the Trocadéro. After dismissing the dairymaid, I telephoned to Bloch, whom I
knew to be on friendly terms with Léa, in order to ask
him. He knew nothing about it and seemed surprised
that the matter could be of any importance to me. I
decided that I must set to work immediately, remembered
that Françoise was ready to go out and that I was not,
and as I rose and dressed made her take a motor-car;
she was to go to the Trocadéro, engage a seat, look high
and low for Albertine and give her a note from myself.
In this note I told her that I was greatly upset by a
letter which I had just received from that same lady on
whose account she would remember that I had been so
wretched one night at Balbec. I reminded her that, on
the following day, she had reproached me for not having
sent for her. And so I was taking the liberty, I informed
her, of asking her to sacrifice her matinée and to join me
at home so that we might take a little fresh air together,
which might help me to recover from the shock. But as
I should be a long time in getting ready, she would oblige
me, seeing that she had Françoise as an escort, by calling

at the Trois-Quartiers (this shop, being smaller, seemed to me less dangerous than the Bon Marché) to buy the scarf of white tulle that she required. My note was probably not superfluous. To tell the truth, I knew nothing that Albertine had done since I had come to know her, or even before. But in her conversation (she might, had I mentioned it to her, have replied that I had misunderstood her) there were certain contradictions, certain embellishments which seemed to me as decisive as catching her red-handed, but less serviceable against Albertine who, often caught out in wrongdoing like a child, had invariably, by dint of sudden, strategic changes of front, stultified my cruel onslaught and re-established her own position. Cruel, most of all, to myself. She employed, not from any refinement of style, but in order to correct her imprudences, abrupt breaches of syntax not unlike that figure which the grammarians call anacoluthon or some such name. Having allowed herself, while discussing women, to say: I remember, the other day, I . . .," she would at once catch her breath, after which "I" became "she": it was something that she had witnessed as an innocent spectator, not a thing that she herself had done. It was not herself that was the heroine of the anecdote. I should have liked to recall how, exactly, the sentence began, so as to conclude for myself, since she had broken off in the middle, how it would have ended. But as I had heard the end, I found it hard to remember the beginning, from which perhaps my air of interest had made her deviate, and was left still anxious to know what she was really thinking, what she really remembered. The first stages of falsehood on the part of our mistress are like the first stages of our own love, or of a religious vocation. They take shape, accumulate, pass, without our paying them any attention. When we wish to remember in what manner we began to love a woman, we are already in love with her; when we dreamed about her before falling in love, we did not say to ourself: This is the prelude to a love affair, we must pay attention!—and our dreams took us by surprise, and we barely noticed them. So also, except in cases that are comparatively rare, it is only for the convenience of my narrative that I have frequently in these pages confronted one of Albertine's false statements with her previous assertion upon the same subject. This previous assertion, as often as not, since I could not read the future and did not at the time guess what contradictory affirmation was to form a pendant to it, had slipped past unperceived, heard it is true by my ears, but without my isolating it from the continuous flow of Albertine's speech. Later on, faced with the self-evident lie, or seized by an anxious doubt, I would fain have recalled it; but in vain; my memory had not been warned in time, and had thought it unnecessary to preserve a copy.

I urged Françoise, when she had got Albertine out of the hall, to let me know by telephone, and to bring her home, whether she was willing or not. "That would be the last straw, that she should not be willing to come and see Monsieur," replied Françoise. "But I don't know that she's as fond as all that of seeing me." "Then she must be an ungrateful wretch," went on Françoise, in whom Albertine was renewing after all these years the same torment of envy that Eulalie used at one time to cause her in my aunt's sickroom. Unaware that Albertine's position in my household was not of her own seeking but had been decided by myself (a fact which, from motives of self-esteem and to make Françoise angry, I preferred to conceal from her), she admired and execrated the girl's dexterity, called her when she spoke of her to the other servants a " play-actress," a wheedler who could twist me round her little finger. She dared not yet declare open war against her, shewed her a smiling countenance and sought to acquire merit in my sight by the services which she performed for her in her relations with myself, deciding that it was useless to say anything to me and that she would gain nothing by doing so; but if the opportunity ever arose, if ever she discovered a crack in Albertine's armour, she was fully determined to enlarge it, and to part us for good and all. " Ungrateful? No, Françoise, I think it is I that am ungrateful, you don't know how good she is to me." (It was so soothing to give the impression that I was loved.) " Be as quick as you can." "All right, I'll get a move on." Her daughter's influence was beginning to contaminate Françoise's vocabulary. So it is that all languages lose their purity by the admission of new words. For this decadence of Françoise's speech, which I had known in its golden period, I was myself indirectly responsible. Françoise's daughter would not have made her mother's classic language degenerate into the vilest slang, had she been content to converse with her in dialect. She had never given up the use of it, and when they were both in my room at once, if they had anything private to say, instead of shutting themselves up in the kitchen, they armed themselves, right in the middle of my room, with a screen more impenetrable than the most carefully shut door, by conversing in dialect. I supposed merely that the mother and daughter were not always on the best of terms, if I was to judge by the frequency with which they employed the only word that I could make out: *m'esas-perate* (unless it was that the object of their exasperation was myself). Unfortunately the most unfamiliar tongue becomes intelligible in time when we are always hearing it spoken. I was sorry that this should be dialect, for I succeeded in picking it up, and should have been no less successful had Françoise been in the habit of expressing herself in Persian. In vain might Françoise, when she became aware of my progress, accelerate the speed of her utterance, and her daughter likewise, it was no good. The mother was greatly put out that I understood their dialect, then delighted to hear me speak it. I am bound to admit that her delight was a mocking delight, for albeit I came in time to pronounce the words more or less as she herself did, she found between our two ways of pronunciation an abyss of difference which gave her infinite joy, and she began to regret that she no longer saw people to whom she had not given a thought for years but who, it appeared, would have rocked with a laughter which it would have done her good to hear, if they could have heard me speaking their dialect so badly. In any case, no joy came to mitigate her sorrow that, however badly I might pronounce it, I understood it well. Keys become useless when the person whom we seek to prevent from entering can avail himself of a skeleton key or a jemmy. Dialect having become useless as a means of defence, she took to conversing with her daughter in a French which rapidly became that of the most debased epochs.

I was now ready, but Françoise had not yet telephoned;
I ought perhaps to go out without waiting for a message.
But how could I tell that she would find Albertine, that
the latter would not have gone behind the scenes, that
even if Françoise did find her, she would allow herself to
be taken away? Half an hour later the telephone bell
began to tinkle and my heart throbbed tumultuously with
hope and fear. There came, at the bidding of an operator, a flying squadron of sounds which with an instantaneous speed brought me the words of the telephonist,
not those of Françoise whom an inherited timidity and
melancholy, when she was brought face to face with any
object unknown to her fathers, prevented from approaching a telephone receiver, although she would readily visit
a person suffering from a contagious disease. She had
found Albertine in the lobby by herself, and Albertine had
simply gone to warn Andrée that she was not staying
any longer and then had hurried back to Françoise.
"She wasn't angry? Oh, I beg your pardon; will you
please ask the person whether the young lady was
angry?" "The lady asks me to say that she wasn't at
all angry, quite the contrary, in fact; anyhow, if she
wasn't pleased, she didn't shew it. They are starting
now for the Trois-Quartiers, and will be home by two
o'clock." I gathered that two o'clock meant three, for
it was past two o'clock already. But Françoise suffered
from one of those peculiar, permanent, incurable defects,
which we call maladies; she was never able either to read
or to announce the time correctly. I have never been
able to understand what went on in her head. When
Françoise, after consulting her watch, if it was two o'clock,
said: "It is one" or "it is three o'clock," I have never

been able to understand whether the phenomenon that occurred was situated in her vision or in her thought or in her speech; the one thing certain is that the phenomenon never failed to occur. Humanity is a very old institution. Heredity, cross-breeding have given an irresistible force to bad habits, to vicious reflexes. One person sneezes and gasps because he is passing a rosebush, another breaks out in an eruption at the smell of wet paint, has frequent attacks of colic if he has to start on a journey, and grandchildren of thieves who are themselves millionaires and generous cannot resist the temptation to rob you of fifty francs. As for knowing in what consisted Françoise's incapacity to tell the time correctly, she herself never threw any light upon the problem. For, notwithstanding the anger that I generally displayed at her inaccurate replies, Françoise never attempted either to apologise for her mistake or to explain it. She remained silent, pretending not to hear, and thereby making me lose my temper altogether. I should have liked to hear a few words of justification, were it only that I might smite her hip and thigh; but not a word, an indifferent silence. In any case, about the time-table for to-day there could be no doubt; Albertine was coming home with Françoise at three o'clock, Albertine would not be meeting Léa or her friends. Whereupon the danger of her renewing relations with them, having been averted, at once began to lose its importance in my eyes and I was amazed, seeing with what ease it had been averted, that I should have supposed that I would not succeed in averting it. I felt a keen impulse of gratitude to Albertine, who, I could see, had not gone to the Trocadéro to meet Léa's friends, and shewed me, by leaving the performance and coming home at a word from myself, that she belonged to me more than I had imagined. My gratitude was even greater when a bicyclist brought me a line from her bidding me be patient, and full of the charming expressions that she was in the habit of using. "My darling, dear Marcel, I return less quickly than this cyclist, whose machine I would like to borrow in order to be with you sooner. How could you imagine that I might be angry or that I could enjoy anything better than to be with you? It will be nice to go out, just the two of us together; it would be nicer still if we never went out except together. The ideas you get into your head! What a Marcel! What a Marcel! Always and ever your Albertine."

The frocks that I bought for her, the yacht of which I had spoken to her, the wrappers from Fortuny's, all these things having in this obedience on Albertine's part not their recompense but their complement, appeared to me now as so many privileges that I was enjoying; for the duties and expenditure of a master are part of his dominion, and define it, prove it, fully as much as his rights. And these rights which she recognised in me were precisely what gave my expenditure its true character: I had a woman of my own, who, at the first word that I sent to her unexpectedly, made my messenger telephone humbly that she was coming, that she was allowing herself to be brought home immediately. I was more of a master than I had supposed. More of a master, in other words more of a slave. I no longer felt the slightest impatience to see Albertine. The certainty that she was at this moment engaged in shopping with Françoise, or that she would return with her at an approaching moment

which I would willingly have postponed, illuminated like
a calm and radiant star a period of time which I would
now have been far better pleased to spend alone. My
love for Albertine had made me rise and get ready to go
out, but it would prevent me from enjoying my outing.
I reflected that on a Sunday afternoon like this little
shopgirls, midinettes, prostitutes must be strolling in the
Bois. And with the words *midinettes, little shopgirls*
(as had often happened to me with a proper name, the
name of a girl read in the account of a ball), with the
image of a white bodice, a short skirt, since beneath them
I placed a stranger who might perhaps come to love me,
I created out of nothing desirable women, and said to myself: "How charming they must be!" But of what use
would it be to me that they were charming, seeing that I
was not going out alone. Taking advantage of the fact
that I still was alone, and drawing the curtains together so
that the sun should not prevent me from reading the
notes, I sat down at the piano, turned over the pages of
Vinteuil's sonata which happened to be lying there, and
began to play; seeing that Albertine's arrival was still a
matter of some time but was on the other hand certain,
I had at once time to spare and tranquillity of mind.
Floating in the expectation, big with security, of her
return escorted by Françoise and in my confidence in
her docility as in the blessedness of an inward light as
warming as the light of the sun, I might dispose of my
thoughts, detach them for a moment from Albertine, apply them to the sonata. In the latter, indeed, I did
not take pains to remark how the combinations of
the voluptuous and anxious motives corresponded even
more closely now to my love for Albertine, from which

jealousy had been absent for so long that I had been able to confess to Swann my ignorance of that sentiment. No, taking the sonata from another point of view, regarding it in itself as the work of a great artist, I was carried back upon the tide of sound to the days at Combray—I do not mean at Montjouvain and along the Méséglise way, but to walks along the Guermantes way—when I had myself longed to become an artist. In definitely abandoning that ambition, had I forfeited something real? Could life console me for the loss of art, was there in art a more profound reality, in which our true personality finds an expression that is not afforded it by the activities of life? Every great artist seems indeed so different from all the rest, and gives us so strongly that sensation of individuality for which we seek in vain in our every day existence. Just as I was thinking thus, I was struck by a passage in the sonata, a passage with which I was quite familiar, but sometimes our attention throws a different light upon things which we have long known, and we remark in them what we have never seen before. As I played the passage, and for all that in it Vinteuil had been trying to express a fancy which would have been wholly foreign to Wagner, I could not help murmuring "*Tristan,*" with the smile of an old friend of the family discovering a trace of the grandfather in an intonation, a gesture of the grandson who never set eyes on him. And as the friend then examines a photograph which enables him to estimate the likeness, so, in front of Vinteuil's sonata, I set up on the music-rest the score of *Tristan,* a selection from which was being given that afternoon, as it happened, at the Lamoureux concert. I had not, in admiring the Bayreuth master, any of the scruples of those people whom, like Nietzsche, their sense of duty bids to shun in art as in life the beauty that tempts them, and who, tearing themselves from *Tristan* as they renounce *Parsifal,* and, in their spiritual asceticism, progressing from one mortification to another, arrive, by following the most bloody of *viae Crucis,* at exalting themselves to the pure cognition and perfect adoration of *Le Postillon de Longjumeau.* I began to perceive how much reality there is in the work of Wagner, when I saw in my mind's eye those insistent, fleeting themes which visit an act, withdraw only to return, and, sometimes distant, drowsy, almost detached, are at other moments, while remaining vague, so pressing and so near, so internal, so organic, so visceral, that one would call them the resumption not so much of a musical motive as of an attack of neuralgia.

Music, very different in this respect from Albertine's society, helped me to descend into myself, to make there a fresh discovery: that of the difference that I had sought in vain in life, in travel, a longing for which was given me, however, by this sonorous tide which sent its sunlit waves rolling to expire at my feet. A twofold difference. As the spectrum makes visible to us the composition of light, so the harmony of a Wagner, the colour of an Elstir enable us to know that essential quality of another person's sensations into which love for another person does not allow us to penetrate. Then there is diversity inside the work itself, by the sole means that it has of being effectively diverse, to wit combining diverse individualities. Where a minor composer would pretend that he was portraying a squire, or a knight, whereas he would make them both sing the same music, Wagner on the contrary allots to each denomination a different reality, and whenever a squire appears, it is an individual figure, at once complicated and simplified, that, with a joyous, feudal clash of warring sounds, inscribes itself in the vast, sonorous mass. Whence the completeness of a music that is indeed filled with so many different musics, each of which is a person. A person or the impression that is given us by a momentary aspect of nature. Even what is most independent of the sentiment that it makes us feel preserves its outward and entirely definite reality; the song of a bird, the ring of a hunter's horn, the air that a shepherd plays upon his pipe, cut out against the horizon their silhouette of sound. It is true that Wagner had still to bring these together, to make use of them, to introduce them into an orchestral whole, to make them subservient to the highest musical ideals, but always respecting their original nature, as a carpenter respects the grain, the peculiar essence of the wood that he is carving.

But notwithstanding the richness of these works in which the contemplation of nature has its place by the side of action, by the side of persons who are something more than proper names, I thought how markedly, all the same, these works participate in that quality of being—albeit marvellously—always incomplete, which is the peculiarity of all the great works of the nineteenth century, with which the greatest writers of that century have stamped their books, but, watching themselves at work as though they were at once author and critic, have derived from this self-contemplation a novel beauty, exterior and superior to the work itself, imposing upon it retrospectively a unity, a greatness which it does not possess. Without pausing to consider him who saw in

his novels, after they had appeared, a *Human Comedy,*
nor those who entitled heterogeneous poems or essays
The Legend of the Ages or *The Bible of Humanity,* can
we not say all the same of the last of these that he is so
perfect an incarnation of the nineteenth century that the
greatest beauties in Michelet are to be sought not so much
in his work itself as in the attitudes that he adopts when
he is considering his work, not in his *History of France*
nor in his *History of the Revolution,* but in his prefaces
to his books?   Prefaces, that is to say pages written after
the books themselves, in which he considers the books,
and with which we must include here and there certain
phrases beginning as a rule with a: " Shall I say? " which
is not a scholar's precaution but a musician's cadence.
The other musician, he who was delighting me at this
moment, Wagner, retrieving some exquisite scrap from
a drawer of his writing-table to make it appear as a theme,
retrospectively necessary, in a work of which he had not
been thinking at the moment when he composed it, then
having composed a first mythological opera, and a second,
and afterwards others still, and perceiving all of a sudden
that he had written a tetralogy, must have felt something
of the same exhilaration as Balzac, when, casting over his
works the eye at once of a stranger and of a father, finding in one the purity of Raphael, in another the simplicity
of the Gospel, he suddenly decided, as he shed a retrospective illumination upon them, that they would be better brought together in a cycle in which the same characters would reappear, and added to his work, in this
act of joining it together, a stroke of the brush, the last
and the most sublime.   A unity that was ulterior, not
artificial, otherwise it would have crumbled into dust

like all the other systematisations of mediocre writers who with the elaborate assistance of titles and sub-titles give themselves the appearance of having pursued a single and transcendent design. Not fictitious, perhaps indeed all the more real for being ulterior, for being born of a moment of enthusiasm when it is discovered to exist among fragments which need only to be joined together. A unity that has been unaware of itself, therefore vital and not logical, that has not banned variety, chilled execution. It emerges (only applying itself this time to the work as a whole) like a fragment composed separately, born of an inspiration, not required by the artificial development of a theme, which comes in to form an integral part of the rest. Before the great orchestral movement that precedes the return of Yseult, it is the work itself that has attracted to it the half-forgotten air of a shepherd's pipe. And, no doubt, just as the swelling of the orchestra at the approach of the ship, when it takes hold of these notes on the pipe, transforms them, infects them with its own intoxication, breaks their rhythm, clarifies their tone, accelerates their movement, multiplies their instrumentation, so no doubt Wagner himself was filled with joy when he discovered in his memory a shepherd's air, incorporated it in his work, gave it its full wealth of meaning. This joy moreover never forsakes him. In him, however great the melancholy of the poet, it is consoled, surpassed—that is to say destroyed, alas, too soon—by the delight of the craftsman. But then, no less than by the similarity I had remarked just now between Vinteuil's phrase and Wagner's, I was troubled by the thought of this Vulcan-like craftsmanship. Could it be this that gave to great artists the illusory appearance of a fundamental originality, incommensurable with any other, the reflexion of a more than human reality, actually the result of industrious toil? If art be no more than that, it is not more real than life and I had less cause for regret. I went on playing *Tristan*. Separated from Wagner by the wall of sound, I could hear him exult, invite me to share his joy, I could hear ring out all the louder the immortally youthful laugh and the hammer-blows of Siegfried, in which, moreover, more marvellously struck were those phrases, the technical skill of the craftsman serving merely to make it easier for them to leave the earth, birds akin not to Lohengrin's swan but to that aeroplane which I had seen at Balbec convert its energy into vertical motion, float over the sea and lose itself in the sky. Perhaps, as the birds that soar highest and fly most swiftly have a stronger wing, one required one of these frankly material vehicles to explore the infinite, one of these 120 horse power machines, mark Mystery, in which nevertheless, however high one flies, one is prevented to some extent from enjoying the silence of space by the overpowering roar of the engine!

For some reason or other the course of my musings, which hitherto had wandered among musical memories, turned now to those men who have been the best performers of music in our day, among whom, slightly exaggerating his merit, I included Morel. At once my thoughts took a sharp turn, and it was Morel's character, certain eccentricities of his nature that I began to consider. As it happened—and this might be connected though it should not be confused with the neurasthenia to which he was a prey—Morel was in the habit of talking about his life, but always presented so shadowy a

picture of it that it was difficult to make anything out.
For instance, he placed himself entirely at M. de Charlus's
disposal on the understanding that he must keep his
evenings free, as he wished to be able after dinner to
attend a course of lectures on algebra. M. de Charlus
conceded this, but insisted upon seeing him after the
lectures. "Impossible, it's an old Italian painting" (this
witticism means nothing when written down like this;
but M. de Charlus having made Morel read *l'Éducation
sentimentale,* in the penultimate chapter of which Fré-
déric Moreau uses this expression, it was Morel's idea of
a joke never to say the word "impossible" without following it up with "it's an old Italian painting") "the
lectures go on very late, and I've already given a lot of
trouble to the lecturer, who naturally would be annoyed
if I came away in the middle." "But there's no need to
attend lectures, algebra is not a thing like swimming, or
even English, you can learn it equally well from a book,"
replied M. de Charlus, who had guessed from the first
that these algebra lectures were one of those images of
which it was impossible to make out anything. It was
perhaps some affair with a woman, or, if Morel was seeking to earn money in shady ways and had attached himself to the secret police, a nocturnal expedition with
detectives, or possibly, what was even worse, an engagement as one of the young men whose services may be
required in a brothel. "A great deal easier, from a
book," Morel assured M. de Charlus, "for it's impossible
to make head or tail of the lectures." "Then why don't
you study it in my house, where you would be far more
comfortable?" M. de Charlus might have answered, but
took care not to do so, knowing that at once, preserving

only the same essential element that the evening hours must be set apart, the imaginary algebra course would change to a compulsory lesson in dancing or in drawing. In which M. de Charlus might have seen that he was mistaken, partially at least, for Morel did often spend his time at the Baron's in solving equations. M. de Charlus did raise the objection that algebra could be of little use to a violinist. Morel replied that it was a distraction which helped him to pass the time and to conquer his neurasthenia. No doubt M. de Charlus might have made inquiries, have tried to find out what actually were these mysterious and ineluctable lectures on algebra that were delivered only at night. But M. de Charlus was not qualified to unravel the tangled skein of Morel's occupations, being himself too much caught in the toils of social life. The visits he received or paid, the time he spent at his club, dinner-parties, evenings at the theatre prevented him from thinking about the problem, or for that matter about the violent and vindictive animosity which Morel had (it was reported) indulged and at the same time sought to conceal in the various environments, the different towns in which his life had been spent, and where people still spoke of him with a shudder, with bated breath, never venturing to say anything definite about him.

It was unfortunately one of the outbursts of this neurotic irritability that I was privileged to hear that day when, rising from the piano, I went down to the courtyard to meet Albertine, who still did not appear. As I passed by Jupien's shop, in which Morel and the girl who, I supposed, was shortly to become his wife were by themselves, Morel was screaming at the top of his

voice, thereby revealing an accent that I had never heard
in his speech, a rustic tone, suppressed as a rule, and
very strange indeed. His words were no less strange,
faulty from the point of view of the French language,
but his knowledge of everything was imperfect. "Will
you get out of here, *grand pied de grue, grand pied de
grue, grand pied de grue*," he repeated to the poor girl
who at first had certainly not understood what he meant,
and now, trembling and indignant, stood motionless before him. "Didn't I tell you to get out of here, *grand
pied de grue, grand pied de grue;* go and fetch your
uncle till I tell him what you are, you whore." Just at
that moment the voice of Jupien who was coming home
talking to one of his friends was heard in the courtyard,
and as I knew that Morel was an utter coward, I decided
that it was unnecessary to join my forces with those of
Jupien and his friend, who in another moment would have
entered the shop, and I retired upstairs again to escape
Morel, who, for all his having pretended to be so anxious
that Jupien should be fetched (probably in order to
frighten and subjugate the girl, an act of blackmail which
rested probably upon no foundation), made haste to depart as soon as he heard his voice in the courtyard. The
words I have set down here are nothing, they would not
explain why my heart throbbed so as I went upstairs.
These scenes of which we are witnesses in real life find
an incalculable element of strength in what soldiers call,
in speaking of a military offensive, the advantage of
surprise, and however agreeably I might be soothed by
the knowledge that Albertine, instead of remaining at the
Trocadéro, was coming home to me, I still heard ringing
in my ears the accent of those words ten times repeated:

"*Grand pied de grue, grand pied de grue,*" which had so
appalled me.

Gradually my agitation subsided. Albertine was on
her way home. I should hear her ring the bell in a moment. I felt that my life was no longer what it might
have become, and that to have a woman in the house like
this with whom quite naturally, when she returned home,
I should have to go out, to the adornment of whose person the strength and activity of my nature were to be
ever more and more diverted, made me as it were a
bough that has blossomed, but is weighed down by the
abundant fruit into which all its reserves of strength
have passed. In contrast to the anxiety that I had been
feeling only an hour earlier, the calm that I now felt at
the prospect of Albertine's return was more ample than
that which I had felt in the morning before she left the
house. Anticipating the future, of which my mistress's
docility made me practically master, more resistant, as
though it were filled and stabilised by the imminent,
importunate, inevitable, gentle presence, it was the calm
(dispensing us from the obligation to seek our happiness
in ourself) that is born of family feeling and domestic
bliss. Family and domestic: such was again, no less
than the sentiment that had brought me such great peace
while I was waiting for Albertine, that which I felt later
on when I drove out with her. She took off her glove for
a moment, whether to touch my hand, or to dazzle me
by letting me see on her little finger, next to the ring that
Mme. Bontemps had given her, another upon which was
displayed the large and liquid surface of a clear sheet of
ruby: "What! Another ring, Albertine. Your aunt *is*
generous!" "No, I didn't get this from my aunt," she

said with a laugh. "It was I who bought it, now that, thanks to you, I can save up ever so much money. I don't even know whose it was before. A visitor who was short of money left it with the landlord of an hotel where I stayed at Le Mans. He didn't know what to do with it, and would have let it go for much less than it was worth. But it was still far too dear for me. Now that, thanks to you, I'm becoming a smart lady, I wrote to ask him if he still had it. And here it is." "That makes a great many rings, Albertine. Where will you put the one that I am going to give you? Anyhow, it is a beautiful ring, I can't quite make out what that is carved round the ruby, it looks like a man's head grinning. But my eyes aren't strong enough." "They might be as strong as you like, you would be no better off. I can't make it out either." In the past it had often happened, as I read somebody's memoirs, or a novel, in which a man always goes out driving with a woman, takes tea with her, that I longed to be able to do likewise. I had thought sometimes that I was successful, as for instance when I took Saint-Loup's mistress out with me, or went to dinner with her. But in vain might I summon to my assistance the idea that I was at that moment actually impersonating the character that I had envied in the novel, that idea assured me that I ought to find pleasure in Rachel's society, and afforded me none. For, whenever we attempt to imitate something that has really existed, we forget that this something was brought about not by the desire to imitate but by an unconscious force which itself also is real; but this particular impression which I had been unable to derive from all my desire to taste a delicate pleasure in going out with Rachel, behold I was now tasting it without having made the slightest effort to procure it, but for quite different reasons, sincere, profound; to take a single instance, for the reason that my jealousy prevented me from letting Albertine go out of my sight, and, the moment that I was able to leave the house, from letting her go anywhere without me. I tasted it only now, because our knowledge is not of the external objects which we try to observe, but of involuntary sensations, because in the past a woman might be sitting in the same carriage as myself, she was not *really* by my side, so long as she was not created afresh there at every moment by a need of her such as I felt of Albertine, so long as the constant caress of my gaze did not incessantly restore to her those tints that need to be perpetually refreshed, so long as my senses, appeased it might be but still endowed with memory, did not place beneath those colours savour and substance, so long as, combined with the senses and with the imagination that exalts them, jealousy was not maintaining the woman in equilibrium by my side by a compensated attraction as powerful as the law of gravity. Our motor-car passed swiftly along the boulevards, the avenues whose lines of houses, a rosy congelation of sunshine and cold, reminded me of calling upon Mme. Swann in the soft light of her chrysanthemums, before it was time to ring for the lamps.

I had barely time to make out, being divided from them by the glass of the motor-car as effectively as I should have been by that of my bedroom window, a young fruit seller, a dairymaid, standing in the doorway of her shop, illuminated by the sunshine like a heroine whom my desire was sufficient to launch upon exquisite adventures, on the threshold of a romance which I might never know. For I could not ask Albertine to let me stop, and already the young women were no longer visible whose features my eyes had barely distinguished, barely caressed their fresh complexions in the golden vapour in which they were bathed. The emotion that I felt grip me when I caught sight of a wine-merchant's girl at her desk or a laundress chatting in the street was the emotion that we feel on recognising a goddess. Now that Olympus no longer exists, its inhabitants dwell upon the earth. And when, in composing a mythological scene, painters have engaged to pose as Venus or Ceres young women of humble birth, who follow the most sordid callings, so far from committing sacrilege, they have merely added, restored to them the quality, the various attributes which they had forfeited. "What did you think of the Trocadéro, you little gadabout?" "I'm jolly glad I came away from it to go out with you. As architecture, it's pretty measly, isn't it? It's by Davioud, I fancy." "But how learned my little Albertine is becoming! Of course it was Davioud who built it, but I couldn't have told you offhand." "While you are asleep, I read your books, you old lazybones." "Listen, child, you are changing so fast and becoming so intelligent" (this was true, but even had it not been true I was not sorry that she should have the satisfaction, failing any other, of saying to herself that at least the time which she spent in my house was not being entirely wasted) "that I don't mind telling you things that would generally be regarded as false and which are all on the way to a truth that I am seeking. You know what is meant by impressionism?" "Of course!" "Very well then, this is what I

mean: you remember the church at Marcouville l'Orgueil-
leuse which Elstir disliked because it was new. Isn't it
rather a denial of his own impressionism when he sub-
tracts such buildings from the general impression in
which they are contained to bring them out of the light
in which they are dissolved and scrutinise like an archaeologist their intrinsic merit? When he begins to paint,
have not a hospital, a school, a poster upon a hoarding
the same value as a priceless cathedral which stands by
their side in a single indivisible image? Remember how
the façade was baked by the sun, how that carved frieze
of saints swam upon the sea of light. What does it matter that a building is new, if it appears to be old, or even
if it does not. All the poetry that the old quarters contain has been squeezed out to the last drop, but if you
look at some of the houses that have been built lately
for rich tradesmen, in the new districts, where the stone
is all freshly cut and still quite white, don't they seem to
rend the torrid air of noon in July, at the hour when the
shopkeepers go home to luncheon in the suburbs, with a
cry as harsh as the odour of the cherries waiting for the
meal to begin in the darkened dining-room, where the
prismatic glass knife-rests project a multicoloured fire
as beautiful as the windows of Chartres?" "How wonderful you are! If I ever do become clever, it will be
entirely owing to you." "Why on a fine day tear your
eyes away from the Trocadéro, whose giraffe-neck towers
remind one of the Charterhouse of Pavia?" "It reminded me also, standing up like that on its hill, of a
Mantegna that you have, I think it's of Saint Sebastian,
where in the background there's a city like an amphi-
theatre, and you would swear you saw the Trocadéro."

"There, you see! But how did you come across my Mantegna? You are amazing!" We had now reached a more plebeian quarter, and the installation of an ancillary Venus behind each counter made it as it were a suburban altar at the foot of which I would gladly have spent the rest of my life.

As one does on the eve of a premature death, I drew up a mental list of the pleasures of which I was deprived by Albertine's setting a full stop to my freedom. At Passy it was in the open street, so crowded were the footways, that a group of girls, their arms encircling one another's waist, left me marvelling at their smile. I had not time to see it clearly, but it is hardly probable that I exaggerated it; in any crowd after all, in any crowd of young people, it is not unusual to come upon the effigy of a noble profile. So that these assembled masses on public holidays are to the voluptuary as precious as is to the archaeologist the congested state of a piece of ground in which digging will bring to light ancient medals. We arrived at the Bois. I reflected that, if Albertine had not come out with me, I might at this moment, in the enclosure of the Champs-Elysées, have been hearing the Wagnerian tempest set all the rigging of the orchestra ascream, draw to itself, like a light spindrift, the tune of the shepherd's pipe which I had just been playing to myself, set it flying, mould it, deform it, divide it, sweep it away in an ever-increasing whirlwind. I was determined, at any rate, that our drive should be short, and that we should return home early, for, without having mentioned it to Albertine, I had decided to go that evening to the Verdurins'. They had recently sent me an invitation which I had flung into the waste paper basket

with all the rest. But I changed my mind for this evening, for I meant to try to find out who the people were
that Albertine might have been hoping to meet there in
the afternoon. To tell the truth, I had reached that
stage in my relations with Albertine when, if everything
remains the same, if things go on normally, a woman
ceases to serve us except as a starting point towards another woman. She still retains a corner in our heart,
but a very small corner; we hasten out every evening
in search of unknown women, especially unknown women
who are known to her and can tell us about her life.
Herself, after all, we have possessed, have exhausted
everything that she has consented to yield to us of herself. Her life is still herself, but that part of herself
which we do not know, the things as to which we have
questioned her in vain and which we shall be able to
gather from fresh lips.

If my life with Albertine was to prevent me from going
to Venice, from travelling, at least I might in the mean
time, had I been alone, have made the acquaintance of
the young midinettes scattered about in the sunlight of
this fine Sunday, in the sum total of whose beauty I
gave a considerable place to the unknown life that animated them. The eyes that we see, are they not shot
through by a gaze as to which we do not know what
images, memories, expectations, disdains it carries, a gaze
from which we cannot separate them? The life that the
person who passes by is living, will it not impart, according to what it is, a different value to the knitting of those
brows, to the dilatation of those nostrils? Albertine's
presence debarred me from going to join them and perhaps also from ceasing to desire them. The man who

would maintain in himself the desire to go on living, and his belief in something more delicious than the things of daily life, must go out driving; for the streets, the avenues are full of goddesses. But the goddesses do not allow us to approach them. Here and there, among the trees, at the entrance to some café, a waitress was watching like a nymph on the edge of a sacred grove, while beyond her three girls were seated by the sweeping arc of their bicycles that were stacked beside them, like three immortals leaning against the clouds or the fabulous coursers upon which they perform their mythological journeys. I remarked that, whenever Albertine looked for a moment at these girls, with a profound attention, she at once turned to gaze at myself. But I was not unduly troubled, either by the intensity of this contemplation, or by its brevity for which its intensity compensated; as for the latter, it often happened that Albertine, whether from exhaustion, or because it was an intense person's way of looking at other people, used to gaze thus in a sort of brown study at my father, it might be, or at Françoise; and as for the rapidity with which she turned to look at myself, it might be due to the fact that Albertine, knowing my suspicions, might prefer, even if they were not justified, to avoid giving them any foothold. This attention, moreover, which would have seemed to me criminal on Albertine's part (and quite as much so if it had been directed at young men), I fastened, without thinking myself reprehensible for an instant, almost deciding indeed that Albertine was reprehensible for preventing me, by her presence, from stopping the car and going to join them, upon all the midinettes. We consider it innocent to desire a thing and atrocious that the other person should desire it. And this contrast between what concerns ourself on the one hand, and on the other the person with whom we are in love, is not confined only to desire, but extends also to falsehood. What is more usual than a lie, whether it is a question of masking the daily weakness of a constitution which we wish to be thought strong, of concealing a vice, or of going off, without offending the other person, to the thing that we prefer? It is the most necessary instrument of conversation, and the one that is most widely used. But it is this which we actually propose to banish from the life of her whom we love; we watch for it, scent it, detest it everywhere. It appals us, it is sufficient to bring about a rupture, it seems to us to be concealing the most serious faults, except when it does so effectively conceal them that we do not suspect their existence. A strange state this in which we are so inordinately sensitive to a pathogenic agent which its universal swarming makes inoffensive to other people and so serious to the wretch who finds that he is no longer immune to it.

The life of these pretty girls (because of my long periods of seclusion, I so rarely met any) appeared to me as to everyone in whom facility of realisation has not destroyed the faculty of imagination, a thing as different from anything that I knew, as desirable as the most marvellous cities that travel holds in store for us.

The disappointment that I had felt with the women whom I had known, in the cities which I had visited, did not prevent me from letting myself be caught by the attraction of others or from believing in their reality; thus, just as seeing Venice—that Venice for which the spring weather too filled me with longing, and which

marriage with Albertine would prevent me from knowing
—seeing Venice in a panorama which Ski would perhaps
have declared to be more beautiful in tone than the place
itself, would to me have been no substitute for the journey
to Venice the length of which, determined without any
reference to myself, seemed to me an indispensable preliminary; similarly, however pretty she might be, the
midinette whom a procuress had artificially provided for
me could not possibly be a substitute for her who with
her awkward figure was strolling at this moment under
the trees, laughing with a friend. The girl that I might
find in a house of assignation, were she even better-
looking than this one, could not be the same thing, because we do not look at the eyes of a girl whom we do
not know as we should look at a pair of little discs of
opal or agate. We know that the little ray which colours
them or the diamond dust that makes them sparkle is
all that we can see of a mind, a will, a memory in which
is contained the home life that we do not know, the intimate friends whom we envy. The enterprise of taking
possession of all this, which is so difficult, so stubborn,
is what gives its value to the gaze far more than its merely
physical beauty (which may serve to explain why the
same young man can awaken a whole romance in the
imagination of a woman who has heard somebody say
that he is the Prince of Wales, whereas she pays no more
attention to him after learning that she is mistaken);
to find the midinette in the house of assignation is to
find her emptied of that unknown life which permeates
her and which we aspire to possess with her, it is to approach a pair of eyes that have indeed become mere
precious stones, a nose whose quivering is as devoid of

meaning as that of a flower. No, that unknown midinette who was passing at that moment, it seemed to me as indispensable, if I wished to continue to believe in her reality, to test her resistance by adapting my behaviour to it, challenging a rebuff, returning to the charge, obtaining an assignation, waiting for her as she came away from her work, getting to know, episode by episode, all that composed the girl's life, traversing the space that, for her, enveloped the pleasure which I was seeking, and the distance which her different habits, her special mode of life, set between me and the attention, the favour which I wished to attain and capture, as making a long journey in the train if I wished to believe in the reality of Venice which I should see and which would not be merely a panoramic show in a World Exhibition. But this very parallel between desire and travel made me vow to myself that one day I would grasp a little more closely the nature of this force, invisible but as powerful as any faith, or as, in the world of physics, atmospheric pressure, which exalted to such a height cities and women so long as I did not know them, and slipped away from beneath them as soon as I had approached them, made them at once collapse and fall flat upon the dead level of the most commonplace reality.

Farther along another girl was kneeling beside her bicycle, which she was putting to rights. The repair finished, the young racer mounted her machine, but without straddling it as a man would have done. For a moment the bicycle swerved, and the young body seemed to have added to itself a sail, a huge wing; and presently we saw dart away at full speed the young creature half-human, half-winged, angel or peri, pursuing her course.

This was what a life with Albertine prevented me from enjoying. Prevented me, did I say? Should I not have thought rather: what it provided for my enjoyment. If Albertine had not been living with me, had been free, I should have imagined, and with reason, every woman to be a possible, a probable object of her desire, of her pleasure. They would have appeared to me like those dancers who, in a diabolical ballet, representing the Temptations to one person, plunge their darts in the heart of another. Midinettes, schoolgirls, actresses, how I should have hated them all! Objects of horror, I should have excepted them from the beauty of the universe. My bondage to Albertine, by permitting me not to suffer any longer on their account, restored them to the beauty of the world. Inoffensive, having lost the needle that stabs the heart with jealousy, I was able to admire them, to caress them with my eyes, another day more intimately perhaps. By secluding Albertine, I had at the same time restored to the universe all those rainbow wings which sweep past us in public gardens, ballrooms, theatres, and which became tempting once more to me because she could no longer succumb to their temptation. They composed the beauty of the world. They had at one time composed that of Albertine. It was because I had beheld her as a mysterious bird, then as a great actress of the beach, desired, perhaps won, that I had thought her wonderful. As soon as she was a captive in my house, the bird that I had seen one afternoon advancing with measured step along the front, surrounded by the congregation of the other girls like seagulls alighted from who knows whence, Albertine had lost all her colours, with all the chances that other people had of securing her for themselves. Gradually she had lost her beauty. It required excursions like this, in which I imagined her, but for my presence, accosted by some woman, or by some young man, to make me see her again amid the splendour of the beach, albeit my jealousy was on a different plane from the decline of the pleasures of my imagination. But notwithstanding these abrupt reversions in which, desired by other people, she once more became beautiful in my eyes, I might very well divide her visit to me in two periods, an earlier in which she was still, although less so every day, the glittering actress of the beach, and a later period in which, become the grey captive, reduced to her dreary self, I required those flashes in which I remembered the past to make me see her again in colour.

Sometimes, in the hours in which I felt most indifferent towards her, there came back to me the memory of a far off moment when upon the beach, before I had made her acquaintance, a lady being near her with whom I was on bad terms and with whom I was almost certain now that she had had relations, she burst out laughing, staring me in the face in an insolent fashion. All round her hissed the blue and polished sea. In the sunshine of the beach, Albertine, in the midst of her friends, was the most beautiful of them all. She was a splendid girl, who in her familiar setting of boundless waters, had—precious in the eyes of the lady who admired her—inflicted upon me this unpardonable insult. It was unpardonable, for the lady would perhaps return to Balbec, would notice perhaps, on the luminous and echoing beach, that Albertine was absent. But she would not know that the girl was living with me, was wholly mine. The vast expanse of blue water, her forgetfulness of the fondness that she had felt for this particular girl and would divert to others, had closed over the outrage that Albertine had done me, enshrining it in a glittering and unbreakable casket. Then hatred of that woman gnawed my heart; of Albertine also, but a hatred mingled with admiration of the beautiful, courted girl, with her marvellous hair, whose laughter upon the beach had been an insult. Shame, jealousy, the memory of my earliest desires and of the brilliant setting had restored to Albertine the beauty, the intrinsic merit of other days. And thus there alternated with the somewhat oppressive boredom that I felt in her company a throbbing desire, full of splendid storms and of regrets; according to whether she was by my side in my bedroom or I set her at liberty in my memory upon the front, in her gay seaside frocks, to the sound of the musical instruments of the sea,—Albertine, now extracted from that environment, possessed and of no great value, now plunged back into it, escaping from me into a past which I should never be able to know, hurting me, in her friend's presence, as much as the splash of the wave or the heat of the sun,—Albertine restored to the beach or brought back again to my room, in a sort of amphibious love.

Farther on, a numerous band were playing ball. All these girls had come out to make the most of the sunshine, for these days in February, even when they are brilliant, do not last long and the splendour of their light does not postpone the hour of its decline. Before that hour drew near, we passed some time in twilight, because after we had driven as far as the Seine, where Albertine admired, and by her presence prevented me from admiring the reflexions of red sails upon the wintry blue of the water, a solitary house in the distance like a single red poppy against the clear horizon, of which Saint-Cloud seemed, farther off again, to be the fragmentary, crumbling, rugged petrifaction, we left our motor-car and walked a long way together; indeed for some moments I gave her my arm, and it seemed to me that the ring which her arm formed round it united our two persons in a single self and linked our separate destinies together.

At our feet, our parallel shadows, where they approached and joined, traced an exquisite pattern. No doubt it already seemed to me a marvellous thing at home that Albertine should be living with me, that it should be she that came and lay down on my bed. But it was so to speak the transportation of that marvel out of doors, into the heart of nature, that by the shore of that lake in the Bois, of which I was so fond, beneath the trees, it should be her and none but her shadow, the pure and simplified shadow of her leg, of her bust, that the sun had to depict in monochrome by the side of mine upon the gravel of the path. And I found a charm that was more immaterial doubtless, but no less intimate, than in the drawing together, the fusion of our bodies, in that of our shadows. Then we returned to our car. And it chose, for our homeward journey, a succession of little winding lanes along which the wintry trees, clothed, like ruins, in ivy and brambles, seemed to be pointing the way to the dwelling of some magician. No sooner had we emerged from their dusky cover than we found, upon leaving the Bois, the daylight still so bright that I imagined that I should still have time to do everything that I wanted to do before dinner, when, only a few minutes later, at the moment when our car approached the Arc de Triomphe, it was with a sudden start of surprise and dismay that I perceived, over Paris, the moon prematurely full, like the face of a clock that has stopped and makes us think that we are late for an engagement. We had told the driver to take us home. To Albertine, this meant also coming to my home. The company of those women, however dear to us, who are obliged to leave us and return home, does not bestow that peace which I found in the company of Albertine seated in the car by my side, a company that was conveying us not to the void in which lovers have to part but to an even more stable and more sheltered union in my home, which was also hers, the material symbol of my possession of her. To be sure, in order to possess, one must first have desired. We do not possess a line, a surface, a mass unless it is occupied by our love. But Albertine had not been for me during our drive, as Rachel had been in the past, a futile dust of flesh and clothing. The imagination of my eyes, my lips, my hands had at Balbec so solidly built, so tenderly polished her body that now in this car, to touch that body, to contain it, I had no need to press my own body against Albertine, nor even to see her; it was enough to hear her, and if she was silent to know that she was by my side; my interwoven senses enveloped her altogether and when, as we arrived at the front door, she quite naturally alighted, I stopped for a moment to tell the chauffeur to call for me later on, but my gaze enveloped her still while she passed ahead of me under the arch, and it was still the same inert, domestic calm that I felt as I saw her thus, solid, flushed, opulent and captive, returning home quite naturally with myself, as a woman who was my own property, and, protected by its walls, disappearing into our house. Unfortunately, she seemed to feel herself a prisoner there, and to share the opinion of that Mme. de La Rochefoucauld who, when somebody asked her whether she was not glad to live in so beautiful a home as Liancourt, replied: "There is no such thing as a beautiful prison"; if I was to judge by her miserable, weary expression that evening as we dined together in my room. I did not notice it at first; and it was I that was made wretched by the thought that, if it had not been for Albertine (for with her I should have suffered too acutely from jealousy in an hotel where all day long she would have been exposed to contact with a crowd of strangers), I might at that moment be dining in Venice in one of those little restaurants, barrel-vaulted like the hold of a ship, from which one looks out on the Grand Canal through arched windows framed in Moorish mouldings.

I ought to add that Albertine greatly admired in my room a big bronze by Barbedienne which with ample justification Bloch considered extremely ugly. He had perhaps less reason to be surprised at my having kept it. I had never sought, like him, to furnish for artistic effect, to compose my surroundings, I was too lazy, too indifferent to the things that I was in the habit of seeing every day. Since my taste was not involved, I had a right not to harmonise my interior. I might perhaps, even without that, have discarded the bronze. But ugly and expensive things are of great use, for they enjoy, among people who do not understand us, who have not our taste and with whom we cannot fall in love, a prestige that would not be shared by some proud object that does not reveal its beauty. Now the people who do not understand us are precisely the people with regard to whom alone it may be useful to us to employ a prestige which our intellect is enough to assure us among superior people. Albertine might indeed be beginning to shew taste, she still felt a certain respect for the bronze, and this respect was reflected upon myself in a consideration which, coming from Albertine, mattered infinitely more to me than the question of keeping a bronze which was a trifle degrading, since I was in love with Albertine.

But the thought of my bondage ceased of a sudden to weigh upon me and I looked forward to prolonging it still farther, because I seemed to perceive that Albertine was painfully conscious of her own. True that whenever I had asked her whether she was not bored in my house, she had always replied that she did not know where it would be possible to have a happier time. But often these words were contradicted by an air of nervous exhaustion, of longing to escape.

Certainly if she had the tastes with which I had credited her, this inhibition from ever satisfying them must have been as provoking to her as it was calming to myself, calming to such an extent that I should have decided that the hypothesis of my having accused her unjustly was the most probable, had it not been so difficult to fit into this hypothesis the extraordinary pains that Albertine was taking never to be alone, never to be disengaged, never to stop for a moment outside the front door when she came in, to insist upon being accompanied, whenever she went to the telephone, by some one who would be able to repeat to me what she had said, by Françoise or Andrée, always to leave me alone (without appearing to be doing so on purpose) with the latter,

after they had been out together, so that I might obtain
a detailed report of their outing. With this marvellous
docility were contrasted certain quickly repressed starts
of impatience, which made me ask myself whether Albertine was not planning to cast off her chain. Certain
subordinate incidents seemed to corroborate my supposi-
tion. Thus, one day when I had gone out by myself, in
the Passy direction, and had met Gisèle, we began to
talk about one thing and another. Presently, not without pride at being able to do so, I informed her that I
was constantly seeing Albertine. Gisèle asked me where
she could find her, since there was something that she
simply *must* tell her. "Why, what is it?" "Something
to do with some young friends of hers." "What friends?
I may perhaps be able to tell you, though that need not
prevent you from seeing her." "Oh, girls she knew years
ago, I don't remember their names," Gisèle replied
vaguely, and beat a retreat. She left me, supposing herself to have spoken with such prudence that the whole
story must seem to·me perfectly straightforward. But
falsehood is so unexacting, needs so little help to make
itself manifest! If it had been a question of friends of
long ago, whose very names she no longer remembered,
why *must* she speak about them to Albertine? This
"*must*," akin to an expression dear to Mme. Cottard:
"in the nick of time," could be applicable only to something particular, opportune, perhaps urgent, relating to
definite persons. Besides, something about her way of
opening her mouth, as though she were going to yawn,
with a vague expression, as she said to me (almost drawing back her body, as though she began to reverse her
engine at this point in our conversation): "Oh, I don't

know, I don't remember their names," made her face, and
in harmony with it her voice, as clear a picture of falsehood as the wholly different air, tense, excited, of her
previous "*must*" was of truth. I did not question
Gisèle. Of what use would it have been to me? Certainly, she was not lying in the same fashion as Albertine.
And certainly Albertine's lies pained me more. But they
had obviously a point in common: the fact of the lie itself, which in certain cases is self-evident. Not evidence
of the truth that the lie conceals. We know that each
murderer in turn imagines that he has arranged everything so cleverly that he will not be caught, and so it is
with liars, particularly the woman with whom we are in
love. We do not know where she has been, what she
has been doing. But at the very moment when she
speaks, when she speaks of something else beneath which
lies hidden the thing that she does not mention, the lie
is immediately perceived, and our jealousy increased,
since we are conscious of the lie, and cannot succeed in
discovering the truth. With Albertine, the impression
that she was lying was conveyed by many of the peculi-
arities which we have already observed in the course of
this narrative, but especially by this, that, when she was
lying, her story broke down either from inadequacy, omis-
sion, improbability, or on the contrary from a surfeit of
petty details intended to make it seem probable. Probability, notwithstanding the idea that the liar has formed
of it, is by no means the same as truth. Whenever, while listening to something that is true, we
hear something that is only probable, which is perhaps
more so than the truth, which is perhaps too probable,
the ear that is at all sensitive feels that it is not correct,

as with a line that does not scan or a word read aloud in mistake for another. Our ear feels this, and if we are in love our heart takes alarm. Why do we not reflect at the time, when we change the whole course of our life because we do not know whether a woman went along the Rue de Berri or the Rue Washington, why do we not reflect that these few hundred yards of difference, and the woman herself, will be reduced to the hundred millionth part of themselves (that is to say to dimensions far beneath our perception), if we only have the wisdom to remain for a few years without seeing the woman, and that she who has out-Gullivered Gulliver in our eyes will shrink to a Lilliputian whom no microscope—of the heart, at least, for that of the disinterested memory is more powerful and less fragile—can ever again perceive! However it may be, if there was a point in common—the lie itself—between Albertine's lies and Gisèle's, still Gisèle did not lie in the same fashion as Albertine, nor indeed in the same fashion as Andrée, but their respective lies dovetailed so neatly into one another, while presenting a great variety, that the little band had the impenetrable solidity of certain commercial houses, booksellers' for example or printing presses, where the wretched author will never succeed, notwithstanding the diversity of the persons employed in them, in discovering whether he is being swindled or not. The editor of the newspaper or review lies with an attitude of sincerity all the more solemn in that he is frequently obliged to conceal the fact that he himself does exactly the same things and indulges in the same commercial practices that he denounced in other editors or theatrical managers, in other publishers, when he chose as his battle-cry, when he raised against them the standard of Sincerity. The fact of a man's having proclaimed (as leader of a political party, or in any other capacity) that it is wicked to lie, obliges him as a rule to lie more than other people, without on that account abandoning the solemn mask, doffing the august tiara of sincerity. The "sincere" gentleman's partner lies in a different and more ingenuous fashion. He deceives his author as he deceives his wife, with tricks from the vaudeville stage. The secretary of the firm, a blunt and honest man, lies quite simply, like an architect who promises that your house will be ready at a date when it will not have been begun. The head reader, an angelic soul, flutters from one to another of the three, and without knowing what the matter is, gives them, by a brotherly scruple and out of affectionate solidarity, the precious support of a word that is above suspicion. These four persons live in a state of perpetual dissension to which the arrival of the author puts a stop. Over and above their private quarrels, each of them remembers the paramount military duty of rallying to the support of the threatened "corps." Without realising it, I had long been playing the part of this author among the little band. If Gisèle had been thinking, when she used the word "must," of some one of Albertine's friends who was proposing to go abroad with her as soon as my mistress should have found some pretext or other for leaving me, and had meant to warn Albertine that the hour had now come or would shortly strike, she, Gisèle, would have let herself be torn to pieces rather than tell me so; it was quite useless therefore to ply her with questions. Meetings such as this with Gisèle were not alone in accentuating my doubts. For instance, I admired Albertine's sketches. Albertine's

sketches, the touching distractions of the captive, moved
me so that I congratulated her upon them. " No, they're
dreadfully bad, but I've never had a drawing lesson in
my life." "But one evening at Balbec you sent word to
me that you had stayed at home to have a drawing lesson." I reminded her of the day and told her that I had
realised at the time that people did not have drawing
lessons at that hour in the evening. Albertine blushed.
" It is true," she said, " I was not having drawing lessons,
I told you a great many lies at first, that I admit. But I
never lie to you now." I would so much have liked to
know what were the many lies that she had told me at
first, but I knew beforehand that her answers would be
fresh lies. And so I contented myself with kissing her.
I asked her to tell me one only of those lies. She replied:
" Oh, well; for instance when I said that the sea air was
bad for me." I ceased to insist in the face of this un-
willingness to reveal.

To make her chain appear lighter, the best thing was
no doubt to make her believe that I was myself about to
break it. In any case, I could not at that moment confide
this mendacious plan to her, she had been too kind in
returning from the Trocadéro that afternoon; what I
could do, far from distressing her with the threat of a
rupture, was at the most to keep to myself those dreams
of a perpetual life together which my grateful heart kept
forming. As I looked at her, I found it hard to restrain
myself from pouring them out to her, and she may perhaps have noticed this. Unfortunately the expression of
such dreams is not contagious. The case of an affected
old woman like M. de Charlus who, by dint of never
seeing in his imagination anything but a stalwart young

man, thinks that he has himself become a stalwart young
man, all the more so the more affected and ridiculous he
becomes, this case is more general, and it is the tragedy
of an impassioned lover that he does not take into account the fact that while he sees in front of him a beautiful face, his mistress is seeing his face which is not made
any more beautiful, far from it, when it is distorted by
the pleasure that is aroused in it by the sight of beauty.
Nor indeed does love exhaust the whole of this case; we
do not see our own body, which other people see, and we
"follow" our own thought, the object invisible to other
people which is before our eyes. This object the artist
does sometimes enable us to see in his work. Whence
it arises that the admirers of his work are disappointed in
its author, upon whose face that internal beauty is imper-
fectly reflected.

Every person whom we love, indeed to a certain extent
every person is to us like Janus, presenting to us the face
that we like if that person leaves us, the repellent face
if we know him or her to be perpetually at our disposal.
In the case of Albertine, the prospect of her continued
society was painful to me in another fashion which I cannot explain in this narrative. It is terrible to have the
life of another person attached to our own like a bomb
which we hold in our hands, unable to get rid of it without
committing a crime. But let us take as a parallel the
ups and downs, the dangers, the anxieties, the fear of
seeing believed in time to come false and probable things
which one will not be able then to explain, feelings that
one experiences if one lives in the intimate society of a
madman. For instance, I pitied M. de Charlus for living
with Morel (immediately the memory of the scene that

afternoon made me feel the left side of my breast heavier than the other); leaving out of account the relations that may or may not have existed between them, M. de Charlus must have been unaware at the outset that Morel was mad. Morel's beauty, his stupidity, his pride must have deterred the Baron from exploring so deeply, until the days of melancholy when Morel accused M. de Charlus of responsibility for his sorrows, without being able to furnish any explanation, abused him for his want of confidence, by the aid of false but extremely subtle reasoning, threatened him with desperate resolutions, while throughout all this there persisted the most cunning regard for his own most immediate interests. But all this is only a comparison. Albertine was not mad.

I learned that a death had occurred during the day which distressed me greatly, that of Bergotte. It was known that he had been ill for a long time past. Not, of course, with the illness from which he had suffered originally and which was natural. Nature hardly seems capable of giving us any but quite short illnesses. But medicine has annexed to itself the art of prolonging them. Remedies, the respite that they procure, the relapses that a temporary cessation of them provokes, compose a sham illness to which the patient grows so accustomed that he ends by making it permanent, just as children continue to give way to fits of coughing long after they have been cured of the whooping cough. Then remedies begin to have less effect, the doses are increased, they cease to do any good, but they have begun to do harm thanks to that lasting indisposition. Nature would not have offered them so long a tenure. It is a great miracle that medicine can almost equal nature in forcing a man to remain in bed, to continue on pain of death the use of some drug. From that moment the illness artificially grafted has taken root, has become a secondary but a genuine illness, with this difference only that natural illnesses are cured, but never those which medicine creates, for it knows not the secret of their cure.

For years past Bergotte had ceased to go out of doors. Anyhow, he had never cared for society, or had cared for it for a day only, to despise it as he despised everything else and in the same fashion, which was his own, namely to despise a thing not because it was beyond his reach but as soon as he had reached it. He lived so simply that nobody suspected how rich he was, and anyone who had known would still have been mistaken, for he would have thought him a miser, whereas no one was ever more generous. He was generous above all towards women,—girls, one ought rather to say—who were ashamed to receive so much in return for so little. He excused himself in his own eyes because he knew that he could never produce such good work as in an atmosphere of amorous feelings. Love is too strong a word, pleasure that is at all deeply rooted in the flesh is helpful to literary work because it cancels all other pleasures, for instance the pleasures of society, those which are the same for everyone. And even if this love leads to disillusionment, it does at least stir, even by so doing, the surface of the soul which otherwise would be in danger of becoming stagnant. Desire is therefore not without its value to the writer in detaching him first of all from his fellow men and from conforming to their standards, and afterwards in restoring some degree of movement to a spiritual machine which, after a certain age, tends to become paralysed. We do not succeed in being happy but we make observation of the reasons which prevent us from being happy and which would have remained invisible to us but for these loopholes opened by disappointment. Dreams are not to be converted into reality, that we know; we would not form any, perhaps, were it not for desire, and it is useful to us to form them in order to see them fail and to be instructed by their failure. And so Bergotte said to himself: " I am spending more than a multimillionaire would spend upon girls, but the pleasures or disappointments that they give me make me write a book which brings me money." Economically, this argument was absurd, but no doubt he found some charm in thus transmuting gold into caresses and caresses into gold. We saw, at the time of my grandmother's death, how a weary old age loves repose. Now in society, there is nothing but conversation. It may be stupid, but it has the faculty of suppressing women who are nothing more than questions and answers. Removed from society, women become once more what is so reposeful to a weary old man, an object of contemplation. In any case, it was no longer a question of anything of this sort. I have said that Bergotte never went out of doors, and when he got out of bed for an hour in his room, he would be smothered in shawls, plaids, all the things with which a person covers himself before exposing himself to intense cold or getting into a railway train. He would apologise to the few friends whom he allowed to penetrate to his sanctuary, and, pointing to his tartan plaids, his travelling-rugs, would say merrily: "After all, my dear fellow, life, as Anaxagoras has said, is a journey." Thus he went on growing steadily colder, a tiny planet that offered a prophetic image of the greater, when gradually heat will withdraw from the earth, then life itself. Then the resurrection will have come to an end, for if, among future generations, the works of men are to shine, there must first of all be men. If certain kinds of animals hold out longer against the invading chill, when there are no longer any men, and if we suppose Bergotte's fame to have lasted so long, suddenly it will be extinguished for all time. It will not be the last animals that will read him, for it is scarcely probable that, like the Apostles on the Day of Pentecost, they will be able to understand the speech of the various races of mankind without having learned it.

In the months that preceded his death, Bergotte suffered from insomnia, and what was worse, whenever he did fall asleep, from nightmares which, if he awoke, made him reluctant to go to sleep again. He had long been a lover of dreams, even of bad dreams, because thanks to them and to the contradiction they present to the reality which we have before us in our waking state, they give us, at the moment of waking if not before, the profound sensation of having slept. But Bergotte's nightmares were not like that. When he spoke of nightmares, he used in the past to mean unpleasant things that passed through his brain. Latterly, it was as though proceeding from somewhere outside himself that he would see a hand armed with a damp cloth which, passed over his face by an evil woman, kept scrubbing him awake, an intolerable itching in his thighs, the rage—because Bergotte had murmured in his sleep that he was driving badly—of a raving lunatic of a cabman who flung himself upon the writer, biting and gnawing his fingers. Finally, as soon as in his sleep it had grown sufficiently dark, nature arranged a sort of undress rehearsal of the apoplectic stroke that was to carry him off: Bergotte arrived in a carriage beneath the porch of Swann's new house, and tried to alight. A stunning giddiness glued him to his seat, the porter came forward to help him out of the carriage, he remained seated, unable to rise, to straighten his legs. He tried to pull himself up with the help of the stone pillar that was by his side, but did not find sufficient support in it to enable him to stand.

He consulted doctors who, flattered at being called in

by him, saw in his virtue as an incessant worker (it was twenty years since he had written anything), in his over-strain, the cause of his ailments. They advised him not to read thrilling stories (he never read anything), to benefit more by the sunshine, which was "indispensable to life" (he had owed a few years of comparative health only to his rigorous seclusion indoors), to take nourishment (which made him thinner, and nourished nothing but his nightmares). One of his doctors was blessed with the spirit of contradiction, and whenever Bergotte consulted him in the absence of the others, and, in order not to offend him, suggested to him as his own ideas what the others had advised, this doctor, thinking that Bergotte was seeking to have prescribed for him something that he himself liked, at once forbade it, and often for reasons invented so hurriedly to meet the case that in face of the material objections which Bergotte raised, this argumentative doctor was obliged in the same sentence to contradict himself, but, for fresh reasons, repeated the original prohibition. Bergotte returned to one of the first of these doctors, a man who prided himself on his cleverness, especially in the presence of one of the leading men of letters, and who, if Bergotte insinuated: " I seem to remember, though, that Dr. X—— told me—long ago, of course—that that might congest my kidneys and brain . . ." would smile sardonically, raise his finger and enounce: "I said use, I did not say abuse. Naturally every remedy, if one takes it in excess, becomes a two-edged sword." There is in the human body a certain instinct for what is beneficial to us, as there is in the heart for what is our moral duty, an instinct which no authorisation by a Doctor of Medicine or Divinity can replace. We know that cold baths are bad for us, we like them, we can always find a doctor to recommend them, not to prevent them from doing us harm. From each of these doctors Bergotte took something which, in his own wisdom, he had forbidden himself for years past. After a few weeks, his old troubles had reappeared, the new had become worse. Maddened by an unintermittent pain, to which was added insomnia broken only by brief spells of nightmare, Bergotte called in no more doctors and tried with success, but to excess, different narcotics, hopefully reading the prospectus that accompanied each of them, a prospectus which proclaimed the necessity of sleep but hinted that all the preparations which induce it (except that contained in the bottle round which the prospectus was wrapped, which never produced any toxic effect) were toxic, and therefore made the remedy worse than the disease. Bergotte tried them all. Some were of a different family from those to which we are accustomed, preparations for instance of amyl and ethyl. When we absorb a new drug, entirely different in composition, it is always with a delicious expectancy of the unknown. Our heart beats as at a first assignation. To what unknown forms of sleep, of dreams, is the newcomer going to lead us? He is inside us now, he has the control of our thoughts. In what fashion are we going to fall asleep? And, once we are asleep, by what strange paths, up to what peaks, into what unfathomed gulfs is he going to lead us? With what new grouping of sensations are we to become acquainted on this journey? Will it bring us in the end to illness? To blissful happiness? To death? Bergotte's death had come to him overnight, when he had thus entrusted himself to one of these

friends (a friend? or an enemy, rather?) who proved too
strong for him. The circumstances of his death were as
follows. An attack of uraemia, by no means serious,
had led to his being ordered to rest. But one of the
critics having written somewhere that in Vermeer's *Street
in Delft* (lent by the Gallery at The Hague for an exhibition of Dutch painting), a picture which he adored and
imagined that he knew by heart, a little patch of yellow
wall (which he could not remember) was so well painted
that it was, if one looked at it by itself, like some priceless
specimen of Chinese art, of a beauty that was sufficient
in itself, Bergotte ate a few potatoes, left the house, and
went to the exhibition. At the first few steps that he
had to climb he was overcome by giddiness. He passed
in front of several pictures and was struck by the stiffness
and futility of so artificial a school, nothing of which
equalled the fresh air and sunshine of a Venetian palazzo,
or of an ordinary house by the sea. At last he came to
the Vermeer which he remembered as more striking, more
different from anything else that he knew, but in which,
thanks to the critic's article, he remarked for the first
time some small figures in blue, that the ground was pink,
and finally the precious substance of the tiny patch of
yellow wall. His giddiness increased; he fixed his eyes,
like a child upon a yellow butterfly which it is trying to
catch, upon the precious little patch of wall. "That is
how I ought to have written," he said. "My last
books are too dry, I ought to have gone over them with
several coats of paint, made my language exquisite in
itself, like this little patch of yellow wall." Meanwhile
he was not unconscious of the gravity of his condition.
In a celestial balance there appeared to him, upon one

of its scales, his own life, while the other contained the little patch of wall so beautifully painted in yellow. He felt that he had rashly surrendered the former for the latter. "All the same," he said to himself, "I have no wish to provide the 'feature' of this exhibition for the evening papers."

He repeated to himself: "Little patch of yellow wall, with a sloping roof, little patch of yellow wall." While doing so he sank down upon a circular divan; and then at once he ceased to think that his life was in jeopardy and, reverting to his natural optimism, told himself: "It is just an ordinary indigestion from those potatoes; they weren't properly cooked; it is nothing." A fresh attack beat him down; he rolled from the divan to the floor, as visitors and attendants came hurrying to his assistance. He was dead. Permanently dead? Who shall say? Certainly our experiments in spiritualism prove no more than the dogmas of religion that the soul survives death. All that we can say is that everything is arranged in this life as though we entered it carrying the burden of obliga-tions contracted in a former life; there is no reason in-herent in the conditions of life on this earth that can make us consider ourselves obliged to do good, to be fastidious, to be polite even, nor make the talented artist consider himself obliged to begin over again a score of times a piece of work the admiration aroused by which will matter little to his body devoured by worms, like the patch of yellow wall painted with so much knowledge and skill by an artist who must for ever remain unknown and is barely identified under the name Vermeer. All these obligations which have not their sanction in our present life seem to belong to a different world, founded upon kindness, scrupulosity, self-sacrifice, a world entirely different from this, which we leave in order to be born into this world, before perhaps returning to the other to live once again beneath the sway of those unknown laws which we have obeyed because we bore their precepts in our hearts, knowing not whose hand had traced them there—those laws to which every profound work of the intellect brings us nearer and which are invisible only —and still!—to fools. So that the idea that Bergotte was not wholly and permanently dead is by no means improbable.

They buried him, but all through the night of mourning, in the lighted windows, his books arranged three by three kept watch like angels with outspread wings and seemed, for him who was no more, the symbol of his resurrection.

I learned, I have said, that day that Bergotte was dead. And I marvelled at the carelessness of the newspapers which—each of them reproducing the same paragraph— stated that he had died the day before. For, the day before, Albertine had met him, as she informed me that very evening, and indeed she had been a little late in coming home, for she had stopped for some time talking to him. She was doubtless the last person to whom he had spoken. She knew him through myself who had long ceased to see him, but, as she had been anxious to make his acquaintance, I had, a year earlier, written to ask the old master whether I might bring her to see him. He had granted my request, a trifle hurt, I fancy, that I should be visiting him only to give pleasure to another person, which was a proof of my indifference to himself.

These cases are frequent: sometimes the man or woman whom we implore to receive us not for the pleasure of conversing with them again, but on behalf of a third person, refuses so obstinately that our protegée concludes that we have boasted of an influence which we do not possess; more often the man of genius or the famous beauty consents, but, humiliated in their glory, wounded in their affection, feel for us afterwards only a diminished, sorrowful, almost contemptuous attachment. I discovered long after this that I had falsely accused the newspapers of inaccuracy, since on the day in question Albertine had not met Bergotte, but at the time I had never suspected this for a single instant, so naturally had she told me of the incident, and it was not until much later that I discovered her charming skill in lying with simplicity. The things that she said, the things that she confessed were so stamped with the character of formal evidence—what we see, what we learn from an unquestionable source—that she sowed thus in the empty spaces of her life episodes of another life the falsity of which I did not then suspect and began to perceive only at a much later date. I have used the word "confessed," for the following reason. Sometimes a casual meeting gave me a jealous suspicion in which by her side there figured in the past, or alas in the future, another person. In order to appear certain of my facts, I mentioned the person's name, and Albertine said: "Yes, I met her, a week ago, just outside the house. I had to be polite and answer her when she spoke to me. I walked a little way with her. But there never has been anything between us. There never will be." Now Albertine had not even met this person, for the simple reason that the person had not been in Paris for the last ten months. But my mistress felt that a complete denial would sound hardly probable. Whence this imaginary brief encounter, related so simply that I could see the lady stop, bid her good day, walk a little way with her. The evidence of my senses, if I had been in the street at that moment, would perhaps have informed me that the lady had not been with Albertine. But if I had knowledge of the fact, it was by one of those chains of reasoning in which the words of people in whom we have confidence insert strong links, and not by the evidence of my senses. To invoke this evidence of the senses I should have had to be in the street at that particular moment, and I had not been. We may imagine, however, that such an hypothesis is not improbable: I might have gone out, and have been passing along the street at the time at which Albertine was to tell me in the evening (not having seen me there) that she had gone a little way with the lady, and I should then have known that Albertine was lying. But is that quite certain even then? A religious obscurity would have clouded my mind, I should have begun to doubt whether I had seen her by herself, I should barely have sought to understand by what optical illusion I had failed to perceive the lady, and should not have been greatly surprised to find myself mistaken, for the stellar universe is not so difficult of comprehension as the real actions of other people, especially of the people with whom we are in love, strengthened as they are against our doubts by fables devised for their protection. For how many years on end can they not allow our apathetic love to believe that they have in some foreign country a sister, a brother, a sister-in-law who have never existed!

The evidence of the senses is also an operation of the mind in which conviction creates the evidence. We have often seen her sense of hearing convey to Françoise not the word that was uttered but what she thought to be its correct form, which was enough to prevent her from hearing the correction implied in a superior pronunciation. Our butler was cast in a similar mould. M. de Charlus was in the habit of wearing at this time—for he was constantly changing—very light trousers which were recognisable a mile off. Now our butler, who thought that the word *pissotière* (the word denoting what M. de Rambuteau had been so annoyed to hear the Duc de Guermantes call a Rambuteau stall) was really *pistière*, never once in the whole of his life heard a single person say *pissotière*, albeit the word was frequently pronounced thus in his hearing. But error is more obstinate than faith and does not examine the grounds of its belief. Constantly the butler would say: "I'm sure M. le Baron de Charlus must have caught a disease to stand about as long as he does in a *pistière*. That's what comes of running after the girls at his age. You can tell what he is by his trousers. This morning, Madame sent me with a message to Neuilly. As I passed the *pistière* in the Rue de Bourgogne I saw M. le Baron de Charlus go in. When I came back from Neuilly, quite an hour later, I saw his yellow trousers in the same *pistière*, in the same place, in the middle stall where he always goes so that people shan't see him." I can think of no one more beautiful, more noble or more youthful than a certain niece of Mme. de Guermantes. But I have heard the porter of a restaurant where I used sometimes to dine say as she went by: "Just look at that old trollop, what a style! And she must be eighty, if she's a day." As far as age went, I find it difficult to believe that he meant what he said. But the pages clustered round him, who tittered whenever she went past the hotel on her way to visit, at their house in the neighbourhood, her charming great-aunts, Mmes. de Fezensac and de Bellery, saw upon the face of the young beauty the four-score years with which, seriously or in jest, the porter had endowed the "old trollop." You would have made them shriek with laughter had you told them that she was more distinguished than one of the two cashiers of the hotel, who, devoured by eczema, ridiculously stout, seemed to them a fine-looking woman. Perhaps sexual desire alone would have been capable of preventing their error from taking form, if it had been brought to bear upon the passage of the alleged old trollop, and if the pages had suddenly begun to covet the young goddess. But for reasons unknown, which were most probably of a social nature, this desire had not come into play. There is moreover ample room for discussion. The universe is true for us all and dissimilar to each of us. If we were not obliged, to preserve the continuity of our story, to confine ourselves to frivolous reasons, how many more serious reasons would permit us to demonstrate the falsehood and flimsiness of the opening pages of this volume in which, from my bed, I hear the world awake, now to one sort of weather, now to another. Yes, I have been forced to whittle down the facts, and to be a liar, but it is not one universe, there are millions, almost as many as the number of human eyes and brains in existence, that awake every morning.

To return to Albertine, I have never known any woman more amply endowed than herself with the happy aptitude for a lie that is animated, coloured with the selfsame tints of life, unless it be one of her friends—one of my blossoming girls also, rose-pink as Albertine, but one whose irregular profile, concave in one place, then convex again, was exactly like certain clusters of pink flowers the name of which I have forgotten, but which have long and sinuous concavities. This girl was, from the point of view of story-telling, superior to Albertine, for she never introduced any of those painful moments, those furious innuendoes, which were frequent with my mistress. I have said, however, that she was charming when she invented a story which left no room for doubt, for one saw then in front of her the thing—albeit imaginary—which she was saying, using it as an illustration of her speech. Probability alone inspired Albertine, never the desire to make me jealous. For Albertine, without perhaps any material interest, liked people to be polite to her. And if in the course of this work I have had and shall have many occasions to shew how jealousy intensifies love, it is the lover's point of view that I have adopted. But if that lover be only the least bit proud, and though he were to die of a separation, he will not respond to a supposed betrayal with a courteous speech, he will turn away, or without going will order himself to assume a mask of coldness. And so it is entirely to her own disadvantage that his mistress makes him suffer so acutely. If, on the contrary, she dispels with a tactful word, with loving caresses, the suspicions that have been torturing him for all his show of indifference, no doubt the lover does not feel that despairing increase of love to which jealousy drives him, but ceasing in an instant to suffer, happy, affectionate, relieved from strain as one is after a storm when the rain has ceased and one barely hears still splash at long intervals from the tall horse-chestnut trees the clinging drops which already the reappearing sun has dyed with colour, he does not know how to express his gratitude to her who has cured him. Albertine knew that I liked to reward her for her kindnesses, and this perhaps explained why she used to invent, to exculpate herself, confessions as natural as these stories the truth of which I never doubted, one of them being that of her meeting with Bergotte when he was already dead. Previously I had never known any of Albertine's lies save those that, at Balbec for instance, Françoise used to report to me, which I have omitted from these pages albeit they hurt me so sorely: "As she didn't want to come, she said to me: 'Couldn't you say to Monsieur that you didn't find me, that I had gone out?'" But our "inferiors", who love us as Françoise loved me, take pleasure in wounding us in our self-esteem.

CHAPTER II

The Verdurins quarrel with M. de Charlus

AFTER dinner, I told Albertine that, since I was out of bed, I might as well take the opportunity to go and see some of my friends, Mme. de Villeparisis, Mme. de Guermantes, the Cambremers, anyone in short whom I might find at home. I omitted to mention only the people whom I did intend to see, the Verdurins. I asked her if she would not come with me. She pleaded that she had no suitable clothes. "Besides, my hair is so awful. Do you really wish me to go on doing it like this?" And by way of farewell she held out her hand to me in that abrupt fashion, the arm outstretched, the shoulders thrust back, which she used to adopt on the beach at Balbec and had since then entirely abandoned. This forgotten gesture retransformed the body which it animated into that of the Albertine who as yet scarcely knew me. It restored to Albertine, ceremonious beneath an air of rudeness, her first novelty, her strangeness, even her setting. I saw the sea behind this girl whom I had never seen shake hands with me in this fashion since I was at the seaside. "My aunt thinks it makes me older," she added with a sullen air. "Oh that her aunt may be right!" thought I. "That Albertine by looking like a child should make Mme. Bontemps appear younger than she is, is all that her aunt would ask, and also that Albertine shall cost her nothing between now and the day when, by marrying me, she will repay what has been spent on her." But that Albertine should appear less young, less pretty, should turn fewer heads in the street, that is what I, on the contrary, hoped. For the age of a duenna is less reassuring to a jealous lover than the age of the woman's face whom he loves. I regretted only that the style in which I had asked her to do her hair should appear to Albertine an additional bolt on the door of her prison. And it was henceforward this new domestic sentiment that never ceased, even when I was parted from Albertine, to form a bond attaching me to her.

I said to Albertine, who was not dressed, or so she told me, to accompany me to the Guermantes' or the Cambremers', that I could not be certain where I should go, and set off for the Verdurins'. At the moment when the thought of the concert that I was going to hear brought back to my mind the scene that afternoon: "*Grand pied de grue, grand pied de grue*,"—a scene of disappointed love, of jealous love perhaps, but if so as bestial as the scene to which a woman might be subjected by, so to speak, an orang-outang that was, if one may use the expression, in love with her—at the moment when, having reached the street, I was just going to hail a cab, I heard the sound of sobs which a man who was sitting upon a curbstone was endeavouring to stifle. I came nearer; the man, who had buried his face in his hands, appeared to be quite young, and I was surprised to see, from the gleam of white in the opening of his cloak, that he was wearing evening clothes and a white tie. As he heard my step he uncovered a face bathed in tears, but at once, having recognised me, turned away. It was Morel. He guessed that I had recognised him and, checking his tears with an effort, told me that he had stopped to rest for a moment, he was in such pain. "I have grossly insulted, only to-day," he said, "a person for whom I had the very highest regard. It was a cowardly thing to do, for she loves me." "She will forget perhaps, as time goes on," I replied, without realising that by speaking thus I made it apparent that I had overheard the scene that afternoon. But he was so much absorbed in his own grief that it never even occurred to him that I might know something about the affair. "She may forget, perhaps," he said. "But I myself can never forget. I am too conscious of my degradation, I am disgusted with myself! However, what I have said I have said, and nothing can unsay it. When people make me lose my temper, I don't know what I am doing. And it is so bad for me, my nerves are all on edge," for, like all neurasthenics, he was keenly interested in his own health. If, during the afternoon, I had witnessed the amorous rage of an infuriated animal, this evening, within a few hours, centuries had elapsed and a fresh sentiment, a sentiment of shame, regret, grief, shewed that a great stage had been passed in the evolution of the beast destined to be transformed into a human being. Nevertheless, I still heard ringing in my ears his "*grand pied de grue*" and dreaded an imminent return to the savage state. I had only a very vague impression, however, of what had been happening, and this was but natural, for M. de Charlus himself was totally unaware that for some days past, and especially that day, even before the shameful episode which was not a direct consequence of the violinist's condition, Morel had been suffering from a recurrence of his neurasthenia. As a matter of fact, he had, in the previous month, proceeded as rapidly as he had been able, a great deal less rapidly than he would have liked, towards the seduction of Jupien's niece with whom he was at liberty, now that they were engaged, to go out whenever he chose. But whenever he had gone a trifle far in his attempts at violation, and especially when he suggested to his betrothed that she might make friends with other girls whom she would then procure for himself, he had met with a resistance that made him furious. All at once (whether she would have proved too chaste, or on the contrary would have surrendered herself) his desire had subsided. He had decided to break with her, but feeling that the Baron, vicious as he might be, was far more moral than himself, he was afraid lest, in the event of a rupture, M. de Charlus might turn him out of the house. And so he had decided, a fortnight ago, that he would not see the girl again, would leave M. de Charlus and Jupien to clean up the mess (he employed a more realistic term) by themselves, and, before announcing the rupture, to "b—— off" to an unknown destination.

For all that his conduct towards Jupien's niece coincided exactly, in its minutest details, with the plan of conduct which he had outlined to the Baron as they were dining together at Saint-Mars-le-Vêtu, it is probable that his intention was entirely different, and that sentiments of a less atrocious nature, which he had not foreseen in his theory of conduct, had improved, had tinged it with sentiment in practice. The sole point in which, on the contrary, the practice was worse than the theory is this, that in theory it had not appeared to him possible that he could remain in Paris after such an act of betrayal.

Now, on the contrary, actually to "b—— off" for so small a matter seemed to him quite unnecessary. It meant leaving the Baron who would probably be furious, and forfeiting his own position. He would lose all the money that the Baron was now giving him. The thought that this was inevitable made his nerves give away altogether, he cried for hours on end, and in order not to think about it any more dosed himself cautiously with morphine. Then suddenly he hit upon an idea which no doubt had gradually been taking shape in his mind and gaining strength there for some time, and this was that a rupture with the girl would not inevitably mean a complete break with M. de Charlus. To lose all the Baron's money was a serious thing in itself. Morel in his uncertainty remained for some days a prey to dark thoughts, such as came to him at the sight of Bloch. Then he decided that Jupien and his niece had been trying to set a trap for him, that they might consider themselves lucky to be rid of him so cheaply. He found in short that the girl had been in the wrong in being so clumsy, in not having managed to keep him attached to her by a sensual attraction. Not only did the sacrifice of his position with M. de Charlus seem to him absurd, he even regretted the expensive dinners he had given the girl since they became engaged, the exact cost of which he knew by heart, being a true son of the valet who used to bring his "book" every month for my uncle's inspection. For the word book, in the singular, which means a printed volume to humanity in general, loses that meaning among Royal Princes and servants. To the latter it means their housekeeping book, to the former the register in which we inscribe our names. (At Balbec one day when the Princesse de Luxembourg told me that she had not brought a book with her, I was about to offer her *Le Pêcheur d'Islande* and *Tartarin de Tarascon,* when I realised that she had meant not that she would pass the time less agreeably, but that I should find it more difficult to pay a call upon her.)

Notwithstanding the change in Morel's point of view with regard to the consequences of his behaviour, albeit that behaviour would have seemed to him abominable two months earlier, when he was passionately in love with Jupien's niece, whereas during the last fortnight he had never ceased to assure himself that the same behaviour was natural, praiseworthy, it continued to intensify the state of nervous unrest in which, finally, he had announced the rupture that afternoon. And he was quite prepared to vent his anger, if not (save in a momentary outburst) upon the girl, for whom he still felt that lingering fear, the last trace of love, at any rate upon the Baron. He took care, however, not to say anything to him before dinner, for, valuing his own professional skill above everything, whenever he had any difficult music to play (as this evening at the Verdurins') he avoided (as far as possible, and the scene that afternoon was already more than ample) anything that might impair the flexibility of his wrists. Similarly a surgeon who is an enthusiastic motorist, does not drive when he has an operation to perform. This accounts to me for the fact that, while he was speaking to me, he kept bending his fingers gently one after another to see whether they had regained their suppleness. A slight frown seemed to indicate that there was still a trace of nervous stiffness. But, so as not to increase it, he relaxed his features, as we forbid ourself to grow irritated at not being able to sleep or to prevail upon a woman, for fear lest our rage itself may retard the moment of sleep or of satisfaction. And so, anxious to regain his serenity so that he might, as was his habit, absorb himself entirely in what he was going to play at the Verdurins', and anxious, so long as I was watching him, to let me see how unhappy he was, he decided that the simplest course was to beg me to leave him immediately. His request was superfluous, and it was a relief to me to get away from him. I had trembled lest, as we were due at the same house, within a few minutes, he might ask me to take him with me, my memory of the scene that afternoon being too vivid not to give me a certain distaste for the idea of having Morel by my side during the drive. It is quite possible that the love, and afterwards the indifference or hatred felt by Morel for Jupien's niece had been sincere. Unfortunately, it was not the first time that he had behaved thus, that he had suddenly "dropped" a girl to whom he had sworn undying love, going so far as to produce a loaded revolver, telling her that he would blow out his brains if ever he was mean enough to desert her. He did nevertheless desert her in time, and felt instead of remorse, a sort of rancour against her. It was not the first time that he had behaved thus, it was not to be the last, with the result that the heads of many girls—girls less forgetful of him than he was of them—suffered—as Jupien's niece's head continued long afterwards to suffer, still in love with Morel although she despised him—suffered, ready to burst with the shooting of an internal pain because in each of them—like a fragment of a Greek carving—an aspect of Morel's face, hard as marble and beautiful as an antique sculpture, was embedded in her brain, with his blossoming hair, his fine eyes, his straight nose, forming a protuberance in a cranium not shaped to receive it, upon which no operation was possible. But in the fulness of time these stony fragments end by slipping into a place where they cause no undue discomfort, from which they never stir again; we are no longer conscious of their presence: I mean forgetfulness, or an indifferent memory.

Meanwhile I had gained two things in the course of the day. On the one hand, thanks to the calm that was produced in me by Albertine's docility, I found it possible, and therefore made up my mind, to break with her. There was on the other hand, the fruit of my reflexions during the interval that I had spent waiting for her, at the piano, the idea that Art, to which I would try to devote my reconquered liberty, was not a thing that justified one in making a sacrifice, a thing above and beyond life, that did not share in its fatuity and futility; the appearance of real individuality obtained in works of art being due merely to the illusion created by the artist's technical skill. If my afternoon had left behind it other deposits, possibly more profound, they were not to come to my knowledge until much later. As for the two which I was able thus to weigh, they were not to be permanent; for, from this very evening my ideas about art were to rise above the depression to which they had been subjected in the afternoon, while on the other hand my calm, and consequently the freedom that would enable me to devote myself to it, was once again to be withdrawn from me.

As my cab, following the line of the embankment, was coming near the Verdurins' house, I made the driver pull up. I had just seen Brichot alighting from the tram at the foot of the Rue Bonaparte, after which he dusted his shoes with an old newspaper and put on a pair of pearl grey gloves. I went up to him on foot. For some time past, his sight having grown steadily weaker, he had been endowed—as richly as an observatory—with new spectacles of a powerful and complicated kind, which, like astronomical instruments, seemed to be screwed into his eyes; he focussed their exaggerated blaze upon myself and recognised me. They—the spectacles—were in marvellous condition. But behind them I could see, minute, pallid, convulsive, expiring, a remote gaze placed under this powerful apparatus, as, in a laboratory equipped out of all proportion to the work that is done in it, you may watch the last throes of some insignificant animalcule through the latest and most perfect type of microscope. I offered him my arm to guide him on his way. " This time it is not by great Cherbourg that we meet," he said to me, " but by little Dunkerque," a remark which I found extremely tiresome, as I failed to understand what he meant; and yet I dared not ask Brichot, dreading not so much his scorn as his explanations. I replied that I was longing to see the room in which Swann used to meet Odette every evening. " What, so you know that old story, do you? " he said. " And yet from those days to the death of Swann is what the poet rightly calls: *' Grande spatium mortalis aevi.'* "

The death of Swann had been a crushing blow to me at the time. The death of Swann! Swann, in this phrase, is something more than a noun in the possessive case. I mean by it his own particular death, the death allotted by destiny to the service of Swann. For we talk of " death " for convenience, but there are almost as many different deaths as there are people. We are not equipped with a sense that would enable us to see, moving at every speed in every direction, these deaths, the active deaths aimed by destiny at this person or that. Often there are deaths that will not be entirely relieved of their duties until two or even three years later. They come in haste to plant a tumour in the side of a Swann, then depart to attend to their other duties, returning only when, the surgeons having performed their operation, it is necessary to plant the tumour there afresh. Then comes the moment when we read in the *Gaulois* that Swann's health has been causing anxiety but that he is now making an excellent recovery. Then, a few minutes before the breath leaves our body, death, like a sister of charity who has come to nurse, rather than to destroy us, enters to preside over our last moments, crowns with a supreme halo the cold and stiffening creature whose heart has ceased to beat. And it is this diversity among deaths, the mystery of their circuits, the colour of their fatal badge, that makes so impressive a paragraph in the newspapers such as this:

"We regret to learn that M. Charles Swann passed away yesterday at his residence in Paris, after a long and painful illness. A Parisian whose intellectual gifts were widely appreciated, a discriminating but steadfastly loyal friend, he will be universally regretted, in those literary and artistic circles where the soundness and refinement of his taste made him a willing and a welcome guest, as well as at the Jockey Club of which he was one of the oldest and most respected members. He belonged also to the Union and Agricole. He had recently resigned his

membership of the Rue Royale. His personal appearance and eminently distinguished bearing never failed to
arouse public interest at all the great events of the musical and artistic seasons, especially at private views, at
which he was a regular attendant until, during the last
years of his life, he became almost entirely confined to
the house. The funeral will take place, etc."

From this point of view, if one is not " somebody," the
absence of a well known title makes the process of decomposition even more rapid. No doubt it is more or less
anonymously, without any personal identity, that a man
still remains Duc d'Uzès. But the ducal coronet does for
some time hold the elements together, as their moulds
keep together those artistically designed ices which Albertine admired, whereas the names of ultra-fashionable
commoners, as soon as they are dead, dissolve and lose
their shape. We have seen M. de Bréauté speak of
Cartier as the most intimate friend of the Duc de
La Trémoïlle, as a man greatly in demand in aristocratic
circles. To a later generation, Cartier has become
something so formless that it would almost be adding to
his importance to make him out as related to the jeweller
Cartier, with whom he would have smiled to think that
anybody could be so ignorant as to confuse him! Swann
on the contrary was a remarkable personality, in both the
intellectual and the artistic worlds; and even although he
had " produced " nothing, still he had a chance of surviving a little longer. And yet, my dear Charles ———,
whom I used to know when I was still so young and you
were nearing your grave, it is because he whom you must
have regarded as a little fool has made you the hero of
one of his volumes that people are beginning to speak of

you again and that your name will perhaps live. If in Tissot's picture representing the balcony of the Rue Royale club, where you figure with Galliffet, Edmond Polignac and Saint-Maurice, people are always drawing attention to yourself, it is because they know that there are some traces of you in the character of Swann.

To return to more general realities, it was of this foretold and yet unforeseen death of Swann that I had heard him speak himself to the Duchesse de Guermantes, on the evening of her cousin's party. It was the same death whose striking and specific strangeness had recurred to me one evening when, as I ran my eye over the newspaper, my attention was suddenly arrested by the announcement of it, as though traced in mysterious lines interpolated there out of place. They had sufficed to make of a living man some one who can never again respond to what you say to him, to reduce him to a mere name, a written name, that has passed in a moment from the real world to the realm of silence. It was they that even now made me anxious to make myself familiar with the house in which the Verdurins had lived, and where Swann, who at that time was not merely a row of five letters printed in a newspaper, had dined so often with Odette. I must add also (and this is what for a long time made Swann's death more painful than any other, albeit these reasons bore no relation to the individual strangeness of his death) that I had never gone to see Gilberte, as I promised him at the Princesse de Guermantes's, that he had never told me what the "other reason" was, to which he alluded that evening, for his selecting me as the recipient of his conversation with the Prince, that a thousand questions occurred to me (as bubbles rise from the bottom of a pond) which I longed to ask him about the most different subjects: Vermeer, M. de Mouchy, Swann himself, a Boucher tapestry, Combray, questions that doubtless were not very vital since I had put off asking them from day to day, but which seemed to me of capital importance now that, his lips being sealed, no answer would ever come.

"No," Brichot went on, "it was not here that Swann met his future wife, or rather it was here only in the very latest period, after the disaster that partially destroyed Mme. Verdurin's former home."

Unfortunately, in my fear of displaying before the eyes of Brichot an extravagance which seemed to me out of place, since the professor had no share in its enjoyment, I had alighted too hastily from the carriage and the driver had not understood the words I had flung at him over my shoulder in order that I might be well clear of the carriage before Brichot caught sight of me. The consequence was that the driver followed us and asked me whether he was to call for me later; I answered hurriedly in the affirmative, and was regarded with a vastly increased respect by the professor who had come by omnibus.

"Ah! So you were in a carriage," he said in solemn tones. "Only by the purest accident. I never take one as a rule. I always travel by omnibus or on foot. However, it may perhaps entitle me to the great honour of taking you home to-night if you will oblige me by consenting to enter that rattle-trap; we shall be packed rather tight. But you are always so considerate to me." Alas, in making him this offer, I am depriving myself of nothing (I reflected) since in any case I shall be obliged to go home for Albertine's sake. Her presence in my house, at an hour when nobody could possibly call to see her, allowed me to dispose as freely of my time as I had that afternoon, when, seated at the piano, I knew that she was on her way back from the Trocadéro and that I was in no hurry to see her again. But furthermore, as also in the afternoon, I felt that I had a woman in the house and that on returning home I should not taste the fortifying thrill of solitude. "I accept with great good will," replied Brichot. "At the period to which you allude, our friends occupied in the Rue Montalivet a magnificent ground floor apartment with an upper landing, and a garden behind, less sumptuous of course, and yet to my mind preferable to the old Venetian Embassy." Brichot informed me that this evening there was to be at "Quai Conti" (thus it was that the faithful spoke of the Verdurin drawing-room since it had been transferred to that address) a great musical "tow-row-row" got up by M. de Charlus. He went on to say that in the old days to which I had referred, the little nucleus had been different, and its tone not at all the same, not only because the faithful had then been younger. He told me of elaborate jokes played by Elstir (what he called "pure buffooneries"), as for instance one day when the painter, having pretended to fail at the last moment, had come disguised as an extra waiter and, as he handed round the dishes, whispered gallant speeches in the ear of the extremely proper Baroness Putbus, crimson with anger and alarm; then disappearing before the end of dinner he had had a hip-bath carried into the drawing-room, out of which, when the party left the table, he had emerged stark naked uttering fearful oaths; and also of supper parties to which the guests came in paper costumes, designed, cut out and coloured by Elstir, which were masterpieces in themselves, Brichot having worn on one occasion that of a great nobleman of the court of Charles VII, with long turned-up points to his shoes, and another time that of Napoleon I, for which Elstir had fashioned a Grand Cordon of the Legion of Honour out of sealing-wax. In short Brichot, seeing again with the eyes of memory the drawing-room of those days with its high windows, its low sofas devoured by the midday sun which had had to be replaced, declared that he preferred it to the drawing-room of to-day. Of course, I quite understood that by " drawing-room " Brichot meant—as the word church implies not merely the religious edifice but the congregation of worshippers—not merely the apartment, but the people who visited it, the special pleasures that they came to enjoy there, to which, in his memory, those sofas had imparted their form upon which, when you called to see Mme. Verdurin in the afternoon, you waited until she was ready, while the blossom on the horse chestnuts outside, and on the mantelpiece carnations in vases seemed, with a charming and kindly thought for the visitor expressed in the smiling welcome of their rosy hues, to be watching anxiously for the tardy appearance of the lady of the house. But if the drawing-room seemed to him superior to what it was now, it was perhaps because our mind is the old Proteus who cannot remain the slave of any one shape and, even in the social world, suddenly abandons a house which has slowly and with difficulty risen to the pitch of perfection to prefer another which is less brilliant, just as the " touched-up " photographs which Odette had had taken at Otto's, in which she queened it in a "princess" gown, her hair waved by Lenthéric, did not appeal to Swann so much as a little "cabinet picture" taken at Nice, in which, in a cloth cape, her loosely dressed hair protruding beneath a straw hat trimmed with pansies and a bow of black ribbon, instead of being twenty years younger (for women as a rule look all the older in a photograph, the earlier it is), she looked like a little servant girl twenty years older than she now was. Perhaps too he derived some pleasure from praising to me what I myself had never known, from shewing me that he had tasted delights that I could never enjoy. If so, he was successful, for merely by mentioning the names of two or three people who were no longer alive and to each of whom he imparted something mysterious by his way of referring to them, to that delicious intimacy, he made me ask myself what it could have been like; I felt that everything that had been told me about the Verdurins was far too coarse; and indeed, in the case of Swann whom I had known, I reproached myself with not having paid him sufficient attention, with not having paid attention to him in a sufficiently disinterested spirit, with not having listened to him properly when he used to entertain me while we waited for his wife to come home for luncheon and he shewed me his treasures, now that I knew that he was to be classed with the most brilliant talkers of the past. Just as we were coming to Mme. Verdurin's doorstep, I caught sight of M. de Charlus, steering towards us the bulk of his huge body, drawing unwillingly in his wake one of those blackmailers or mendicants who nowadays, whenever he appeared, sprang up without fail even in what were to all appearance the most deserted corners, by whom this powerful monster was, evidently against his will, invariably escorted, although at a certain distance, as is the shark by its pilot, in short contrasting so markedly with the haughty stranger of my first visit to Balbec, with his stern aspect, his affectation of virility, that I seemed to be discovering, accompanied by its satellite, a planet at a wholly different period of its revolution, when one begins to see it full, or a sick man now devoured by the malady which a few years ago was but a tiny spot which was easily concealed and the gravity of which was never suspected. Although the operation that Brichot had undergone had restored a tiny portion of the sight which he had thought to be lost for ever, I do not think he had observed the ruffian following in the Baron's steps. Not that this mattered, for, ever since La Raspelière, and notwithstanding the professor's friendly regard for M. de Charlus, the sight of the latter always made him feel ill at ease. No doubt to every man the life of every other extends along shadowy paths which he does not suspect. Falsehood, however, so often treacherous, upon which all conversation is based, conceals less perfectly a feeling of hostility, or of sordid interest, or a visit which we wish to look as though we had not paid, or an escapade with the mistress of a day which we are anxious to keep from our wife, than a good reputation covers up—so as not to let their existence be guessed—evil habits. They may remain unknown to us for a lifetime; an accidental encounter upon a pier, at night, will disclose them; even then this accidental discovery is frequently misunderstood and we require a third person, who is in the secret, to supply the unimaginable clue of which everyone is unaware. But, once we know about them, they alarm us because we feel that that way

madness lies, far more than by their immorality. Mme.
de Surgis did not possess the slightest trace of any moral
feeling, and would have admitted anything of her sons
that could be degraded and explained by material interest,
which is comprehensible to all mankind! But she forbade them to go on visiting M. de Charlus when she
learned that, by a sort of internal clockwork, he was inevitably drawn upon each of their visits, to pinch their
chins and to make each of them pinch his brother's. She
felt that uneasy sense of a physical mystery which makes
us ask ourself whether the neighbour with whom we have
been on friendly terms is not tainted with cannibalism,
and to the Baron's repeated inquiry: "When am I going
to see your sons again?" she would reply, conscious of
the thunderbolts that she was attracting to her defenceless
head, that they were very busy working for examinations,
preparing to go abroad, and so forth. Irresponsibility
aggravates faults, and even crimes, whatever anyone may
say. Landru (assuming that he really did kill his wives)
if he did so from a financial motive, which it is possible to
resist, may be pardoned, but not if his crime was due to
an irresistible Sadism.

*In the French text of 'La Prisonnière',
Volume I. ends at this point.*